HER LOVE WAS NOT BLIND

From the moment Amelia laid eyes upon Lord Verwood, she saw right through his pretense of being a loyal servant of the Crown.

Unfortunately, Amelia was the only one.

Even her normally sensible brother, Peter, went along with all the rest of society in being captivated by this man's charm, taken by his obvious intelligence and strength, and won over by the limp Verwood claimed to have acquired in fighting abroad.

Only Amelia was sure that the limp was a lie, as was the name he went by and the title he claimed. But if Amelia had discovered that Lord Verwood was too good to be true, she was also finding out he was too attractive to resist. . . .

The Ardent Lady Amelia

SIGNET REGENCY ROMANCE
COMING IN AUGUST 1990

Sheila Walsh
The Arrogant Lord Alastair

Katherine Kingsley
A Natural Attachment

Barbara Allister
The Frustrated Bridegroom

The Ardent Lady Amelia

by
Laura Matthews

A SIGNET BOOK

SIGNET
Published by the Penguin Group
Penguin Books USA Inc., 375 Hudson Street,
New York, New York 10014, U.S.A.
Penguin Books Ltd, 27 Wrights Lane,
London W8 5TZ, England
Penguin Books Australia Ltd, Ringwood,
Victoria, Australia
Penguin Books Canada Ltd, 2801 John Street,
Markham, Ontario, Canada L3R 1B4
Penguin Books (N.Z.) Ltd, 182–190 Wairau Road,
Auckland 10, New Zealand

Penguin Books Ltd, Registered Offices:
Harmondsworth, Middlesex, England

First published by Signet, an imprint of New American Library, a division of
Penguin Books USA Inc.

First Printing, February, 1984
10 9 8 7 6 5 4 3 2

 REGISTERED TRADEMARK—MARCA REGISTRADA

Printed in the United States of America

For Lois Walker, with thanks.

— 1 —

"There's something we need to discuss, Amelia," he said, leaning against the mantelpiece and gazing solemnly in his sister's direction. His hair, which had been carefully cut in the fashionable Brutus style, was at the moment slightly disarranged from working one hand nervously through it. The fifth Earl of Welsford, however, was not particularly concerned with his appearance at the moment, though he had been known to spend the proper amount of time over his toilette on the odd occasion. His dark brown eyes were narrowed thoughtfully as he struggled for the perfect way to phrase what he intended to be a command. Knowing his sister as well as he did, he felt sure the matter of delivery was of paramount importance. She was not likely to sit quietly and accept a dictum from him.

Lady Amelia Cameron regarded him with one slightly lifted brow, as though amused by his hesitation. If she hadn't known it unsettled him, she probably wouldn't have done it, but there, he had that paternalistic gleam in his eyes, which could only mean some nasty sort of regulation was about to be handed down. The more discomposed he was, the better, from her point of view, because then he was likely to blurt out quite the wrong kind of brotherly advice, and she would be able to dismiss it without a qualm. He meant well, of course, and he was four years her senior, though young at five-and-twenty to have come into the title, let alone be her sole surviving relative from their immediate

7

family. Aunt Trudy was a God-send, to be sure, but it wasn't like having one's own mother and father. . . . Lady Amelia's lifted eyebrow abruptly fell.

"I say, Amelia," the earl muttered, "no need to take on that Friday face. I wasn't going to scold you, heaven knows. It's just . . ." He shrugged a pair of wide shoulders, his mouth twisting ruefully. "I hadn't given enough thought to what you've been doing . . . about the spying, I mean. It suddenly occurred to me that it's not at all the thing for you to be nosing out information. You could put yourself in danger." One of his long, muscular hands came up as though to ward off her protest. "I know you don't do anything particularly hazardous in itself. There never seemed the least harm in having you ask a few questions here and there. But now I see it could cause suspicion in the wrong places, don't you know. And where there's suspicion, there's danger. Anyone who would be supporting the French cause in England isn't likely to be just your amiable dandy. They take this business as seriously as I . . . we do, and they wouldn't hesitate to play some wretched trick on you. Believe me, I've appreciated the bits and pieces you've been able to pick up. More often than not they've proved more important than what I've come across, but, hell, Amelia, it's just not the sort of thing a lady *does*."

His sister had sat quietly through the entirety of his speech, her hands busy with a piece of tatting. Now she looked up and smiled at him. "Really, Peter, you'd think I skulked around gin palaces in the dead of night, the way you talk. I've never done a thing more than listen to some fool talk too much when he was a bit disguised. If I can relay something of interest to you, at least it repays me for having my feet stomped on during a country dance, which is more than I get for listening to most of the intoxicated gentlemen I meet at balls and parties. What's put this flea in your ear? Danger? Nothing could be further from the truth. I dare say most of them are too far gone to even remember dancing with me, let alone spilling something they shouldn't have. And how often have I been able to bring you something of use? Maybe three times in the last two years. You'd think I made a regular occupation of listening at keyholes in disreputable houses."

A log rolled forward in the fireplace and Peter kicked it back with his booted foot. He continued to stare into the grate, not really noticing the brass andirons or the cheerful blaze. It was early April, with spring taking its time in warming London and the surrounding countryside. At Margrave, his country seat, the leaves would be sporting a fresh green and there would be the sweet smell of new growth in the air. Surely Amelia wouldn't mind going to Margrave at this time of year. How they'd both loved it there as children! He grimaced at the smoke-blackened bricks and straightened his shoulders.

"I know you haven't done anything you'd consider dangerous, my dear," he said, turning to face her with a smile. "But a man might very well remember later what he let slip to you, and desperately regret it. We aren't dealing with softhearted fellows. Anyone who would betray his own country has a decidedly vicious streak in him, Amelia. I think you'd be better off out of London for a while."

She regarded him with genuine surprise. "Out of London? During the season? Whatever can you be thinking of, Peter?"

"Your safety," he grumbled.

"Nonsense. Lord, I'm surrounded by footmen who'd take a cudgel to anyone who crossed his eyes at me! There was never anyone so well protected as I am, never out of sight of some worthy protector. Escorted everywhere I go, pampered in the most disgusting fashion. Mother would never have approved of such cosseting, you know."

The reference to their revered parent made him wince. "I'm convinced neither Mother nor Father would have approved of what I've allowed you to do, Amelia. And that's the crux of the matter."

But he didn't meet her eyes and Amelia sat silent, waiting for him to continue. The tick of the grandfather clock in the corner and the hiss of the fire were the only sounds in the room. When he didn't speak, she cocked her head at him and asked, "What is it, Peter? What's come up to alarm you? Was it something I passed on from the rowing party? I've never heard so many loose tongues in my life, but I didn't think there was anything of significance there."

"It wasn't the rowing party."

"Then what was it?"

He glared at her across the room. "It doesn't have to have been anything in particular. I'm just saying I don't want you asking any questions anymore, or listening to those loose tongues. And maybe for now it would be a good idea if you went to Margrave."

The door to the room had opened without his noticing, and what appeared to be a disembodied head yelped, "Go to Margrave? During the season? Your wits must have gone begging, Peter." Gertrude Harting pushed the door farther open and steamed into the room, her graying curls quivering with indignation. Everything about her was round, from the sausage curls she sported, right down to her plump, short feet. "I was going to ask if I could interrupt your discussion, but I can see you've need of a more mature head in this little gathering. You can't be serious about Amelia leaving London at this time of year. Why, there wouldn't be a soul in Sussex to have a cup of tea with. And what's more, there are two very distinguished gentlemen who are showing a decided partiality for her this season. You can't walk out on that kind of interest."

"Two?" Amelia asked, grinning. "Surely there are three."

"I don't count Rollings. He's not the least distinguished. In my day we'd have called him a fortune hunter."

"That's what we still call them," Peter murmured.

"Such a sweet man," Amelia mused, regarding a porcelain shepherdess on the mantel with mock wistfulness. "Such distinguished manners, such manly carriage, such a winning way about him. Why, I believe he's been willing to tear himself away from the card table at least once at each entertainment just so he could dance with me. How very flattering! I don't believe he's done it for any other young woman."

"None of the rest of them will dance with him," Peter suggested.

"Well, one feels sorry for the poor fellow. Such exquisite taste and not the money to support it. Did you see his waistcoat at the Brimptons'? The subtlety of it very nearly took my breath away. Black and gray stripes! I tell you even Brummell can't duplicate that kind of elegance. I had thought of a similar one for you for your birthday next month, Peter."

Her brother scowled at her. "You know I wouldn't be caught dead in that kind of finery, Amelia. Let's not stray from the matter under discussion. Margrave is delightful at this time of year. You and Aunt Trudy could do with a little country air after so long in the city. I dare say the pace of the season is wearing on Aunt Trudy."

Trudy, who never bestirred herself more than absolutely necessary, gave him a fierce look from under the bushy eyebrows of which she was inordinately proud. "You're talking pure drivel," she snorted. "Few things are more pleasing to me than taking Amelia about to the various entertainments. To hear you talk, one would think I was getting on for eighty, rather than forty. With two years to go, at that. Not that you need mention my age to anyone," she hastened to add, patting the plump curls around her face before continuing.

"I see all my friends at the balls and dinners. There's nothing strenuous about sitting on one of those little gilt chairs and catching up on the latest gossip, I assure you. Sometimes one wishes the chairs were a little larger . . . But that's neither here nor there. Have you never watched your sister at a ball? Never a dance unspoken for, I promise you. She is greatly admired, as one might expect, with that glorious honey-colored hair, and those enormous violet-colored eyes, and that aristocratic nose. All the Camerons have the most amazing noses. She certainly didn't inherit it from the Harting side."

Amused, and slightly embarrassed, by the extravagant praise, Amelia interjected a change of subject. "Did you plan to come to Margrave with us, Peter?"

"Why, no." He ran a finger along the carving of the mantelpiece, only reluctantly looking up to meet her gaze. "I have commitments in town."

"As we do," Trudy remarked with a sniff. "Summer's the time to go to Margrave, when the sea breezes aren't making it insufferable. Why, at this time of year it would be dead as a doornail. No company to be found for miles around."

"Except that of spies and smugglers," Amelia added with a mischievous wink at her brother. "There are probably all sorts of French agents wandering around the Sussex coast looking for good spots for Napoleon to land a new invasion fleet. And smugglers who have routine contact with the French while importing brandy and silks. Oh, we'd have a marvellous time."

"Bath, then," Peter said. "Bath is a marvellous place for a holiday. The air is a great deal more salubrious than that of London, and there's plenty of company to be found there."

"Humph." Trudy punctuated her contempt with a disgusted flick of her pudgy fingers. "Retired military men and droning, elderly clergymen. Bath is for the old, the infirm, and the upstarts. Not at all like it was in my day. I remember my first visit there, when I was just eighteen. I suppose even then its glory was fading, but, my, how elegant everything looked to me. All the ladies and gentlemen dressed in the first stare of fashion, the bells continually announcing the arrival of some new worthy to town, the chairmen scurrying up the hills like mountain goats." She gave a reminiscent sigh and lifted her shoulders in a gesture of regret. "But it's nothing like it was. Oh, there are those who still go there, and they still have the assemblies, but it's not the same. It doesn't hold the attraction it did for the young people, you see. And Amelia needs to be where there are young people."

"Eligible men, she means," Amelia clarified, grinning across at Peter. "Aunt Trudy is determined to see me married this season."

Trudy glared at her. "I should think so! With a little effort you could have brought more than one fellow to the sticking point, my girl. What is it you're waiting for? You're not as young as you once were. Men want the ones just out of the schoolroom, you mark my words. The more set in your ways you get, the less interested they are. They want a miss they can shape to their liking. Pretty manners and a good heart aren't enough."

Amelia heaved a sorrowful sigh. "I fear it's already too late for me, Aunt Trudy. Biddable as I am, twenty-one is too advanced an age."

"Biddable!" Peter exclaimed. "I can't think when I've met a less biddable female. And twenty-one is still practically in leading strings. What does anyone know at twenty-one? It's an age when older, wiser heads should prevail," he said meaningfully, leaving himself open to Trudy's misunderstanding.

"Indeed it is," she remarked, smugly surveying the two of them. "So I'm sure Peter will listen to my counsel about Amelia. Under no circumstances should she leave London when things are looking so promising for her here. It would be the greatest folly to remove her. The chances of finding a suitable match in Sussex are nonexistent, I assure you, and in Bath . . . well, you must understand that the *quality* wouldn't be there."

Peter swallowed an exasperated sigh. Trudy was not a party to his activities, or even to Amelia's. The poor woman would be horrified at the thought of even a little circumspect information-gathering by his sister. Her disapproval was a foregone conclusion, even though, as Amelia had pointed out, there was very little she was in a position to do to serve "The Cause," as she sportingly called it. Peter sometimes wondered if she took the matter seriously, or if she only undervalued it so he would consider her low-key attitude absurdly harmless. Which he had done until Verwood had called him on it.

Oh, God, he was expecting Verwood any moment and he didn't want Amelia and Trudy to still be with him when the fellow arrived. Peter had planned to be finished with this business and safely ensconced in the library by nine for the appointed meeting. He shifted restlessly to one side, trying to catch a glimpse of the grandfather clock without seeming to as he tugged down a cuff under the tight-fitting blue coat he wore. Trudy was awaiting his reply to her remarks (which he couldn't remember) and Amelia was placidly working on her tatting, seemingly unconcerned. The muted sound of a knock on the front door reached them. "I have work to do in my study," he said abruptly. "We'll discuss the matter another time."

"What is there to discuss?" Trudy asked, offended. "Surely I've convinced you it would be most unwise for Amelia to leave London now."

"Yes, yes. I can see that." His brown eyes came to rest on Amelia's gently smiling face. "There was another matter Amelia and I had to settle, but it will have to wait."

Even as he hastened to the door connecting the drawing room with the library, Bighton flung open the door from the hall, announcing, "Lord Verwood." The gentleman who entered stood several inches taller than the butler, and carried himself with the kind of bearing one expected in a military man. He entered the room without hesitation, though a slight limp was apparent in his firm step. Masses of unruly black curls had obviously resisted all efforts to train them into the semblance of a stylish coiffure, or perhaps it was merely that he hadn't bothered to rearrange them after removing his hat. He wore a blue coat, rather old-fashioned in its cut, and buff pantaloons that strained over his muscular thighs. His neckcloth was tied in a neat but un-fashionable manner, as though he had attended to the matter himself, in no patient endeavor to be done with the task.

Altogether not an entirely imposing figure, Amelia decided as she studied the stranger. For he was a stranger to her. She had a very good memory for names and faces, and if she'd seen him at all, previously, it could only have been in a crowd. Certainly he'd never been introduced to her. She couldn't very well have forgotten his impressive height or the fierceness of his nearly black eyes, or even the suppressed energy that seemed to radiate from him. He didn't appear the sort of man who would suffer fools gladly, or even run tame at a polite social gathering. A man of action, she thought, not without amusement. A soldier not of the parade-ground variety, but of battle. She wondered how Peter had met him.

"Ah, Verwood," Peter said, seeming at something of a loss. "I thought we'd meet in the library. Should have told Bighton. Well, never mine. We can go through here."

If he thought by indicating the door he was going to escape without an introduction, he was sadly out. Trudy was not in the habit of watching young men wander through "her" drawing room without a proper greeting. "I don't believe we've met," she said, extending her fingers just slightly in the newcomer's direction.

Verwood's alert eyes instantly swung toward her and he executed a stiff, if minuscule, bow as Peter mumbled, "Aunt Trudy, Lord Verwood. Verwood, my aunt, Gertrude Harting." From her seat just opposite Trudy, Amelia watched in fascination as the man's eyes took in every detail of Trudy's appearance with the intensity of a beam suddenly loosed from a lantern in the dark. Though his countenance changed not a whit, Amelia had the distinct impression he'd formed an immediate judgment of the older woman, penetrated to some essential core of her, and extracted a definition he would not forget. It was an unnerving observation and she rather hoped Peter wouldn't bother introducing the dark fellow to her.

But in an instant the black eyes shifted to Amelia, subjecting her to the same sort of scrutiny as Peter reluctantly spoke her name. "Lady Amelia," he murmured in a voice as deep as a coal pit and about as warm. This was not the manner in which Amelia was used to being treated by gentlemen and she couldn't help the slight irritation which burgeoned in her bosom. She was aware that one of her brows rose slightly, though she had no control over it, but she couldn't possibly know that her long, thin nose, which Trudy had so recently called aristocratic, actually twitched. If Lord Verwood considered this an extraordinary circumstance, he gave no indication of it. His bow to her was, if possible, even slighter than that to Gertrude, but there was no apparent disrespect in it. One so stiff, after all, might fall over were he to incline himself too far, Amelia decided.

"Verwood," Trudy was saying, her brow wrinkled with thought. "I remember a Vernon in Hampshire, but no

Verwoods. And he was a baronet, if I'm not mistaken. What part of the country are you from, Lord Verwood?"

"Derbyshire."

Trudy had expeced a little more information than that, but she was undaunted. "And you still have a home there, do you?"

"To the best of my knowledge."

If he had said it with a twinkle in his eyes, Amelia might have warmed to him, but no, his face and those unnerving black eyes were as politely cool as ever. Trudy persisted. "Have you family there?"

"No."

"Ah, then they're here with you in London," Trudy surmised in the face of his unwillingness to be more forthcoming.

"No."

Which left her knowing precisely nothing. He might have family (a wife) who weren't either in Derbyshire or in London, or he might have no family (a wife) at all.

"Do you plan a long stay in London?"

"I haven't any idea, as yet."

"Have you a house here?"

"Yes."

"In South Street," Peter offered, to propitiate her bursting curiosity.

Trudy sat back a little in her chair, nodding as though satisfied. "There are some acceptable houses in South Street. For myself, I like the squares, but not everyone can live on one of them. South Street has the advantage of being so close to the park," she added kindly.

"There is that."

"Do you ride?"

"Yes, ma'am." Verwood stood at his ease, never shifting his eyes from Trudy to any other member of the small group. He looked as though he were prepared to withstand her inquisitive assault for hours, unperturbed. Amelia refused to join the questioning, or even to make some inoffensive remark. From where she sat she could observe the rugged strength of his sun-browned face, the broad set of his shoulders. Definitely a military man, she decided. Probably wounded, accounting for the limp. A few years in the army could have roughed his polish, though she personally doubted that he'd ever had any. She'd seldom run into a man with less-agreeable manners, though one couldn't exactly fault him for impoliteness. She didn't observe brusqueness very often in her circles. Perhaps that's why she'd never seen him before.

"The Candovers are from Derbyshire," Aunt Trudy remarked. "I imagine you know them."

"Yes."

"Well, splendid. Then we'll probably see you at their ball next week."

Verwood's eyes for the first time left Trudy's to swing questioningly at Peter, who shrugged and said, "My sister and aunt aren't planning on leaving town after all."

"I should think not!" Trudy cried. "In the middle of the season! I never heard anything so tottyheaded. This is precisely the perfect time to *be* in London." She smiled graciously at Verwood. "So we'll no doubt see you at the Candovers' next week."

"Yes, ma'am."

Peter had had quite enough of the cross-examination, and felt a little more had been revealed than he could have wished. "I hope you'll excuse us, Aunt Trudy, but Lord Verwood has called on a business matter and I shouldn't like to keep him longer than necessary."

"Why, of course, dear boy. I wouldn't think of intruding on such a subject. You might take him into the library."

Amelia grinned at her brother's exasperation, but he merely pursed his lips in response. Lord Verwood followed him to the door before turning to bid the ladies a pleasant evening.

"Rather a strange man," Trudy confided when they'd gone.

Amelia continued to stare at the closed door. "Very strange indeed," she agreed.

— 2 —

There was a toasty fire burning in her room when Lady Amelia arrived there an hour later. Her brother was still closeted with Lord Verwood, and Aunt Trudy had agreed an early night would be good for them. Sundays were invariably enervating, with very little activity outside the house after church. Lady Amelia couldn't very well stroll about the area with Trudy, since Trudy never strolled. And she didn't like to take a footman away from the house because most of the servants had the day off. Occasionally there was a ride in the park, if Peter was free, but he'd been away all day today, only returning in the evening.

She felt restless from the lack of exercise and paced up and down her room. The air was still too chilly to open a window and let in a refreshing breeze. If the Shiptons had been able to join them for a quiet dinner, the day wouldn't have passed so slowly, but Clarissa had contracted some trifling illness and refused to stir so far as the three houses that separated their two domiciles. It was one of Clarissa's few faults, this overenthusiasm for pampering herself with any slight indisposition, and Amelia tried to take it in her stride. There were times, however, when it proved the greatest nuisance. One's friends should be more considerate, she thought ruefully.

The absence of entertainment was not, of course, the only thing she had on her mind. Peter's odd pronouncements, and his odd friend, were far more pressing to her at the moment than a small disappointment of company. Whether she acknowledged it to him or not, she did rather fancy herself useful in gathering information, and she had no intention of giving up her quietly adventurous life. There were things she heard that he wasn't likely to hear, things that might have, and indeed on occasion *had* had, some bearing on England's struggles with the French. Granted, she had uncovered no nefarious plots which would have undone her country, but she had been able to obtain tidbits of information that had proved useful.

The way in which she obtained this information was not precisely as simple as she'd let on to Peter. But then, he wouldn't have approved of her slightly unorthodox methods, so it was better he didn't know. True, inevitably the gentlemen in question were decidedly foxed when they let their tongues run away with them, but they needed a little encouragement in the right direction. After all, they were more inclined to spout amorous bits of nonsense than details of renewed French preparations for an invasion. And one couldn't just come out and ask if they happened to know anything about Napoleon's plans. It was necessary to have them in the proper mood, and then show a great deal of bravado about how Napoleon would never dare to attack the English on their own soil, to get a rise out of someone. Most of the men she'd gotten in the proper mood hadn't known the first thing about a French invasion, or anything else, for that matter.

Lady Amelia stopped in front of the looking glass above her dressing table and considered her reflection for a moment. Her hair was dressed simply for a quiet Sunday at home, with none of the elaborate curls and falls she allowed Bridget to arrange when she was going out for the evening. Still, the honey-colored tresses looked perfectly acceptable, pulled back softly and arranged in a knot on the crown of her head. She released the pins and returned them to the red lacquer box on the table, letting her hair escape down over her shoulders. Loose, it looked even softer, brushing gently against her rosy cheeks, curling toward the hollow of her throat.

Her mother's hair had been much the same color. Amelia dropped to the velvet-colored stool and picked up the framed miniature that always sat facing her on the table. There was no miniature of her father, but a three-quarter-length portrait of him in the gallery, a copy of the one at Margrave, beside a matching one of his wife. Amelia could see other resemblances between herself and her mother, but she had inherited her father's determined chin and ruddy coloring. Lady Welsford had been delicate, in her person and in her health. Amelia might have looked more like her if she hadn't been so tall and sturdy. The violet eyes were the same, and the finely molded lips, but the configuration of the face was wholly different. Instead of her mother's fragile beauty, Amelia had a more robust, wholesome appearance, which was perhaps no less striking, but it would never call forth the same sort of protective response the world at large had felt for Lady Welsford.

Only they hadn't been able to protect her. Not in the end. Amelia set down the miniature and picked up a hairbrush, drawing it vigorously though her long hair again and again. Sometimes it took total concentration to blot out the memory of her last view of her mother and father, both waving quite cheerfully from the other carriage. She could remember her own anxiety as she allowed Peter to assist her back into their carriage for the hurried drive to Calais. He had assured her, over and over, that their parents would be close behind them and that there was no reason to suspect any problem just because they were out of sight.

It was a frantic time, especially so for a seventeen-year-old girl who had expected a pleasure trip to Paris with her family, and ended up alone with her brother on the packet boat back to England. She had insisted that they wait for the earl and countess, but he had said, "They'll get the next packet, Amelia. Father told me not to wait for them if they weren't here on time." There was so much commotion, so much tenseness among their fellow passengers, that Amelia could barely sit still during the rough passage. And then they had waited at an English inn for the next packet, which didn't come. Hours and hours they waited, Peter going out frequently for any news he could glean, finally returning to tell her, "Napoleon has ordered the arrest of all British travellers in France. We were the last packet to make it out safely."

"But he can't do that!" she had insisted, her cheeks flushed, tears welling in her eyes. "What will become of them?"

"They'll be all right," he replied, squeezing her cold hands. "He wouldn't dare treat them badly, Amelia. It's just a gesture of revenge. The government will have them released within a few days. You can be sure of it."

Peter was wrong—not about the treatment, but about the release of their parents. The interned British travellers were still in France now, four years later. Most of them. Peter had worked diligently to have his parents freed, and had finally managed, because of their aristocratic standing, to purchase their freedom. But the actual exchange had come too late. Unaccustomed to the straitened living conditions, Lady Welsford had contracted an illness which had eventually killed her, with her husband, weakened from his grief and the long hours of caring for her, soon following. Their bodies were returned to England and buried in the family crypt at Margrave in the spring of 1804 on the day Amelia turned eighteen, almost nine months after her last sight of them.

It had been possible for some of the interned British to escape, but at great struggling with their souls, for the French had exacted a vow from them not to escape, in return for decent living conditions. The earl had felt bound by his word, refusing the assistance Peter sent clandestinely before he arranged for a legal freedom. Amelia frequently wondered how her father must have felt when his wife died, the agony of knowing they might have been safely in England by then. Not that she blamed him. If he had given his word, he would keep it. She blamed Napoleon and the French for the whole tragic situation. And she went on blaming them, year after year, doing the only thing she could to help bring about the downfall of the savage who ruled that country.

Her rage had calmed into a more manageable anger. When her worst fears were realized, she found a new strength in herself to cope with the grief, a new outlet through Peter's work with the War Department for her burning desire to have some part in the effort to displace Napoleon. Her exasperation with her own government's lack of wisdom in prosecuting the war was frequently as strong as her indignation with the French. But Peter, for all his elegance and sophistication, had learned a great deal during his attempts to secure his parents' release, and he used his knowledge now to best effect. There was little chance, at this point, of an invasion. Those fears were gradually dying, but there were other rumors abroad which could prove beneficial to the cause, and Amelia had no intention of letting them pass her by without some effort to latch on to them.

So this new attitude of Peter's was upsetting. Not only was he trying to exclude her from some chance to be useful, he was threatening to banish her from life in London. Since their parents' death, they had spent most of their time in the city, unable to tolerate for long the unhappy associations at Margrave. Two months in the summer and two in the winter were ordinarily the total of their year's stay in Sussex. Amelia was ready to spend more time there, but not now, when the season was in progress, bringing with it the best possible time for uncovering something of interest. If Peter had planned to go there himself, she would have been willing to go along as his hostess, she supposed, but he had no intention of going anywhere with her. His aim was apparently her exile.

Amelia couldn't conceive why her brother had so suddenly taken the perverse notion into his head that she was in some danger. She made a face at herself in the mirror and set the silver-backed hairbrush carefully on the mahogany dressing table. Lord Verwood certainly had not evinced the slightest interest in her honey-colored hair or her violet eyes or her aristocratic nose! Her brow puckered in thought. But he had shown some interest in the fact that she and her aunt weren't going to be out of town. Now, why would he even think of such a thing? Peter had only brought it up this

evening, for heaven's sake. It was possible, barely, that Peter
had mentioned his intention of sending his sister out of town
to Lord Verwood on some previous occasion—but why? So
far as Amelia knew, Peter was only recently acquainted with
his lordship, who had not even been introduced to her until
this evening. It seemed unlikely her name would have arisen
in a discussion between the two men at all.

The more Amelia thought about the matter, the more
convinced she became that it was quite the other way
around. For some reason which she could not begin to
imagine, Lord Verwood had been the one to suggest to Peter
that she be sent out of town! The concept held a ring of truth
to her, though she couldn't put her finger on any reason why
it should. Verwood was an army man—she would have
sworn to it. One became familiar with the mannerisms, with
the stiff bearing, with the preoccupation such gentlemen
exhibited. Amelia stood up and began to pace around the
room again, taking no notice of anything but her thoughts.

Several possibilities occurred to her. The first was that
Lord Verwood was not what he proclaimed himself. That he
was a villain intent on duping her brother in some way.
Though this seemed unlikely, it had a certain appeal to her,
since she felt decidedly offended with the gentleman. If he
were the cause of this breach between her brother and herself, he might very well be up to no good. On the other
hand, Peter was rather a shrewd judge of character, constantly on the lookout for imposters. Which didn't necessarily make Lord Verwood an acceptable acquaintance.
Peter might be using him for his own purposes.

What seemed more likely was that the two of them were
working together. That wouldn't have surprised Amelia in
the least. Peter never gave her much of a clue as to what he
was up to. If there were some danger involved in his current
work, he might want her out of town to be on the safe side.
Well, it wasn't likely she would leave town if Peter was in
some kind of predicament! But knowing that, he might very
well have schemed to get her to leave on her own account.

Amelia's head was beginning to whirl with the possibilities. The fire in the grate had burned low, casting a

reddish glow in the dimly lit room. From a distance she heard the closing of a door and guessed, from the dull thud, that it was the heavy oak front entry. She padded across to the window that overlooked the street and twitched back the draperies a few inches.

A man stood on the stoop, carelessly adjusting the curly-brimmed beaver to an unfashionable angle before stuffing his hands in his pockets. Certainly not Peter! No gentleman with any pretensions to distinction distorted his coat with balled hands in his pockets, even when it was cold out and he didn't have a pair of gloves with him. Surely Lord Verwood had worn a pair of gloves, even for a casual evening call on Peter. Actually, Amelia could see them hanging precariously from his pocket as he stepped down onto the pavement and stomped along Grosvenor Square, his limp less apparent from this height. What an odd sort of man he was! Not even a carriage waiting for him. Though South Street wasn't that far away, it was a particularly chilly evening, with the constant threat of rain clearly proclaimed in the heavy skies.

Amelia dropped the draperies back into place when he had disappeared from sight. There seemed no time like the present, since she was fully awake and still fully clothed, to approach Peter with the mystery Lord Verwood presented. She could hear his familiar tread on the stairs and hastened to open her door. "Peter? I'd like to have a word with you before you go to bed," she whispered across the echoing hall.

Her voice had startled him, and the candleholder in his hand jerked slightly, illuminating a worried frown on his handsome features which he immediately dispersed with a brief smile. "Still up, Amelia? I thought you'd have been asleep hours ago."

Leaving the door open, Amelia retreated into her room, waiting for him to follow. She took a seat in one of the two chairs at the far end used as a sitting area. Peter followed more slowly, lowering himself almost reluctantly onto the seat and placing the brass candleholder on the small oval table between them. The light it cast did not greatly brighten the large room which ran across half the house front. Peter looked tired in its feeble light.

"Are you exhausted?" Amelia asked, concerned. "Did that ridiculous man upset you?"

His head came up abruptly. "Ridiculous man? Do you mean Verwood?"

"Who else? I'd have a care of him if I were you, Peter."

"I haven't the first idea what you're talking about. There's nothing even faintly ridiculous about Verwood, for God's sake. Where did you get that idea?"

Amelia smiled and shook her head. "Oh, you wouldn't notice, Peter. He looks as though he raided someone's wardrobe from ten years ago, and his manners could stand a great deal of improvement. Most of your friends are more amiable."

His shoulders lifted in an elaborate shrug. "He's not much concerned with making an impression, I suppose, but there's nothing about him to cause concern."

"Tell me about him," Amelia urged, tucking her feet up under her. "Where did you meet him?"

Peter made a dismissive gesture with one hand. "At one of the clubs, I imagine. There's nothing of importance to know about him. What we really ought to talk about, my dear, is you. I can see I'm not going to get Trudy to leave town during the season, but at the very least I want you to stop doing anything other than being the charming young society belle. It wasn't wise of me to let you get involved in this cloak-and-dagger stuff, and I want you to accept my decree on the matter. With the change in government last month, things are a little tricky at best. Anything you did might be misconstrued, and I can't take a chance of that happening."

"He put you up to this, didn't he?" Amelia demanded, her voice bitter. "There's so little I can do, and your mysterious Lord Verwood wants to have me out of the picture entirely, doesn't he?"

"Who said Verwood had anything to do with this? Don't be a gudgeon, Amelia. I'm only thinking of our own good. Enjoy yourself. It's time you started thinking about marriage, though I hate to sound like Trudy on the subject. You've been too wrought-up about the French threat and French injustices to give much consideration to your own life. Mother would have expected me to help you find some sort of respectable match. No, don't glare at me that way. I haven't any intention of pushing you into something you don't want, but if you don't consider the possibility soon, you're going to find yourself left behind, my girl. Haven't you formed the slightest tendre for one of those exquisite gallants who are forever squiring you and Trudy about?"

"Certainly not! Do you take me for an idiot? There's not a one of them who understands the first thing about politics or the war. You could put their brains in a peapod and they'd rattle around. Do you think I'd be content with some fop who only knows how to steal polite conversation from last night's dinner party? You wouldn't believe how inane some of them are, Peter. On Friday you get a rehash of the more brilliant gems dropped by their friends on Thursday, and sometimes you wonder if they even understand them. Or they talk about wagers on sporting events, or their rotten luck at the gaming tables."

"They can't all be that bad." Peter laughed and then leaned toward her with an earnest expression. "You're not really looking, Amy. And that's because you've been so caught up in this little game of ours. I don't want to see you waste your life. Heaven knows how long this painful war will last, and if you wait until it's resolved to find yourself a husband, you could be an old lady. Mother would have wanted you to marry and have a family of your own. That's not such a bad prospect, is it? There's very little you can't do when you're married that you can when you aren't. In fact, I should think there were quite a few more things you *could* do."

"Oh, I intend to marry one day," she replied wearily, "though I think it's a great pity that's all one gets to do with one's life."

He raised a quizzical brow at her. "What sort of thing do you have in mind?"

"I'd like to run the government, I think. Something on

that order. Being a soldier is too brutal, and being in trade would be too tame. But running the country would be just the thing to satisfy my impulses to see that things are done right, don't you think?" she asked, grinning at him.

"Just so. Well, we'll look for a gentleman of a political disposition for you, then. You can influence him in your own inimitable way."

"Hardly the same thing as running the government myself," Amelia retorted with a sniff.

Peter smiled and rose from his chair, giving her shoulder a pat before he picked up the candleholder. "I wouldn't put that past you either, my dear," he murmured. "Sleep well."

Only when he had gone did Amelia realize how little information he'd given her on Lord Verwood. Well, she was perfectly capable of finding out a few things herself. And Peter had undoubtedly overlooked the fact that she hadn't *promised* not to continue her former activities. There was so little she could actually do. Peter could ride off on the spur of the moment, accountable to no one but himself, while she was forced to sit at home drinking tea and making polite conversation with the most incredible dullards.

As she undressed for the night, she wished she hadn't sent Bridget to bed already, and then grimaced at her own readiness to rely on all the trappings of luxury she encountered every day. When Peter went off on one of his missions, he didn't take his valet and a portmanteau full of starched cravats. He was apparently as at home in a fisherman's hovel on the coast as he was in the house in Grosvenor Square, when the situation required it. Amelia doubted her own ability to be so flexible and crawled into bed without using the warming pan, just to toughen herself. But the sheets were frightfully cold and she bounced back out of the four-poster bed to retrieve the warming pan. So much for her noble experiment, she thought ruefully as she finally lay down in the warm bed. She fell asleep only slightly chastened.

— 3 —

A strange thing happened after that night. Whereas Amelia
could not recall having seen Lord Verwood at a solitary
entertainment previous to that time, now she saw him everywhere. He was at evening parties, at routs, at assemblies, at
balls, at breakfasts. He was there in Hyde Park when she
went riding or driving, he was in Bond Street when she went
shopping. He was even, occasionally, in the house in Grosvenor Square.

Not that he paid the least attention to her. If they
chanced actually to face each other, he would give her an icy
sort of smile and murmur her name, as though he could
barely recollect it. He never stood up with her for a dance,
nor brought her a glass of ratafia, though she saw him dance
a few times, despite his limp, and bring other young women
beverages, though he hardly accomplished the task in the
approved gallant manner.

It annoyed her to see that, after the first few days, he
dressed just like all the other elegant gentlemen. Amelia
couldn't feel that he looked comfortable in the tight pants
and the exquisite coats, but no one else seemed to notice.
His neckcloths were now arranged with all the fanciful falls
and knots one could possibly wish—not too high, always a
sparkling white. Amelia decided he must have acquired a
valet, a teasing remark which she tried out on her Aunt
Trudy.

"A valet?" the older woman grunted. "Well, of course he'd have a valet, Amelia. Every proper gentleman has a valet."

"I thought you didn't regard him as quite a proper gentleman. You said yourself that he was odd."

"Odd? Not a bit of it. I've seen him absolutely everywhere this past week, and there's not a thing out of the ordinary about him. He doesn't talk a great deal, to be sure, but then, you're always complaining about the gentlemen who blather on about nothing. I should think you'd find him a refreshing change."

As Trudy had not particularly noticed that Lord Verwood never spoke to her at all, Amelia had no intention of enlightening her. "Has he told you more about himself?"

Trudy gave her a haughty glance. "I'm not one to press where a gentleman wishes to preserve his privacy. His silence is no more than a healthy reserve. We discussed architecture at Lady Morestead's ball, and he was eminently knowledgeable on the subject. I haven't the least doubt that his own home is Jacobean, since he is most informed on that subject. One can learn a great deal by simply reading between the lines, my dear."

From her friend Clarissa Shipton, Amelia was able to find out very little about the viscount. "Verwood?" she said as she studied one of her shoes, wiggling it back and forth and comparing it with the other. "You know, I do think the left one looks slightly larger, Amelia. And it's a bit loose on my foot. I'm going to have to take it back, I'm afraid, and they'll never be able to match it perfectly. Mother says he's from Derbyshire. He's been in the army, though she couldn't find out whether he'll be returning or not. In Egypt, I believe it was. Now, why would they fight in Egypt when Napoleon's in Europe?"

Amelia made no attempt to explain the ramifications of the fiasco in Egypt, since she knew Clarissa wasn't really interested. That Mrs. Shipton, a woman whose reputation for knowing everything about everyone was as well known as her astonishing penchant for wearing all of her jewelry at once, didn't know more about Verwood surprised and alarmed Amelia. "Did your mother find out if he was married?"

"Married?" Clarissa abruptly allowed both feet, which had been swinging in the air for her inspection, to snap back against the floor. This was almost an accomplishment for her, since she was so tiny that in many chairs her feet didn't even reach the ground. "Are you interested in him, Amelia?"

"No, of course I'm not interested in him. That is, not personally. I just feel there's a great deal of mystery about him. No one seems to know anything at all."

"I've seen him around with your brother. Why don't you ask him?"

"I *have* asked him. Peter told me absolutely nothing. You wouldn't think Lord Verwood could just mingle in society with no one knowing where he came from, or who he was, would you?"

"Well, I dare say Peter's vouched for him, my dear. He doesn't look very mysterious—Verwood. Just sort of stiff and uncompromising. Not a comfortable chap, if you know what I mean. Did you think the title wasn't real?"

"Oh, no. Peter seems to believe in it, and Peter isn't easily fooled. Couldn't your mother find out anything else?"

"My dear Amelia, what are you suggesting?" Clarissa demanded with a twinkle in her eyes. "Surely you don't think Mama is inquisitive! Hardly more so than Miss Harting, I promise you." Clarissa laughed and tapped one of her shoes against the floor. "I don't see what's so interesting about Lord Verwood, anyhow. His face is quite sun-browned and rather . . . rough. And those eyes. I had the odd feeling he could tell what I was thinking when he looked at me. Perhaps I won't return the shoes after all. You didn't notice the difference, did you?"

Amelia was soon frustrated by this type of response to her queries. No one seemed to know or care from whence Lord Verwood had sprung. For all they noticed, he might have hatched full-blown from an ostrich egg. There seemed little curiosity engendered by his sudden appearance in society, and not even much speculation as to whether he would be an appropriate match for one of the eligible young ladies making her debut that season. The latter might have been caused by his obvious lack of interest in the debutantes, but Amelia suspected the dearth of curiosity stemmed directly from Verwood's own handling of people who questioned him too closely. He had an uncanny habit of turning the tables on them, asking questions they would have preferred unraised.

Ellis Winchfield, one of her supposed suitors, seemed the most unlikely person to be able to provide some background on the viscount, but Amelia, out of perseverance, posed her standard question to him as they stood together after a country dance at the Candovers' ball. "Verwood, you say? Known him for years. That's to say, I knew him years ago. Haven't seen him since I was fifteen."

"Where did you meet him?" Amelia asked.

"Well, at school, of course. He was a few years older, come to think of it, so it may be I haven't seen him since I was thirteen."

Amelia remained calm, and patient, and dogged. "What school was that, Mr. Winchfield?"

"Why, Harrow, of course. Surely you knew I went to Harrow."

"Now that you mention it. . . . I understand he's from Derbyshire."

"Wouldn't be surprised. Lot of the lads were."

"Did you know him well?"

"Not to speak of. Only knew him at all because he was great at games, you know. Lord, it makes me shudder to think how all those boys ran around in the mud. We'd stand there and cheer for them while they knocked their brains out and got filthy as pigs. I don't know what it is about some boys, that they want to exhaust themselves that way and ruin their clothes. I never took part in that sort of thing. Well, it stands to reason, doesn't it?"

Amelia nodded and allowed herself to be claimed for the next dance.

It was progress of a sort. Lord Verwood had gone to

Harrow and he was good at sports. She wasn't surprised that he was good at sports, only that he could have escaped from Harrow without learning more polished manners. While she conversed with her partner, and executed the steps of the boulanger, it occurred to her that she hadn't taken the most logical step of all in trying to find out about him: asking her host and hostess of the evening. The Candovers were from Derbyshire, and Lord Verwood had actually confessed to an acquaintance with them. What more logical source for information?

Sir Arthur and Lady Candover were not particularly well known to her. He was a tall, emaciated-looking fellow with graying hair, and she was rather nondescript and painfully shy. They were not frequent visitors to London, being quite content to spend their time in the country. But they had spawned a bevy of daughters, and arrived in the city for a season as each of the young ladies reached the proper age to be launched into society.

The girls themselves never seemed to have the slightest difficulty contracting a suitable alliance. They were as a rule attractive and pretty-behaved youngsters, obedient but without that docile quality that frequently irritated Amelia in new debutantes. The current daughter, Genevieve, had not quite outgrown a coltish sort of awkwardness, but she was all the more appealing for it, with her eager eyes and her ready smile.

Since it was Genevieve's big day, Amelia didn't wish to detract from it by taking up any of the young woman's time, and she decided to approach Lady Candover instead. Sir Arthur might have done just as well, considering his wife's shyness, but he was constantly surrounded by a group of sporting gentlemen whom Lady Amelia had no intention of intruding upon. That was his standard protective measure on these occasions, since he was not inclined toward social gatherings in general, and Lady Candover sometimes seemed at a loss without his support. Amelia considered it almost a kindness to spend some time with the woman.

Lady Candover stood on the edge of a group of matrons, watching her daughter dance with a stalwart young man a

few years her senior. Genevieve's two married sisters were in
the group as well, both of them large with child. Amelia
supposed, with an inward sigh, that Genevieve would be in a
similar condition by a year from now. It wasn't difficult to
cut Lady Candover off from the others. With a smile and a
kindly comment that Genevieve was a charming girl, she
placed herself between the baronet's wife and her daughters.

"Oh, Lady Amelia, how good of you to say so," Lady
Candover murmured. "It's such a nerve-racking time, isn't
it, waiting to see if a child will take? But I do think she's
going on very well, don't you?" A flood of color rushed up
into her cheeks suddenly. Amelia couldn't understand the
cause until the older woman stammered, "Not that you
didn't take. . . . That is, anyone could see you were immensely admired from the first time you put in an appearance in London society. Why, you'd have been the talk of
the town if Sally Cheriton hadn't come out the same season.
I mean, you *were* the talk of the town, of course, but Sally
Cheriton was always doing such outrageous things, wasn't
she? And Lady Caroline. People always make such a fuss
over the obstreperous ones. They don't seem to notice those
who are well-behaved."

It was possibly the longest speech Lady Candover had yet
made in society, but her words did not, somehow, seem to
comfort her for what she considered a grievous faux pas.
Amelia quickly interjected a word as her hostess prepared to
further muddle the matter. "I understand Lord Verwood is
from Derbyshire."

Lady Candover looked utterly confused, and then relieved. "Why, so he is. Sir Arthur knows him very well. Or,
maybe not so well. They do know one another. That is, I'm
sure they've met before."

"Then his home is not, perhaps, too far from yours?"

"A matter of twenty miles, I should think. No, closer to
twenty-five, as he's beyond Chesterfield."

"That's a fair distance in the country," Amelia acknowledged. "I don't suppose you've ever been to his home."

"No, never. Some years ago I met his mother, but she's
gone now. His father, too. I don't believe they approved of

his going into the army, as an only child, you know. There was some talk that his father would get him a seat in the House, just to keep him occupied and out of the army, but nothing came of it."

This was just the sort of thing Amelia wanted to learn, and she pressed for more detail. "Did he actually stand for a seat?"

"I don't think so. He was an impatient young fellow, I believe, and couldn't be bothered with waiting around for a safe seat. But I could be wrong," she added hastily. "That's just county gossip."

"Have you heard anything of him since he returned? Was he wounded?"

Lady Candover was vague on the subject. "I heard he was in Derbyshire recuperating for a while. Or was that Tom Owlsbury? Perhaps both of them. They were friends as boys, or so I surmise. The Owlsburys have all been a little wild. Nothing extravagant! Just the usual playfulness as youngsters."

"Did Mr. Owlsbury go to school with him at Harrow?"

"Harrow? Dear me, no. The Owlsburys never have two pennies to rub together. Maybe that's what makes them so wild," Lady Candover said thoughtfully.

"And Lord Verwood," Amelia pursued, fearful of losing Lady Candover's attention, "is he married?"

The older woman blinked at her. "Married? Oh, I shouldn't think so. When would he have had the time to marry? Unless he chose some exotic woman while on his travels."

Which made his army career sound like the Grand Tour, Amelia thought, discouraged. "I take it you haven't seen him previously in London."

"Goodness, no. We weren't on the kind of terms where he'd be likely to leave a calling card. We did just hear that he was in the city, though, and thought it proper to send an invitation for this evening."

"Do you happen to remember how you heard he was in town?"

Lady Candover gave her a puzzled, indeed a very

peculiar, look, before shrugging her shoulders. "Heavens, I haven't the slightest idea. One just does hear, doesn't one?"

"Yes, of course," Amelia agreed in the most demure manner possible. "He's rather a friend of my brother's, you see. I thought possibly Peter mentioned it to you."

"Ah, perhaps." Lady Candover clearly felt the subject wasn't of the least interest. "If you'll excuse me, Lady Amelia, I should just speak to Mrs. Woolbridge for a moment."

"Certainly." Amelia watched the older woman struggle through the crowd toward a matron with what must have been two dozen ostrich plumes in her frizzy white hair. People did think you were awfully peculiar if you asked unusual questions. Poor Lady Candover patently believed there was something strange about Amelia's interest in Lord Verwood, but she was too polite to say so. Amelia decided it was time to abandon her efforts for the evening, and enjoy herself, as Peter had suggested. She placed herself in a spot where the searching Mr. Rollings would see her, and accepted the next dance.

But that was the first evening she had the distinct impression Lord Verwood was watching her. Until then it had seemed only peculiar that he happened to appear wherever she went. Even if two people moved in the same circles, it was highly unlikely one would run into the other so often, but since that seemed to be the case, for a week Amelia had accepted it. At the Candovers' she began to have doubts. Twice when she glanced over at the viscount, he was looking at her. Such a thing had happened before, of course. There were a certain number of gentlemen who found her attractive, and had been known to follow her progress during the course of an evening. But those men invariably approached her at some point and begged the favor of a dance. Lord Verwood never even spoke to her, and pretended, when she happened to catch his eye, that he didn't see her at all. A very strange and annoying circumstance.

Lady Amelia did not attend exactly the same functions as her brother. If that had been the case, she wouldn't have been as surprised to see Verwood here and there, with Peter. But when she and Trudy decided to go to the Hampworths' rather than the Comptons', there Verwood was, with his unruly black hair and his fierce eyes, standing in a corner watching her again. It was really too much, and yet there wasn't a thing Amelia could do about it. Once, while she was dancing (and listening to the most outrageous compliments from Rollings), she glanced over to see Verwood speaking with Aunt Trudy. He was, of course, long gone by the time she rejoined her aunt.

"What did Lord Verwood want with you?" she asked when she got her aunt alone.

Trudy frowned at her from under a confection of lavender-and-pink lace of which she was particularly fond. "He didn't *want* anything, my dear girl. The merest civility brought him over to speak with me."

"And what did you speak about?"

Her aunt sniffed. "The most ordinary things, I assure you. What's gotten into you, Amelia? Have you formed a tendre for the fellow? I wouldn't do that, you know. These military types are the devil to land. They're used to being in charge, and they don't want anyone who'll speak up to them. Have you ever been in Mrs. Ovington's house? Well, it would open your eyes. Everything is run with the greatest precision because her husband was once in the Horse Guards. And not very recently, you may be sure. She's always in the greatest dither that he'll find something amiss. No, no, you wouldn't want to consider an alliance in that direction."

"An alliance! Your mind must be gathering wool, Aunt Trudy. I haven't the slightest romantic interest in Lord Verwood! In fact, I think there's something peculiar about him." Amelia could feel the color rising to her cheeks and willed it down as she plied a fan briskly just below her face. "How could you think I'd developed a tendre for him? He's never even spoken to me, let alone danced with me."

"Ah, I see how it is," Trudy murmured with a complacent nod of her colorful head. "You resent his indifference to you. Well, I shouldn't let that bother me. One can see clearly enough that he's not one for the ladies. Whom has he stood up with this evening? Marissa Hampworth? That's only to be expected; it's her ball. And Julia Binderton? I saw Colonel Binderton lead him straight over to the girl. No getting out of that sort of spot, now, is there?" Trudy pursed her lips in an imitation of thought. "He did bring refreshments to that pretty little Bissett girl. Now, she's just the kind of girl an army man might cotton to. Fluff straight through from her head to her toes. Pretty as a picture, of course."

"Have you been watching him all night?" Amelia demanded. Trudy wasn't usually so knowledgeable about which gentleman had danced with which lady.

"One can't help but notice him," Trudy grumbled. "He's half a head taller than most of the people in this room."

Only Beningbrough topped him, it was true. Perhaps that was the reason he seemed so obvious. Amelia had thought it must be his air of negligent disrespect for the proceedings. Even dressed appropriately, he exhibited none of the elegance of his fellowman. There was something unpolished about him; a bluntness that was not, perhaps, unattractive, but it certainly wasn't the standard in society gentlemen. His features, too, were aggressively rugged, suffering from none of the pampered softness of his associates. And the size of his hands! One could not imagine how a fragile champagne glass managed to escape unshattered from his grip.

Amelia was not particularly aware that she'd been staring at him, her violet eyes narrowed under furrowed brows. The fan in her hand had stilled and come to rest unconsciously against the bare skin above her jonquil gown. It was, though unstudied, a rather provocative pose, since she quite automatically carried herself with remarkable assurance and often stood with one hip thrust slightly forward, a posture which had long recommended itself to her because it eased the tiredness caused by dancing.

Because her mind was wandering over the few facts she'd learned about him, Amelia didn't really notice that Verwood was moving toward her until he had almost covered the distance between them. Her mind snapped back to the present with an unpleasant jolt. Whatever must he think of her? His expression was especially grim, even for him, as he closed the remaining distance.

Whom was she supposed to be joining the country dance with? For a moment her mind refused to dredge up a name, and then, with relief, she realized it was Bepton. She cast a frantic glance about her, but could see him nowhere. Verwood stood in front of her now, his brows raised in query, the line of his mouth straight and uncompromising. There was a faintly sardonic note to his voice when he spoke.

"Lady Amelia? Was there some problem?"

"Goodness no, Lord Verwood." She wasn't at all comfortable under his scrutiny. He made her feel decidedly gauche, and Lady Amelia was not accustomed to feeling gauche. An outrageous scheme entered her mind, and without giving herself time to consider its consequences, she said archly, "I dare say you've forgotten you solicited my hand for this country dance."

— 4 —

His eyes narrowed only slightly. There was no other indication of his reaction, one way or the other. He bowed slightly to her, saying, "I do beg your pardon, Lady Amelia. Shall we?"

She accepted his proffered arm. There didn't seem to be anything else to do, though she was now feeling slightly nervous about what she'd done. What if he didn't know the steps for this particular country dance? Well, it would serve her right if he fumbled his way through the whole thing. When she was standing in the ladies' line, opposite him, she found it difficult to meet his eyes, but forced herself to appear completely at ease.

"Where did you serve in the army, Lord Verwood?" she asked.

"Most recently, in Egypt."

"Is that where you were wounded?"

"I was wounded in the leg."

For the merest fraction of a second she saw a gleam of humor in the fierce black eyes, but it was gone so quickly she could almost believe she had imagined it. "Well, yes," she muttered, "I could tell by your limp."

Their hands were joined, at shoulder height, as they promenaded down the line. The other dancers were watching them, naturally, so it was not a propitious moment for him to ask, with astonishment, "Do I have a limp?"

Amelia was ordinarily quite a graceful dancer. If, during

her first season, she had not been designated as a diamond of the first water, she had at least been acknowledged as the most accomplished and elegant dancer of all the young women who made their bows that year. She stumbled now, flushed with embarrassment. If she had met his eyes, she would have again seen that flash of humor, but she was too mortified to even look at him as they parted to continue down opposite sides of the lines. By the time she reached her spot, however, she had decided it was impossible he didn't know he had a limp, and she stared across at him for the brief moment before she joined hands with the second gentleman in the line. There was nothing to be read in his face now but indifference.

Her desire to question him had abated completely. When they were joined by the dance again, she remained mute, waiting for him to offer some pleasantry, if he was able. He didn't seem to even realize that such an effort was called for, but listened unabashedly to the couple next to them, interjecting a remark now and then, something that smacked of good-natured raillery. Amelia began to wish she'd never come to the ball.

It was a great effort to thank him for the set. She mumbled something wholly unintelligible as he led her back to Aunt Trudy, but he merely stopped abruptly to ask in a determinedly patient voice, "I beg your pardon? There's so much noise here; I didn't catch what you said."

"I said *thank you*," she hissed through clenched teeth.

"My pleasure, I'm sure. I trust you know you can rely on me anytime to rescue you from such an awkward situation. These Bond Street beaux can't be trusted to remember their names after a few glasses of champagne. Who was it stood you up?"

Amelia glared at him and said nothing.

"It doesn't matter," he said, sounding obnoxiously hearty. "Peter would do the same for me, if there were the need. Quite a good chap, your brother. I'm sure he has your best interests at heart. Not every young woman could say that about a sibling. I hope, in future, he considers your welfare before even that of his country, and I hope you have the good sense to follow his advice."

His eyes had that all-knowing look now, as though he could see right into her mind. (And didn't approve of what he saw there.) "Please don't trouble yourself on my account, Lord Verwood," Amelia said with an angry toss of her head. "It must be a great strain for you to say so much all at once, and I assure you I'm perfectly capable of attending to my own welfare."

"If you believe that, you're less astute than I gave you credit for being," he murmured. Then he bowed stiffly and turned on his heel.

She refused to watch him walk away, but turned to her aunt instead. Trudy, unable to hear their exchange, though she had tried, said, "I thought he'd never asked you to dance."

"He never has," Amelia replied, with what she hoped was a mysterious smile. She immediately turned to her next partner, who was already standing at her elbow. "Ah, Mr. Gray. It's frightfully warm in here, isn't it? Would you mind if we get a glass of champagne before we join the set?"

In the carriage, on the way home, Amelia sat back against the squabs and listened, more or less, to her aunt's commentary on the evening. Trudy had a way of making each evening sound the same as the last, which, Amelia realized, wasn't very far from the truth. To be sure, the company varied minimally, the decorations changed from place to place (but not significantly), the food was distinctly similar, and the music identical. On the other hand, it was the most interesting time of year, during the season. There were more private parties, as well as more public events, to keep one from boredom. But when you were enduring your third season as a marriageable young woman, the similarity of events was rather daunting.

Amelia hadn't been brought out until she was nineteen, owing to the circumstances surrounding her parents' incarceration and death. Looking back, she could remember how

excited she'd been that first season, ready for some gaiety in
her life, anticipating the romantic advances of elegant
gentlemen and the intelligent friendship of similarly minded
young women. There had been grave disappointments. So
much had seemed frivolous rather than fun, after a while.
Only at small, intimate parties had there been real conversation. Only through Peter's allowing her to help in his
work had she felt useful.

More than ever Amelia was convinced Lord Verwood was
the one who'd changed Peter's mind about letting her help.
He had as much as said so when he brought her from the
dance floor to Aunt Trudy. Since he most assuredly took no
personal interest in her, why would he have interfered in the
first place? It occurred to Amelia as she stared out into the
dark London night that the most likely reason was that she
had somehow stumbled onto something important, and he
didn't want her to learn more. Was that because of concern
for her safety—or because she might find out something dis-
advantageous to him?

Trudy gave an impatient tug to the sleeve of Amelia's blue
velvet redingote. "We're home, Amelia. Where's your mind
wandering?"

"Not very far," Amelia sighed, following her aunt out of
the carriage and up the stairs into the house in Grosvenor
Square.

Alexander Thomas Alresford, Viscount Verwood, did not
stay long at the Hampworths' after Lady Amelia and her
aunt took their leave. In spite of the huge crowd, he was
aware when they left because he seldom let Lady Amelia out
of his sight. This was from no personal fondness for the
young lady. He didn't, after all, know her very well, and he
had not, as some of the Bond Street beaux were fond of
proclaiming (to anyone who would listen, *about* anyone who
had happened to catch their fancy), been stricken by her
enormous violet eyes or her dazzling smile. His concern was
purely and simply that she would get herself in trouble and
ruin Peter's endeavors, and his own. It had seemed safest to

suggest her leaving town, but as she wouldn't, he could easily keep an eye on her.

Actually, there was another facet to the problem, one which he had not even broached to Peter when he'd discussed the matter. It was, in many ways, irrelevant. At least to Verwood. To Peter it would no doubt seem very relevant indeed. It concerned Lady Amelia's methods of extracting information.

The Hampworths had a house in Berkeley Square, a reasonable walk to South Street. Verwood had, in fact, walked there, and intended to walk back home, but he was feeling restless when he left the overheated mansion. So instead of turning into Hill Street, he walked around the square and down Berkeley Street to Piccadilly.

A chuckle escaped him when he remembered poor Lady Amelia's embarrassed flush when she'd mentioned his limp. Of course he knew he had a limp. The owner of a bum leg could hardly be oblivious of such a nuisance. The wound was healing, and his doctor assured him the limp would eventually disappear, but he couldn't resist the urge to embarrass Lady Amelia, after the way she'd manipulated him into dancing with her. Verwood didn't much like dancing, especially with the limp. Oh, he'd done it, of necessity, a number of times during the last week. That didn't mean he enjoyed it.

Berkeley Street joined Piccadilly just beyond Green Park, and Verwood turned left toward St. James's Street, where any number of activities went forth day and night. There were Brooks's and White's, for the Whigs and Tories, respectively, where gambling would go on until all hours. He passed Hoby's, where he'd had his military boots made, and now, reluctantly, his Hessians. There was a grocer's at number 3 and Lock's the hatter's at number 6. Lock's charged exorbitant amounts for their beplumed and gold-laced shakos, as though all Hussars and Dragoons were good for a fortune. Hotels dotted the street, too—Symon's, Ellis's, Fenton's, and Reddish's.

Verwood was headed for Boodle's, across the wide

thoroughfare from Brooks's. Since his return to London he'd
steered clear of either of the politically affiliated clubs. The
Ministry of All Talents which had formed after Pitt's death
the preceding year had not proven very talented after all.
The only thing they'd accomplished was the abolition of the
slave trade, which was a worthy achievement, but hardly
enough when it should have addressed itself to the
Napoleonic dangers on the Continent. Their prosecution of
the war was lethargic, and Verwood hadn't been much distressed to witness their downfall.

It remained to be seen whether the wholly Tory adminis-
tration under the old Duke of Portland would be any more
successful. "All of Pitt's friends without Pitt," as Moore had
said. Already Lord Granville Gower had been sent off to
Russia and Sir Arthur Paget to the Aegean. The government had ordered up transports, and reached agreement
with Russia and Prussia. But everything moved so slowly
with a parliamentary system.

Verwood had seen the unconscionable waste of men in
Egypt, which was still going on. He had agreed with Sir John
Moore that a military expedition was necessary to support
the forcing of the Dardanelles, but the Cabinet had instead
ordered Lieutenant General Fox to land six thousand troops
in Egypt. Under Major General Mackenzie Fraser they had
taken Alexandria, but had subsequently suffered hor-
rendous losses at Rosetta. And now Fraser's forces were
blockaded in Alexandria. Only time would tell whether the
new government would be more forceful in its efforts, and
more realistic in its use of its limited resources.

Wounded at Rosetta, Verwood had been lucky enough to
find transport back to England after resigning his
commission. There seemed little point in continuing,
disabled, with the misdirected forces. He had begun to conceive that his influence at home would be more useful than
in the field. There were not enough militarily knowledgeable men here to understand the best advice they were
getting from the field, in the voices of Sir John Moore and
Sir Arthur Wellesley. He intended to see that they listened
more seriously to that advice.

But more than that. Verwood handed his hat and gloves to the footman who approached him at Boodle's. Lamps burned in the hallway but no sound penetrated from behind the heavy wooden doors on either side. "Is Lord Welsford here this evening?" he asked, thinking it just possible Peter would have escaped some boring entertainment to come.

"No, milord, I haven't seen him." The footman draped Verwood's coat over his arm, careful to avoid wrinkling it.

"Monsieur Chartier, then?"

"Yes, he's in the room on the right."

Verwood was led to an enormous room, its Axminster carpet mellow in the light from several crystal chandeliers. There were large round green-baize-covered tables down the street side of the room, and smaller square tables opposite. A lamp stood on each of the larger tables, while the smaller were in partial shadow, though the play at them seemed no less serious. He nodded to Tytherly, who was paired off with a gentleman Verwood had never met, probably playing piquet. He didn't stop to find out, but cast his gaze over the fuller tables, where he felt sure he would find Chartier.

The Frenchman was only recently arrived in London, within the month, he said. Which was one of the things about him that interested Lord Verwood, since he had himself seen the fellow two months previously leaving Dr. Braithwait's house in Golden Square. Dr. Braithwait had his surgery in his home, through a separate entrance at the side of the house. Verwood had become quite familiar with it during the period when the worst of his sufferings were over, but he was instructed to drop by weekly so the good doctor could check his progress.

On the day he'd seen Chartier, he'd been suffering some pain, and had stopped beside the railings to give the leg a short rest. He'd taken two balls at Rosetta, one in the thigh and one in the knee. The wound in his thigh had healed quickly, but the knee injury, though not as disastrous as it might have been, continued to plague him because of the constant strain placed on that joint by walking. Not that Braithwait had counselled him against exercise; the doctor had insisted he must use it to keep it from stiffening completely.

It was when he was leaning over to rub the aching knee that he happened to glance through the railings at the sound of a door closing. A man came out of Dr. Braithwait's surgery, a very ordinary man, so far as Verwood could see. He was obviously well-dressed, young, with neatly brushed hair and attractive features. Verwood hardly noticed him, except when the young man inadvertently stepped in dog dirt on the pathway and gave vent to a very Gallic exclamation and shrug. The fellow was still scraping his boot against the pavement as he passed Verwood, whom he didn't notice at all.

If the viscount hadn't happened to be introduced to the young man two months later, he would never have recollected the incident. But in the course of their conversation Chartier happened to mention he'd only recently (within the month) come to stay in London. In conjunction with his obviously French background, this struck Verwood as rather suspicious, and he asked if Chartier had never been to London before.

"Oh, many times, many times," the fellow replied cheerfully. "My sister and I live in Hampshire, with relatives. But I have come to stay in London, and soon, soon, I will bring her here as well."

So the matter might have ended, except that it nagged at Verwood. When he asked Dr. Braithwait about Chartier, the good doctor insisted he'd never met the man. A thorough check of his records, which the viscount urged, revealed no listing of his name. Verwood decided it wouldn't hurt for him to form an acquaintance with the elusive Frenchman. A false name, a deliberate lie—there might be a reasonable explanation, but the viscount couldn't offhand think of one that satisfied him.

They had met at Boodle's, and it was to Boodle's that Verwood went to seek out the young Frenchman. His observations led him to several conclusions. The Frenchman gambled, and he seldom walked away from the tables a loser. But even Verwood couldn't find any reason to believe he cheated. Chartier never stayed in a game if the stakes became to high; he drank moderately and handled his cards shrewdly. When he lost, he merely shrugged his shoulders and said with a smile, "Tomorrow will be better."

His main purpose did not seem to be the gambling, actually, but making contacts with his fellow gamblers. These companions approved of his droll wit, of his self-deprecating good nature. Verwood could not discover who had put him up for membership, but he did know there was none of the sly gossip that ordinarily followed a not-up-to-snuff new denizen of the hallowed club. Which spoke for the man's charm more than for his antecedents. Verwood was unable to find any member of the regular French community in London who was familiar with him.

One evening, when the play had become too high at his table, Chartier was about to leave when Verwood approached him with an offer of a hand of piquet. The younger man smiled and shrugged. "My pockets are not so plump this evening."

"I've no stomach for high play myself," the viscount assured him. "Just a quiet game by the fire."

Chartier had quickly assented, making a point of offering the sofa closest to the hearth to his companion. Though this deference to his age (he was twenty-eight, to the fellow's twenty-three or -four, he supposed) and the ungainliness of his crippled condition annoyed Verwood, he smiled as Chartier took the straight-backed chair opposite and asked, "Can I offer you a brandy?"

"*Merci, non.* I have just had the port," he said with an arch raising of his brows, "and the stomach it would rebel at anything."

"Yes, it's heavy," Verwood agreed as he cut for the deal. "I've never had much of a taste for port myself."

They played a desultory game, talking unenthusiastically of the weather and politics and society. Chartier won the first game in five quick hands. His brow was wrinkled with a thoughtful frown as he fingered the cards in the new hand he was dealt. "I had intended to bring my sister to London," he said finally. "But now I am not sure. It would not be good for her, the—how shall I say it?—the lax attitude I've discovered here."

Verwood played a card as he said, "I shouldn't think there was anything to worry about, Chartier. Every young woman I've ever seen has been surrounded by a bevy of chaperones."

"There are chaperones, yes. My cousin could come as Veronique's chaperone, but that would not be good enough, I fear. My sister is not used to company, she is not used to the casual attitude of the London society. She has a purity, my Veronique, which would, I think, be sullied in this city."

"Oh, I doubt that. She'd be well-protected."

"No, no, you do not understand. One who is so naive would be certain to be influenced by the attitude of those around her."

"She's not likely to consort with ladies of damaged reputation," Verwood said, smiling at the thought.

"But even the highest, the greatest of the ladies, haven't the modesty of a properly brought-up young French girl," Chartier insisted, leaning forward to more fully catch the viscount's attention. "Me, I know. You dance with a young woman once, twice, and she allows you to take liberties with her."

"That's never been my experience," Verwood said, sounding almost regretful.

"Yes, yes, it happens. Instead of a dance, she will go to the balcony with you, behind the curtains where no one can see her. Her chaperone is perhaps in the card room or engaged in conversation with the other chaperones. Even the sister of an earl, who seems the model of propriety. I don't say I am blameless. No, no, but the wine, the music, the violet eyes, the hair of gold, one can be carried away, *non?*"

"Hmm. Yes, I suppose so."

"I am not telling tales. No lady's name would ever pass my lips. I am a little smitten by this lady, I admit, and I take her to the balcony. But does she run away when I take a liberty? No. Does she perhaps slap my face and call me a rogue? No. Does she protest her youth and innocence? No and no. So. If

I were to bring my cherished sister to such a society, might she not adopt these London morals? I could not take such a chance."

Verwood assured him once again that no harm would come to his sister in London, and wondered why he was the one chosen to receive this unusual tale. He was not familiar with the description of Lady Amelia at the time, but it didn't take him long to discover the only earl's sister who fit the description. Fortunately, in the discovery he also found Peter, who shared his commitment to the war against the French. Verwood did not, of course, tell Peter of the imputation on Lady Amelia's character. Well, one really couldn't with such a devoted brother. But he did convince Peter that there was some danger in Amelia's activities, that they might of necessity place her in awkward situations. Reluctantly, Peter agreed.

Still, Verwood had taken it on himself to keep an eye on Lady Amelia. Not on account of her unorthodox behavior, but because he wanted to make sure she was obeying Peter's dictum. He had made note of her discussions with Ellis Winchfield and Lady Candover. Well, it would keep her out of harm's way trying to find out something disreputable about himself, for he never doubted that was her goal. And it couldn't, unless she thought he was a spy, be considered in the same league with what she'd been doing. The possibility that she thought he was a spy amused him and he very nearly laughed out loud until he remembered where he was.

He brought his attention back to the room, scanning it once again for Chartier. For the last week he hadn't run into the Frenchman at Boodle's and he had been relieved to hear the footman say he was present this evening. Just as his eye settled on the young man at the farthest table, Chartier rose and collected his winnings. As he came toward Verwood, his face broke into a charming smile.

"Ah, my lord," he said, "I have taken your advice, after much searching of my soul. I have brought my sister Veronique to London and hope to have the honor of presenting her to you in the near future."

— 5 —

Amelia studied, with something less than approval, the new hairstyle Bridget had arranged for her. The ringlets which were reflected in the mirror gave her too frivolous an appearance, but it was getting late and she'd have to leave them for the time being. She smiled at the girl and said, "Yes, thank you, that will be fine for this evening. But they make me look more like eighteen than twenty-one, don't you think?"

"They're all the rage, Lady Amelia, and you look very pretty." Bridget cocked her head to one side, considering. "Perhaps they don't just perfectly *suit* you, but they soften your chin, you know."

A twinkle appeared in Amelia's eyes. Bridget would never come right out and say that such a determined chin hardly belonged on a maiden her age, but Amelia was aware of it. Long ago she had accepted this fatal flaw in her otherwise acceptable appearance. There had been times when she'd wondered if it wasn't a blessing in disguise. Men had tended to take her a little more seriously than the other young women, and the matrons had tended to assume a high-minded aspect to her behavior.

There were points in which she was both serious and high-minded, but they weren't necessarily where others thought they were. She didn't, for instance, take seriously the wagers and sporting events gentlemen were often so profoundly interested in, though she was perfectly willing to lend them her attention when they spoke of these matters. Nor was she high-minded about preserving the sacrosanct precincts of the ton from encroachers and dilettantes. It was, after all, amongst the encroachers and dilettantes that she was most likely to come across information of use to Peter. Not that her archenemies were likely to be such trifling fellows, but only the trifling fellows were foolish enough to run off at the mouth! Amelia felt sure her real adversaries were a much more complicated and sophisticated lot, and at times she was relieved that she hadn't run into any of them.

What she *was* serious and high-minded about were her projects for the worthy suffering of London. Having come of age, she had at her disposal a handsome income, the whole of which she could scarcely use on her own ornamentation and amusement. It should not be supposed that she doled out her benevolence merely for the pleasure of living up to her excessive income. No, Amelia felt the severe injustice of living in luxury while so many around her among London's teeming poor could scarcely eke out a living.

The prescribed method for aiding these victims of want was to subscribe to various worthy causes—orphanages, schools, homes for unmarried pregnant women. And Amelia did her share of this sort of charity giving, as her mother before her had. But there was something altogether too straightforward and distant about that kind of help. One could, of course, visit an orphanage in one's white gloves and plumed hats, and hear the children say "Thank you" in an unnerving chorus. Amelia found no gratification in that sort of contact.

She had searched her soul to find a more personal way to be of assistance. And also to make sure that it wasn't a matter of pride which led her to want to be involved in the lives of those she helped. Perhaps, she thought, she simply wanted the satisfaction of hearing thanksgiving solely aimed at herself. This seemed quite a likely possibility, so she had made it a rule that her intercession in any given matter was handled by Robert, a strapping footman who held the terrors of London's less-desirable areas as naught. She remained nameless to her beneficiaries, though Robert did not. There were occasions, such as now, when this proved to be a little tricky.

Bridget had adjusted the last ringlet to her satisfaction when there was a light tap at Amelia's door. Since Trudy always entered without bothering to knock, Amelia thought it was probably Peter, trying to speed up her progress. He had kindly agreed to accompany them to the Chithursts', though Amelia assumed he would not stay there long. He'd mentioned a "late meeting," which invariably meant something to do with his activities for the War Department.

"Come in."

Robert opened the door slightly and stood there looking acutely embarrassed. "I'm sorry to bother you, Lady Amelia, when you're about to go out. It's the boy Carson. He says his mama is horridly sick."

"Is he here?"

"Yes, in the kitchen."

"I'll come to see him."

Tommy Carson was one of her special projects. The minister of a parish church in St. Giles Rookery had brought him to her attention. His father was dead and his mother had three other, younger children to care for and feed. The Reverend Sidney Symons, whom she had met at an orphanage, had mentioned him to her one day as an example of how the youngsters in the slums started to go bad. When there was no honest money forthcoming, they took to begging or to crime to help support their families. The little money his mother could make from bringing in laundry was insufficient for her family. At eight, Tommy had taken to the tricks of the streets, pickpocketing mostly, at which he was very skilled.

"His mother's an upright woman," Reverend Symons had said, "and it's nearly breaking her heart what he's doing, but she can't refuse the money and see her children suffer. What's she to do? Tommy's always been a good boy, but he sees himself as having to provide for the family now his father is gone. There's no honest way an eight-year-old can earn enough to help out."

Amelia had given the matter a great deal of thought. It would have been simple enough to drop a pile of money on the Carsons. The price of a silk scarf would probably feed them for a month. But it wasn't a lasting solution, and it didn't take into account the necessity to wean the boy from his newfound life of crime. Together with the reverend she'd come up with a plan: she would pay the boy for attending school, and his siblings as they reached school age. The hours school covered, together with the time the children needed to spend doing chores in their home, would keep Tommy off the streets and consequently honest, Amelia hoped. So far the plan had worked fairly well, with Mrs. Carson's cooperation.

As she descended the main staircase in her dancing slippers, the doorbell sounded, but she paid no attention to it. She wasn't expecting anyone, and if Peter or Trudy were, they hadn't told her. There was a commotion coming from the kitchen area, an anguished wailing that reached clear through the door. She was headed in that direction when the door burst open and a small urchin came barrelling through, his face stained with tears and his childish voice raised in a call for Robert, who preceded Amelia by only a few paces.

Suddenly the hall seemed to be full of people. Peter emerged from his study on one side of the hall, Trudy from the drawing room beyond. Bighton was just ushering Lord Verwood through the front door. Robert scooped the frantic boy up in his arms, saying, "It's all right, lad. I was just coming."

A chorus of voices asked, "What's going on here?" Tommy noticed the crowd for the first time and shrank back against Robert, scrubbing at his eyes with small fists. Into the uncomfortable silence that followed, Amelia stepped forward and motioned Robert to set the boy down.

"There's nothing to alarm yourselves about. This is Tommy Carson and he and I are going to go into the Blue Room to see what can be done about his problem." She offered her hand to the child, who blinked at her uncertainly before laying his in it. "Robert, I'll probably need you," she remarked as she led the child toward a door across the hall from where they were all standing.

"For God's sake, Amelia," Peter protested.

Without replying, she drew the boy into the Blue Room, with Robert following, and nodded for him to close the door. "Now, then," she said, "tell me exactly what's happened with your mother, Tommy."

"She's so sick . . ." He gulped. "I think she's dying."

"Have you sent for a doctor?"

"We don't know a doctor, ma'am, and there isn't the money to pay for one."

"Well, Reverend Symons knows a doctor. Did you send for him?"

The boy nodded vigorously. "He wasn't at home. His housekeeper wouldn't help me. I didn't know where else to go."

"I see. Tell me about your mother's condition. What I mean is, how does she look? How is she acting?"

"She's all white and moaning and grabbing her stomach. Twice she's thrown up, and there was blood in it." Tommy's eyes were wide and he looked about to cry again.

Amelia turned to Robert. "Dr. Wells has gone into St. Giles Rookery before for me. See if you can get him. If not, try Dr. Harper. Take Tommy with you and stay with his mother until the situation is under control. I'll be responsible for any expenses, of course, but you'd better take this." She dug in her reticule and produced several pound notes. "Do what's necessary to have the children taken care of temporarily . . . if Mrs. Carson should have to go into hospital."

She turned her attention back to the boy. "Robert is going to take care of everything, Tommy. He'll bring a doctor for your mother. He'll find someone to take care of you and your brothers and sister while your mother's ill. I want you to be a brave boy and help him all you can. Will you do that?"

"Yes, ma'am. Thank you." His voice wavered slightly. "What if . . . my mother . . . ?"

Amelia hugged his small frame against her. "Let's be hopeful, Tommy. Sometimes things look worse than they are. You've kept up your end of the bargain about school, and we won't let you down . . . or your family. Hurry along, now; your mother needs help."

After they were gone, Amelia remained standing in the Blue Room for a few minutes, staring at the closed door. So many suffering people. How little she could do for them, how few of them she even heard about. She stiffened her slumping shoulders and fixed a smile firmly on her lips before going out into the hall. To her surprise, she found all three people waiting there, presumably expecting an explanation. She had no intention of giving one.

"I'm sorry to have kept you waiting," she said, addressing her remark somewhere between Peter and Trudy, and purposely not glancing toward Lord Verwood at all. "I'll just get my wrap."

"Oh, no, you don't!" Peter exclaimed. "I'd like to know what that was all about, Amelia."

"Why, nothing," she said, raising innocent eyes to his. "The boy is a protégé of mine. There's some trouble in his family and I've arranged for Robert to take care of it. I won't be a moment."

"You'll have to change your dress," Trudy said ominously. "There appears to be a stain on it."

Amelia glanced down at the damp mark left by the child's tears. "It's nothing. By the time we get to the party it will be dry."

Unsatisfied, but unwilling to comment further in front of their visitor, Peter and Trudy watched her hasten toward the stairs. Lord Verwood, for his part, did a rapid calculation concerning whether the urchin was young enough to be Lady Amelia's child, and decided it was impossible. Then he contemplated the chances that the boy had something to do with Lady Amelia's prohibited activity. This seemed much more likely and he frowned as he watched her graceful tread up the stairs. She really was an amazingly attractive woman, with the most delightful figure. From this angle her obstinate chin did not cause any doubts. Her profile was almost classic, after all, and Verwood studied it—and the rest of her—until she disappeared around the corner upstairs.

Trudy muttered something that sounded like "Troublesome chit!" and rolled back to the drawing room, leaving the men standing in the hall. Peter found himself under close scrutiny by his new friend and threw up a hand in mock despair. "Don't ask me what it was all about. I haven't the slightest idea. But I *don't* think it had anything to do with that other matter. One never knows what Amelia's about, you know. She has all sorts of secret plots afoot. Nothing disreputable or dangerous, I assure you. She just seems to like to keep her own counsel; it makes her feel less . . . oh, smothered, I suppose."

"She called the boy her protégé," Verwood reminded him.

"Yes, well, I think she's had something to do with a minister in St. Giles Rookery," Peter confessed. "One of these fellows who runs an orphanage and points out promising boys for the support of wealthy patrons."

"Hmm." Verwood looked totally unconvinced, and he didn't like the sound of Lady Amelia having "something to do" with a minister. Not all men of the cloth were above suspicion, after all. "St. Giles Rookery is not a place one would like to see one's sister frequent."

"Amelia never goes there unaccompanied," Peter protested. "Robert always goes with her, and undertakes any number of commissions for her."

Robert, so far as Lord Verwood was concerned, was less above suspicion than any minister could ever be. Why, the fellow must be as large as a prizefighter, and was, in addition, more handsome than most of the actors one saw at Drury Lane. He looked like a soldier in that elegant Welsford livery, not like a common chore-runner. Verwood's imagination seemed to be turning more lurid by the moment, and he brought himself back to reality with a stern effort. "She's your sister, Peter," he said. "I'm sure you know how to keep a rein on her."

Not wanting to confess that he'd never had the slightest

idea how to do such a thing with the ardent Amelia, Peter merely shrugged and said, "She's a very levelheaded girl, Alexander, for all her enthusiasms. Very generous, too, you know."

Though Peter referred to her charity, Verwood had other sorts of visions of generosity and carefully repressed a shudder. A time would come, he feared, when he would have to be more blunt with Peter about Lady Amelia's indiscretions. However, when he brought up the matter, he wanted to have a little more information, so he determined on a course of continuing to watch the young lady. Delay, he realized, might be hazardous in her case, but he was not a man given to acting on misguided impulse. He moved, when he did, with the proper grounding, and with considerable force.

The party of four drove to the Stratfords' in thoughtful silence, broken occasionally by a civil remark from one or the other of those in the carriage. Trudy, who had not been consulted on the viscount's accompanying them, was a little put out with her nephew, though she did her best not to show it. Amelia's mind was wholly occupied with the emergency at the Carsons', but she had long since trained herself to disguise this sort of concern, knowing precisely what was expected of her at an evening entertainment. One more ball would be no more difficult to manage than any other facet of her very social life.

The Stratfords lived on Portman Square in a magnificent house notable for its towerlike domed staircase and an ingeniously designed group of rooms planned *en suite* and carefully contrasted in shape, character, and proportion. The decoration of them consisted in the slimmest of pilaster orders supporting a minimal entablature and almost no cornice under the restrained riches of an Adams ceiling. Pastel colors of green, beige, and pink provided a mute background for the swirl of guests clothed in their finest gowns and magnificently cut coats. Everything was understated elegance, a refreshing change from some of the overly ornamented houses in which Amelia found herself.

The guests, too, were the cream of the ton. The Stratfords had no need to prove their social prominence by inviting everyone in London, for the inevitable "crush." Their festivities were always well-attended but the list of guests was never so long as to make the rooms crowded or uncomfortable. Amelia had always admired this flaunting of social convention, though she supposed it might merely indicate an overweening pride on their part, an implicit declaration that they refused to associate with less than the best people.

Which was why she was surprised to see M. Chartier at the gathering. There was, in her mind, question enough about whether Lord Verwood would have been there if he hadn't accompanied them. Had he actually received an invitation, or had Peter accepted the invitation for them, indicating that Verwood was Amelia's escort? An interesting speculation, and one which Amelia might have mentally pursued if she hadn't been so struck with M. Chartier's presence. She was astonished that the Stratfords even knew him, let alone invited him to their ball.

For M. Chartier claimed no title, though half the Frenchmen in London seemed to do so without much cause. He was new on the scene, and not above suspicion, in Amelia's eyes. In London one didn't question a man's loyalties simply because he was French, of course. The French aristocracy certainly had little good to say about Napoleon, but there were those whose attachment to their heritage made it seem beneficial for the French nation to conquer as much of the Continent as possible, Napoleon notwithstanding.

Amelia's first exchanges with M. Chartier had convinced her it would be worthwhile to learn a little more about him. A Frenchman living on the south coast could do a great deal of damage to the English, if he had a mind to. There was also his Gallic excitability to arouse her curiosity. He spoke passionately on any subject that surfaced, from horse racing to the more curious customs of English society, such as the fact that the kissing of ladies' hands had gone out of style here. M. Chartier considered it a travesty that such a time-honored tradition should be so callously set aside.

There were other things about him which disturbed her:

his obvious attempt to ingratiate himself with gentlemen who were knowledgeable about the English position regarding the war with France; his lack of friendship with other French émigrés; his shifty eyes. This last bore no small amount of weight with her. Amelia was convinced you could tell a great deal about a person by his eyes.

After the episode on the balcony, M. Chartier had changed his attitude toward her. He had never once looked her straight in the eye. Strange, that. For the last week or so, she hadn't seen him at all, and had rather hoped he'd disappeared from the London scene altogether. But, no, here he was with a beautiful girl in tow, a sparkling-eyed French beauty whom he identified, to Peter and Lord Verwood, as his sister, Veronique Chartier. M. Chartier seemed reluctant to introduce her to Amelia, though he had very little choice in the matter. He managed not to meet her eyes, and to mumble her name.

Amelia was surprised to hear Lord Verwood addressed with great familiarity by the Frenchman. M. Chartier was smiling and bowing and generally fawning all over the place when he got to the viscount. "This is my sister, of whom I have spoken to you, milord. You were so kind as to give me your advice concerning her introduction to London, and I'm pleased that you are one of the first gentlemen to whom I present her."

If Amelia expected the viscount to depress this sort of pretension, she was much mistaken. He greeted Mademoiselle Chartier with more finesse than she had previously believed him capable of, and went so far as to congratulate M. Chartier on having so lovely a relative. Really, it was quite sickening. But what distressed her most of all was Peter.

At five-and-twenty, the Earl of Welsford seemed to have entirely escaped being touched by even the greatest beauties of the day. A very eligible bachelor, he had spent large amounts of time dallying with this young lady and then that one. He had a reputation for charm and wit; his looks were admired; his title and wealth were the envy of many. Amelia had known several women who would have been thrilled to elicit the kind of look Peter now gave Mademoiselle Chartier. It was compounded of frank admiration, a dreamy kind of awe, and, worst of all, just the slightest element of surprise.

"Has anyone solicited the first set with you, Mademoiselle Chartier?" he inquired.

"No, milord," she replied, her eyes modestly downcast.

"Then I wonder if you would do me the honor."

The biggest, bluest eyes Amelia had ever seen slowly swept up to meet his gaze. They were filled with innocence, humor, even a touch of self-mockery. "Nothing would please me more," she sighed, and offered him her hand.

As Amelia watched them walk onto the dance floor, she felt a momentary touch of alarm and found that her own gaze automatically lifted to Lord Verwood. He let out an inaudible exclamation as he, too, watched the couple, and then turned brusquely to her to ask, "Shall we join this set, Lady Amelia?"

None of his polite phrases for her, of course. He almost made it sound as though she expected him to ask her, which she certainly did not. She was unaware that her nose twitched, but she was aware of her voice answering, "If you wish, milord."

His intent, she soon found, was to place them next to Peter and the lovely Veronique.

— 6 —

Mlle. Chartier's English was perfect, with only the faintest trace of an accent. Oh, but that trace was delicious. It even appeared, somehow, in her laughter, which was warm and spontaneous. Without the least observable effort to do so, she had all the gentlemen in the set hanging on her every word. Her excitement about being at the ball, about being in London, about meeting all these fascinating people, was more than evident—but not in a naive gushing of childish phrases. No, it showed in her eyes, which glowed with the thrill of it all. Her healthy pink cheeks radiated it and her voice echoed with its undercurrent.

Not that she put herself forward in any way by speaking out of turn, or by speaking at all unless spoken to. But Peter questioned her, gently probing into her background and her interests. Verwood, too, though it was none of his duty, addressed remarks to her. Which of course meant that his undivided attention wasn't aimed at Amelia, who couldn't have cared less. She was not, however, quite used to being ignored by her partner and had an insane desire to flirt with one of the other gentlemen in the set, except that such a course of action would have discomposed some other lady.

And she was curious to hear what the French girl had to say for herself. Amelia was convinced that M. Chartier was up to no good, and this introduction of his sister (was she really?) into society merely made her more suspicious. True, there was some similarity between the brother and sister, the same brown hair and blue eyes, a resemblance even in the delicate molding of the faces. On the other hand, her eyes weren't the least shifty. Her gaze met that of each gentleman who addressed her with a becoming shyness which managed still to be open and friendly.

Peter was at his most adroit, a blend of sophistication and charming wit. Yet Amelia could see real interest in his eyes as he asked, "Have you lived near Bournemouth long, Mlle. Chartier?"

"Almost four years. My cousins are English and their family has lived there for hundreds of years." Her cheeks dimpled as she smiled at him. "I thought at first the place must be haunted, with all the strange noises at night, but it proved to be only the sea."

"Is the property right on the coast, then?" Verwood asked with a great show of indifference.

"Oh, yes. I can look out my bedroom window and see the water."

"How delightful," Amelia contributed. "There are only a few rooms at Margrave where the water can be seen, and none of them are the major bedchambers. But we can hear the sound. I find it immensely soothing."

"Margrave is in Sussex," Peter explained.

Mlle. Chartier nodded her understanding. "I believe Sussex is quite lovely."

"Have you never been there?" Verwood asked.

"Oh, no. I've scarcely been out of Hampshire since I came to England."

The dance separated the two couples and Amelia studied Verwood's face for some sign of his reason for questioning Mlle. Chartier. He had adopted a rather peculiar expression, one Amelia assumed was meant to convey to any interested observer that he was rather taken with the young girl. But he had it all wrong. Probably, Amelia felt, because he had no idea what it was like to feel smitten by anyone.

"I had no idea you were so intimately acquainted with M. Chartier that he would seek your advice on his sister's introduction to London," she remarked. He gave her a sharp glance but said nothing, so she continued. "I find it rather odd that he would consult you. After all, what could you know of a young lady's introduction to London society? You've only come here recently yourself and presumably know nothing of such matters as a debutante's dress or the proper way for her to conduct herself. If you gave sufficient thought to the matter, I suppose you could tell him which invitations were best to accept," she suggested, sounding markedly skeptical. "On the other hand, I rather doubt he has a great number of invitations from which to choose. In fact, I was astonished to find him here this evening."

"Why?"

His bluntness was a wonderful goad. "Because, my dear Lord Verwood, he is new in town, the other French émigrés don't recognize him, and his fortune isn't known. That would ordinarily make him rather suspect amongst the ton, and especially by the Stratfords. Perhaps you spoke for him to them?"

"I barely know them myself," he murmured as he turned away from her to link arms with the woman to his left.

Which merely confirmed her suspicion that Lord Verwood had come on her own invitation as her escort. Really, it was too bad of Peter to do that without getting her approval. She wouldn't have given it. Lord Verwood was not at all her idea of a comfortable escort. When he paid attention to her at all, it was with a barely concealed disapproval. It seemed quite conceivable to her that there was something not altogether aboveboard about the viscount, despite his friendship with Peter. He was also on friendly terms with the Frenchman, after all. But since he'd managed to get himself there with them, she decided it was as good an opportunity as any to see if she could uncover something significant about him. So when they were rejoined by the dance, she offered him her most charming smile.

"I imagine you have some ideas on the prosecution of the war that are a little different from the Cabinet's," she said. "Are you in agreement with Sir John Moore?"

"Yes. I think he's the most knowledgeable man around. But it was wise of the new government to send Gower and

Paget off. Unfortunately, they're probably too late, and there's not a large enough contingent on the Continent to help the summer campaign."

"Do you think the Russians are doomed, then?"

"Almost of a certainty. And if they are, Napoleon will make the most of their defeat, to exclude England from trading on the Continent."

"Would that be disastrous for us?" she asked, fluttering her eyelashes.

"It would make things very difficult," he said, looking pointedly at the crown of her head.

"Who would be the ones to profit?"

He shrugged. "Smugglers, unscrupulous men in trade who weren't too particular about their loyalties. England needs her continental trade."

"I suppose the money-lenders would be cheated of their investments abroad."

"Probably."

The dance came to a vigorous conclusion. Amelia fanned her face ostentatiously and said, "My, it's warm in here. I should just like to step out on the balcony for a moment, if you wouldn't mind continuing our discussion there."

He stared at her for a moment, then took her elbow and steered her toward the open glass doors at the far end of the room. Amelia was surprised by the strength of his grip. She felt more like his prisoner than a woman luring a man to a tête-à-tête. His heavy black brows were lowered so incredibly far down that they looked in danger of obscuring his vision. For a moment she felt a touch of panic and looked around to see where Trudy was, or even Peter, but neither of them was in view. Lord Verwood gave her a little nudge when she hesitated at the threshold of the balcony.

It was not warm outside, though the chill night air was not what made Amelia shiver. Lord Verwood came close to her, too close, backing her into the darkest corner of the ivy-hung space. He blocked her view of the ballroom with the bulk of his body, making her feel shut off from any means of escape. Nonsense, she tried to tell herself. There was no need to escape from him. He was a friend of her brother's, a gentleman. He wouldn't dare put into practice any of those things his eyes were blazing with—would he?

"It's colder out than I thought," she murmured, turning her head aside from his gaze. "I think perhaps I'll go back in."

He didn't move to make way for her. "I thought you wished to continue our discussion."

"Some other time, perhaps. Really, Lord Verwood, it's quite cold here."

"Nonsense. I can keep you warm," he said. And moved to put his arm around her shoulders.

Amelia gave a tiny squeak of dismay and slipped out from under the looming limb, only to find herself pressed up against the wall with him not five inches from her. "Sir! I beg to remind you who I am," she protested. "I'm not in the habit of letting gentlemen put their arms around me."

"Aren't you?"

"Of course not!" She cast a glance over the balcony and decided it was too far to jump over. "My aunt will be worried about me."

"You should have thought of that before you suggested one of your 'intrigues.' "

His face was as implacable as ever, the dark eyes glittering in the moonlight. Amelia jabbed a finger at his chest, declaring, "I'm going in."

"You must do as you wish, of course." He caught her hands in his large, roughened ones and bent to claim her lips with an unnervingly brief ardency. Amelia turned her head aside and yanked back her hands. In a quavering voice she insisted, "Please step aside, Lord Verwood."

"Why, certainly," he said, sounding surprised. "Wasn't there room for you to pass? I do beg your pardon, Lady Amelia."

The whole episode was ludicrous. She could see now that he was mocking her, that he'd never had any intention of doing more than frightening her for bringing him out on the balcony. Well, what could he possibly have done out there with dozens of people in calling distance? He had used the occasion to make her feel foolish, and she had stepped right into his trap. Amelia was not used to having people behave so outrageously toward her and she lifted her brows as she wedged herself past his body (which he'd moved only slightly).

"Your manners could stand improvement," she snapped. "Perhaps years in the army have dulled your sense of what is fitting in a gentleman."

"Ah, that would be it," he agreed. "I've been away so long I didn't even know it was customary for young women to invite gentlemen out onto the balcony alone with them."

"It was only for a breath of air! The ballroom was exceedingly warm and the dancing energetic."

"I'm surprised that one set should have so heated you, Lady Amelia," he remarked, trailing behind her into the room.

She refused to reply. Trudy was across the room from her, deep in conversation with one of her cronies. Amelia skirted the dance floor, where another set was in progress. Behind her she could hear Verwood limping along, an exaggerated shuffling that was surely calculated to draw attention to himself, and her. Well, she wasn't going to have any part of his antics. Let him make a spectacle of himself. No one could possibly know she'd been with him, though someone might wonder why she would be crossing the floor by herself.

"You're going too fast for me," he said, much too loudly, and in a wretchedly plaintive voice. "My injury makes me limp, you know."

"Your injury is a hoax," she hissed, turning to glare at him. "I don't want you following me about."

"I have to return you to your aunt. She's been worried about you," he said, his eyes flashing with unholy merriment. "If you would just have pity on my infirmity . . ."

"It's your *mind* that's infirm, Lord Verwood." Amelia quickened her pace, and he quickened his, with discreet groans of soldierly fortitude that reached her quite distinctly.

Trudy glanced up briefly when Amelia arrived breathless at her side. "Ah, there you are," she said, wagging her head. "I wondered where you'd gotten to." She lowered her voice to add, "You shouldn't walk so fast with poor Lord Verwood, my dear. His injured leg, you know."

It was a great temptation for Amelia to say something cutting about poor Lord Verwood's leg. She restrained herself only because she felt certain it was exactly what he expected her to do. He was watching her with slightly hooded eyes now, his expression unreadable, waiting to be dismissed. Amelia thanked him for the set, politely, because Trudy might be listening, though it seemed unlikely, since she had nodded briefly to Verwood and resumed her discussion with her neighbor.

The dance in progress was only half-finished and there was no one around to solicit her hand for the next. Nor was there an unoccupied seat near her aunt so she could sit down. Amelia wanted Verwood to go away, but he refused to budge when it would mean leaving her standing there alone. He was, after all, her escort for the evening, she realized, and it wouldn't do for him to abandon her in such an awkward position.

"Perhaps we might seek a bit of refreshment," he suggested.

"Thank you, no. You go ahead, Lord Verwood. I'll be quite all right."

He continued to stand at her side, one leg slightly bent to take his weight off it. Amelia wondered if it really did hurt, if he were in some pain. She glanced around surreptitiously for two chairs in the immediate vicinity, but there were none available. The Stratfords were notorious for dispensing with such frivolities, expecting their guests to dance and mingle and only seat themselves out of sheer exhaustion or old age and infirmity.

"Why did the boy come to you tonight?" Verwood asked suddenly, startling her.

She hesitated. "His mother was very ill."

Verwood lifted one skeptical brow. "Why would he bring that matter to your attention, Lady Amelia?"

"I'm acquainted with the family through a clergyman in St. Giles Rookery." She said it dismissively, hoping he would drop the subject. She should have known better.

"Does this clergyman frequently put you in touch with families there?"

"Occasionally."

"For what purpose?"

Amelia was spared the necessity of answering him by the arrival of M. Chartier and his sister, who was still pink from the dance which had just ended. She smiled shyly at Amelia and kept her eyes lowered when Viscount Verwood spoke to her.

"She is besieged," M. Chartier said cheerfully. "But I told her, 'Veronique, you must save a dance for Lord Verwood, who has taken the time to advise your brother on your welfare.' She has already committed herself for supper, but this dance she has saved."

"I'm grateful," Verwood assured her in a voice so gentle Amelia scarcely recognized it. "Perhaps we could find a glass of ratafia before the next set begins."

With a small bow to Amelia, he walked off with Mlle. Chartier on his arm, leaving Amelia with the young lady's brother. In spite of the fact that Amelia believed there was every possibility M. Chartier was a French spy, she didn't at all like being left alone with him. He fidgeted when he was around her. He hadn't always done that, in fact had at one time seemed inordinately pleased to spend any time in her company, but all that had changed after she'd spent a half-hour out on a balcony with *him*.

Most of the homes in which she was entertained had some sort of balcony on which to accomplish an intimate questioning of someone who was suspect. M. Chartier was most certainly suspect, but when she had been alone with him he'd been too ardent to pay much attention to her queries. He had grabbed her hand and pressed kisses from her wrist to the tips of her fingers, declaring all the while how devoted he was to her. Because of his distraction, and Amelia's right to know where he stood if he were putting himself forward as a suitor, Amelia had swallowed her annoyance and asked, "Have you returned to France since you immigrated to England?"

He turned her hand over and slurped on her palm. "Why

should I go to France?" he murmured. "It is in England that I find everything wonderful—like you, lovely Lady Amelia."

"Yes, but you must miss some of your friends there," she insisted. "Aren't you in contact with anyone in France?"

His small, elegant shoulders lifted in a shrug. "No one of importance."

"Then perhaps you have old friends among the other French émigrés."

"None."

Amelia took her hand away. "That's rather odd, isn't it?"

"Odd? Odd? What is odd about it?" he demanded, making an attempt to reclaim her hand. "My family is very old and has never associated with these upstarts. Every one of them comes to England, where the aristocracy is revered, and says they are of good family. Who is to know? Me, I know. None of them are a patch on the Chartier family. I will not lower myself to play their kinds of tricks. It is not that my family lacks their distinction," he said, glancing behind them to assure himself he wasn't overheard. "Quite the contrary. But when we came to England we did not bring with us French trappings. That was my decision. Leave the worthless behind, I said to my sister. The English are a nation who recognize aristocratic blood. They will recognize us."

Much to her surprise, he then placed his hands on her shoulders, staring intently into her eyes. "You recognized me, didn't you?"

Amelia had no idea what he was talking about. "Um. Well. I could tell you were of good family."

"Ah, you see! Certainly you could tell. I knew you would be able to tell."

"Yes, but if you had to leave everything in France . . ."

His eyelid twitched. Or at least that's what Amelia thought for a moment before she realized it was a grotesque wink. "No, no, you must not think I have lost everything in France. I can reclaim my inheritance just like that," he said, making an unsuccessful attempt to snap his fingers.

"But it's there—in France?" she persisted.

A guarded expression closed over his face. "I cannot say. I

tell no one, no one, even those nearest and dearest to me." He brushed back a wisp of her honey-colored hair and stroked the cheek that he exposed. "Even the dearest," he repeated, whispering in her ear.

"You're quite right to tell no one," she assured him. "I was merely thinking it would be dangerous for you to travel to France these days. It would worry me to think of you being in danger."

He was delighted and moved by this absurd untruth. So moved, indeed, that he said, "There is little danger to *me*," and kissed her. Amelia did not welcome his kiss, but this had happened before and she knew it was the best time to press her advantage.

"Oh, I can't think it is safe for you in France," she said, demurely lowering her eyes. "Only Napoleon's supporters are safe there."

"You mustn't worry yourself on my behalf," he insisted. His eyes were amorously softened in the pale moonlight, very close to her. "I have contacts. I can come and go when I please, without fearing harm."

"You must be very clever to manage," she said admiringly.

Flattered, he waved this off with a careless gesture. "One must be, in these times, Lady Amelia. Once, I—"

Amelia could have cried that they were interrupted right then by an inebriated buck who lurched out onto the balcony for a breath of air. But she couldn't be caught in such a position with M. Chartier and turned her back on the newcomer as she slid past and back into the ballroom. She had expected further revelations from the Frenchman on future occasions, and was at first surprised when he took to avoiding her. Then it seemed clear to her that he felt he had said too much and for his safety had determined not to have any contact with her whatsoever. It never occurred to her that he disapproved of her letting him kiss her. No one else ever had.

Unfortunately, he was now placed in a position where he had to confront her whether he liked it or not, because of Lord Verwood's hasty retreat with Mlle. Chartier. As he seemed incapable of introducing any topic for conversation, Amelia said, "Your sister is quite lovely, M. Chartier. How old is she?"

He paused before answering her. "Eighteen years," he said finally, presumably deciding this was not hazardous information to convey.

"I suppose she misses France."

"Not at all!"

His vehemence amused Amelia, but she merely nodded. "Perhaps she came here young enough to make England seem her home."

"But of course! She loves England! She hardly remembers France at all." Couples were beginning to form in rows for the next set and he eagerly grasped the opportunity to end their tête-à-tête. "Would you care to dance, Lady Amelia?"

"Thank you."

His method of dancing was particularly energetic, leaving little room for conversation, and that of the most mundane matters. Amelia shrugged off her disappointment and progressed from M. Chartier to Mr. Winchfield, from Mr. Winchfield to Mr. Rollings, from Mr. Rollings to Sir William Conrady (another of her supposed suitors), and on through the evening. Her three suitors held varying degrees of disinterest for her. Winchfield stood in line to a barony, but he was foolish and inane. Sir William was ten years her senior, but might have been thirty for all his stuffy rectitude. And of course Rollings was a delightful scamp—but a fortune hunter of limited intelligence.

Amelia paid scant attention to any of them. She did note that Lord Verwood danced only the once with Mademoiselle Chartier, but that Peter danced with her twice. Verwood did not approach Amelia again until the end of the evening, ready to escort them home, and then he didn't speak directly to her, but to Trudy and Peter.

When they reached the house in Grosvenor Square, Amelia felt exhausted, and disturbed by Verwood's subtly ignoring her. It was not that she wanted him to pay her any attention, of course. On the other hand, she disliked being ostracized. Somehow he managed not even to say good night directly to her, though she looked straight at him. He was busy pressing Trudy's hand and patting Peter on the shoulder.

Amelia would have liked to go to her room, but first sought out the footman Robert, only to learn that he had not as yet returned from his errand. In her bedchamber she intended to wait up until she could find out about her protégé and his mother, but she fell asleep in a chair by the window, not waking until the light of early morning streamed through the curtains.

— 7 —

The house was still, Amelia thought drowsily. No sounds of stirring yet from the floor below. She pushed the curtains aside and the full impact of a gorgeous spring day burst upon her. The sun was golden through the fresh new leaves of the trees behind the house, birds chirped and sang in the branches. She opened the window to catch the faint breeze with its smell of dewy earth and awakening vegetation. Leaning out, she breathed deeply, filling herself with the promise of the glorious day. There was something at the back of her mind that teased at her, fluttered in her sleep-numbed brain, but she ignored it for the delight of the moment.

It was the perfect day for an early ride in Hyde Park, while no one was around. The grass would be wet still, and a brilliant green. Early-spring flowers would be poking through, some of them bravely unfurling their rich colors. Just the sort of day, she found herself thinking, when it would be heavenly to ride along Rotten Row and suddenly come abreast of a gentleman who made one's heartbeat quicken, whose challenging black eyes excited a thrill of anticipation, whose unruly black hair might still be damp from a bath, curling healthily about his head. Oh, she would smile and exclaim at the sheer beauty of the morning, knowing he'd think her a little naive, but knowing, too, that he would be feeling the electricity in the air.

They would ride along together, casting furtive glances at

each other from time to time, talking perhaps of days they remembered from their childhoods, days in the country when nature around them was lush and ripening into the fullness of harvest, summer days, autumn days. He would not be impervious to her enthusiasm, her sheer exuberance. She would see he had a softer side, one where they could share an affinity for things beneath the surface trimmings. He would smile at her—had he ever smiled at her?—and restrain himself from clasping her hand where it rested in the lap of her riding habit as her mare walked sedately along the path.

Spring was for this sort of daydream, this excitement racing through the blood, this wistful desire for something special and rare. Perhaps they would ride beneath the trees, turning slightly off the Row and stopping their horses under the bower of emerging leaves. If there was no one around, he might hold out his hand, and she would place hers in it. There would be a warmth in his touch. She could feel it as the sun caressed her cheeks; it would be as welcome as the breeze through her hair. Would he kiss her?

Yes, he would kiss her, but what kind of kiss would it be? As soft as a butterfly landing on the skin? Firmer. There would be some pressure behind it, sternly controlled passion even, softened to her innocence. His eyes would speak to her of what he held back, his lips of what he was unable to rein in. Mmmm. It would not be brief, she decided. Awkward, on horseback, but possible. Her mare was very patient—too patient, she had frequently told Peter. But now she appreciated this patience, the animal placidly remaining in one spot, one hidden spot off the Row where no one could see them.

Perhaps it would be better if they dismounted and walked under the trees? Then he could hold her hand as they strolled, and stop to kiss her whenever she lifted her face to his. But no, this time it would be best to remain on horseback. Another time she could consider the possibilities of a stroll through a sun-dappled woods. It wasn't the kind of day when you wanted things to move too quickly. You wanted them to be slow, stretched out over time so that every moment could be savored. His kiss, for instance, could go on, in her mind, for an hour and she'd be quite content.

There was a crunching noise from the gravel path beneath her window and Amelia looked down to see the kitchen maid carrying a bucket of water that she poured conscientiously on the border of earth that had produced dozens of swaying yellow daffodils. The girl wore a blue scarf over her hair and hummed to herself as she returned slowly toward the house, no doubt relishing the short break out in the spring weather. Amelia very nearly called down to ask her to inform the stable boy that she would be riding out directly, when two things suddenly occurred to her.

One was that Tommy Carson's mother had been very sick the previous evening.

The other was that the gentleman about whom she'd been daydreaming was none other than Lord Verwood, archenemy.

Amelia quickly withdrew her head from the window and brought the sash down with unnecessary force. How could she possibly have forgotten Tommy's mother? And what in the devil was she doing daydreaming about Lord Verwood like some moonling? He had done nothing but irritate her since the first time they'd met. He had mocked her and ignored her and exasperated her every moment she'd spent in his company. Plus which, he stood some chance of being a political as well as a personal enemy.

It was the way he'd looked at her last night, of course. And that brief kiss. Probably she had dreamed of that mocking kiss, and simply woven it into her waking fantasy. Full moons and spring days had a lot to answer for! Amelia refused to believe it was any more than the strange combination of events. How could it be? An air of mystery clung about Lord Verwood, and a strong suggestion of masculinity, but Amelia wasn't given to developing tendres for mysterious, masculine strangers who kissed her to teach her a lesson. In fact, she wasn't given to developing tendres at all.

The last time she'd been smitten with a male was when she was thirteen years old and thought a neighbor at Margrave,

Rodney Cartwright, was the most dashing creature on earth. Rodney had been twenty at the time and given to every excess of male fashion, including extraordinarily high shirt points, extravagantly arranged neckcloths, and boots so highly polished that they reflected one's image. Though it was given out in the neighborhood that Rodney was attending Oxford, Amelia had learned from him that he'd been sent down for some childish prank (she could no longer remember what it was), and he kept close to home until he was reinstated. Since Peter had been away at school at the time, Rodney had spent many hours with her, having no other friends in the vicinity.

There hadn't been anything physical in their relationship, except the one time he had kissed her, just before returning to Oxford. Amelia had been far too young to consider, ahead of time, the possibility that he would kiss her. It had seemed to happen so naturally, when he had said good-bye and was about to mount his horse. He'd suddenly leaned forward and pressed his lips to hers, withdrawing after a moment to say, "It's a damned shame you're so young, Amy." Then he rode away without looking back.

For a year she'd dreamed about him, and about that kiss—night dreams, daydreams. She was quite sure she was in love with him. He came home very seldom, and when he did, she did not see him alone after that. And then he married, a woman he'd met in London during the season, and Amelia had thought her heart was broken. But she had learned that wounds like that healed, a lesson that seemed to shield her somehow from impetuously "falling" for other men. If it was a protective measure, it was also a practical one.

Look at Rodney Cartwright now, for instance. There wasn't a thing about him that she admired anymore, really. She had long since decided his extraordinary style lacked taste, and he was given to drinking and gambling still, as though he'd not outgrown his adolescence. He took no interest in the small estate on which he and his family lived, and paid little attention to what was going on in the rest of the country. Such a waste. He had seemed so promising.

That kiss, though, was another matter. The kiss, she hadn't forgotten. She had suffered a number of kisses in the last few years—in the service of her country, as she thought of it. None of them could hold a patch to Rodney's kiss . . . because she had been attracted to him, had felt a great affection for him, had perhaps in her schoolgirl way even loved him then. Well, she hadn't loved anyone since, and she hadn't had the least desire to be kissed by anyone. Until now. And this was surely an aberration. Lord Verwood's kiss had not been the same sort of thing at all. It was neither in the line of duty nor in the way of an attachment. Yet it had moved her somehow. . . .

Amelia shook off the lingering mists of bemusement and turned to her toilette. There were more important things to think about than the reprehensible Lord Verwood. She had to find out from Robert what had happened at the Carsons'.

Robert had returned only an hour previously and had decided to stay up until he'd had a chance to talk with Lady Amelia before seeking a little rest. She found him sitting in the kitchen over a strong, hot cup of coffee, the remains of a sizable breakfast on the plate in front of him on the deal table. He didn't look as though he'd been up all night. His livery was still neat and his hair freshly brushed, and he didn't look the least surprised to see her arrive in the kitchen at seven in the morning. He rose instantly and bowed to her.

"Good morning, Robert. How's Mrs. Carson?"

"Dr. Wells thinks she'll pull through. He's put her in hospital, and I stayed with the children until he sent a woman to care for them. She's a motherly sort of person, very good with the youngsters. I left her some money and told her I'd be by this afternoon to see how everything was going."

"Good. I'll come with you."

"It's a rough neighborhood, milady."

"I dare say. Still, I should like to go with you. About three, perhaps? You should get some sleep now."

Robert bowed his agreement and Amelia retreated to the breakfast room for tea and toast, a slice of ham, and an

orange. It was still early when she finished, and she was
again tempted by the sun streaming through the windows.
Sparkling light glinted off the knife on her plate and
separated through the crystal glass into a rainbow on the
snowy damask cloth. There were few times in London when
she felt this springtime enchantment stirring in her blood,
and she decided not to waste the opportunity. She flung
down her napkin and rang for a footman.

"Please send a message to the stable that I'll be riding
Cleo in about fifteen minutes. I'll want Jason to accompany
me." Amelia hastened out the door the footman held open
for her and ran up the stairs two at a time.

Lord Verwood watched as Lady Amelia rode through the
Grosvenor Gate and past the rows of trees on either side. She
adjusted the skirts of an emerald-green riding habit over the
pommel of the sidesaddle and set her horse to a gentle
canter, the groom trailing after her at a respectful distance.
Verwood followed at a greater distance, not wishing to be
seen, but intent on finding out whether she was out so early
for some sort of assignation. The tale of the sick mother the
night before hadn't seemed the least plausible to him.

She was a delightful sight, Lady Amelia, with her bronze
hair streaming out behind her as she rode. And she rode
very well. There was none of the stiffness one associated with
young women who feared horses, nor even particularly the
haughtiness one sometimes saw in women who prided themselves on their riding ability. Here was a simple elegance in
the pleasure of cantering across the dewy grass on a perfect
spring morning. Verwood found himself not unmoved by
the sight.

There were few people out yet, only one or two others on
horseback, and a few gentlemen strolling along the paths.
Lady Amelia skirted the ring, heading down toward the Serpentine. Verwood maintained the distance between them,
so he could not see her clearly, but he could imagine the
color in her cheeks, the sparkle in her eyes. His own mount
was impatient to be given his head, but Verwood held him
back. If it hadn't been necessary to find out what she was

doing, he would have liked to ride up to her and simply pass the time of day. On a morning like this he might not have teased her in quite the same way he had the night before.

More likely, though, he would have been tempted to pay homage to her, something he had not the least intention of doing. Verwood thought himself entirely lacking in the proper graces to carry on a light flirtation, but he was tempted, as he watched Lady Amelia's charming progress toward a stand of trees beyond the water, to give it a try. He would, after all, need some sort of practice if he were to spend much time in London society. . . .

She slowed her horse as she approached the trees and looked about her in a way that seemed furtive to Verwood. Fortunately, he was directly behind her, though quite a way, and her swinging glance to left and right did not encompass him. At the edge of the grove she slid from her mount and tossed the reins to her groom before walking purposefully toward the leafy bower.

Verwood felt sure this was where her assignation was to be. The growth was dense and in a moment she disappeared from sight behind the outer row of trees. He set his horse to the gallop, approaching the wood from the north, as she had entered from the west. There was not a soul in sight, save her waiting groom, and no horse tied in the trees that he could see. Verwood swung from his saddle out of sight of the groom and led his horse into the obscurity of the trees, wrapping the reins tightly around the lowest branch he could find.

Sunlight penetrated several yards into the trees, then was more sketchy, with patches falling through spaces between the overhanging limbs and leaves. Verwood made his way quickly and quietly in the direction he presumed Lady Amelia would be, treading carefully on the fallen twigs and the shoots of new grass. At another time he might have noticed the wildflowers nestled around the ancient trees, but now he was too preoccupied with his mission to pay them any heed. What he listened for was the murmur of voices, to direct him to the meeting place, but all he heard was the trill of birdsong.

He very nearly walked right into the small, sun-dappled clearing where Lady Amelia stood leaning against a tree, her bonnet swinging by its ribbons in her hand. If she hadn't been lost in thought, she would surely have heard or seen him, but she seemed oblivious of his presence. Her head rested against the rough bark of the tree; her gaze toward the branches above was absent, almost dreamy. A whimsical smile lifted the corners of her lips. It's an assignation with a lover, he thought, unsettled.

But no one came, and she continued to stand there, the sun falling on her creamy skin. She didn't give the appearance of eagerly waiting for someone, paid no attention to the scuffle of small animals in the undergrowth, never cast her gaze about in search of the errant swain. Verwood was totally confused by her seeming indifference to the inexplicable nonappearance. *He* would have shown up if she'd . . .

He stopped the absurd thought before it could be finished. Either Lady Amelia was still indulging in her information-gathering activities, or she was a rather loose young lady, and in either case it was his duty to keep an eye on her. For Peter's sake. Verwood didn't relish the responsibility, of course. It would be most uncomfortable eavesdropping on a pair of lovers, and highly distasteful for him to carry the tale to Peter. Well, he wouldn't have to do that, if it was a lover she planned to meet. He could have a talk with her himself, letting her know he was aware of her activities and sternly insisting that she desist under threat of his revealing them to her brother. But if it was a conspirator she met, he wouldn't have the least compunction in approaching Peter about the matter.

After a while Lady Amelia sighed and walked away from the tree. Verwood carefully concealed himself where he could still catch a small glimpse of her adjusting the bonnet over her shining hair. She tied the ribbon at a smart angle under her chin, picked some wildflowers that grew at her feet, and headed back out of the wood. Was that it? Was she leaving? Verwood found it difficult to believe the determined young woman would give up so easily on her planned meeting, so he followed at a cautious distance and actually saw her aided onto her mare by the patient groom. She did not look around her to see if anyone were coming, but rode off at a sedate pace toward the reservoir.

Verwood remained standing in the shadows for some time after she was out of sight. None of it made any sense to him. Whether she was waiting for a conspirator or a lover, she should have been impatient, agitated, something other than the placid, dreamy creature she had appeared in the woods. Was he wrong about her? Verwood was willing to consider the possibility, but he thought it highly unlikely. There was M. Chartier's direct and unequivocal statement; there was Lady Amelia's acknowledged clandestine activity in the past, the advent of the child from St. Giles Rookery last night. Too much to be simply overlooked.

It occurred to him, in a suspiciously welcome burst of inspiration, that the logical thing for him to do was to spend more time in her company. Only by being closer to the situation was he going to be able to judge for himself just what Lady Amelia was, and what she wasn't. He would pretend to court her, never getting himself in so deeply that he could not extract himself with honor, but deep enough so he came to know what depths those violet eyes hid from the casual observer.

The only difficulty he was likely to encounter was Lady Amelia's obvious dislike of him. A small matter, he thought ruefully as he hurried back to his horse through the woods. One he could no doubt overcome with his nonexistent charm, his sterling lack of polite conversation, and his impressively un-Corinthian looks. To say nothing of his limp.

There were a lot more people around when he emerged from the woods and mounted his horse. The spring day had drawn them, at an unprecedentedly early hour for some of the ton. He hadn't been surprised to find Lady Amelia there, but he took care now to avoid anyone he might know as he cantered his horse across the grass to where she was approaching the Grosvenor Gate.

She paid no attention to the approaching hoofbeats, but

showed a surprising confusion on his coming alongside and speaking to her. The color in her cheeks deepened and she looked about her rather anxiously, as though she were alarmed at being seen with him. "Good morning, Lord Verwood." Her gaze seemed centered on his face, but he didn't have the impression she was meeting his eyes.

"I trust you slept well last night," he offered, wondering what one *did* say to set up a flirtation.

"Very well, thank you."

They had come through the Grosvenor Gate and were crossing Park Lane. "I hope the boy's mother is better this morning."

"She's in hospital, but the doctor thinks she'll recover."

Verwood searched her face for some sign of the charade he felt this must be, but Lady Amelia was frowning absently at the house they passed. He was startled when they reached the corner and she said, reining her horse left onto Upper Grosvenor Street, "Have a pleasant day, sir."

"I thought I'd accompany you home."

She gave him a sharp look but inclined her head in agreement. The color had receded slightly from her cheeks, but her eyes still skittered about in an uncomfortable way, unwilling to linger on his face.

"If I . . . upset you last night, I apologize," he said, thinking perhaps she was still annoyed with him for that foolhardy kiss. On the balcony he'd suddenly had a vision of her in similar circumstances dozens of times, trying to wheedle information from her companions by bribing them with kisses, or worse. Hadn't Chartier said precisely that? And she *had* been trying to get information from him. But she had reacted more like a Fury to his kiss than the docile maiden Chartier had painted, who didn't protest at all. Maybe getting information from him wasn't worth accepting his advances.

"The sooner last night is forgotten, the better," she muttered. Her hands on the reins clenched more tightly for a moment and she stared straight ahead to the corner of Grosvenor Square.

Verwood softened his voice to a most persuasive tone. "I'd

be infinitely grateful if you could see your way clear to forgetting it. Is it asking too much to depend on your charity, Lady Amelia?"

Her eyes finally lifted to his face, still half-suspicious. Apparently satisfied with what she saw there, she said, "I'm sure it's already forgotten. We needn't mention it again."

"Certainly not," he agreed, and smiled at her. He found he wished to erase those little frown lines above her nose, to coax some warmth into her violet eyes. Her lips, in the spring sunshine, looked even more tempting than they had the night before, but he brushed aside the thought to apply himself to cajoling her into a better humor toward him. "You're an excellent rider, Lady Amelia. I fear, though, that your mare isn't quite as young and energetic as she used to be."

"Yes," she said, stroking the horse's neck fondly, "I'm afraid it's time to retire her. I've mentioned it to Peter, but he's been too busy to take me along to Tattersall's. Poor Cleo deserves to spend the rest of her days in a pasture. London makes her nervous nowadays."

"On Monday I saw a fine bay mare at Tattersall's. One of Hampnett's, I believe. They say he's rolled himself up again and is selling his whole stable. I'd be happy to look into it for you, if you'd allow me."

"That's kind of you," she replied, uncertain. "Perhaps if you were to mention the mare to Peter . . ."

"Of course."

They had reached the earl's house and Verwood quickly dismounted to offer his assistance to Lady Amelia. She swung one knee free of the hook and the other foot free of its stirrup, but hesitated when he held his hands out to her. His smile became gently quizzical and she placed her hands in his before sliding to the ground. For a moment they stood gazing into each other's eyes. Then he pressed her fingers and released them, saying, "I shall call soon, if I may."

Amelia caught her lip uneasily between her teeth before shrugging slightly. "If you wish," she said softly. "Good morning, Lord Verwood." Without waiting for a response, she grabbed the skirts of her habit in both hands and hurried up the stairs.

— 8 —

Trudy was standing in the large entry hall when Amelia
came down that afternoon to meet Robert for their excursion to St. Giles Rookery. One of Trudy's favorite costumes
was a high-waisted gold-and-white-striped day dress that
seemed to balloon out from her on all sides. She was observing herself complacently in the gilded glass over an
ornate table on which rested the silver tray for visiting cards.

"Where are you going?" she asked, eyeing Amelia's pelisse
in the mirror.

"I'm off with Robert to see the child who was here last
night. His mother's in hospital and I want to make sure the
children are well-cared-for and lack nothing. I won't be
long."

"Really, my dear, you can't go into some appalling area of
town, even with Robert. Send him to assess the situation."

Amelia smiled placidly. "I assure you I'll be perfectly safe
with Robert, Aunt Trudy. No one ever so much as looks at
me askance when I'm with him."

Trudy gripped one billowing panel of her dress and
smoothed it down. "I'm sure Robert can accomplish any
errand on his own, dear. You really can't expose yourself to
the kind of squalor there's bound to be where that child
lives."

"It's already arranged."

"It can be unarranged," Trudy informed her, frowning at
Amelia's reflection.

There were not many occasions on which the two strong-willed women clashed, but Amelia could see that this was going to be one of them. She was about to put forth arguments in her behalf when the knocker sounded. Bighton came unhurriedly through the green baize door at the end of the hall, bowed slightly to the two women who faced each other obstinately, and progressed to the front door, where he admitted none other than Lord Verwood.

"Ah, a guest," Trudy murmured. "You really can't leave with a guest just come."

"He's come to see Peter." Amelia felt certain this wasn't really the case.

"No, indeed. He's come to see you. Peter is out."

"But he doesn't *know* Peter is out," Amelia suggested.

Trudy glared at her. "He brought you home from the park this morning. I saw him from the breakfast parlor. In any case, we must surely entertain him."

"*You* may entertain him," Amelia muttered. "I have other matters to attend to." But she smiled pleasantly as Verwood advanced toward them, saying, "I'm afraid you've missed my brother, sir, and I was just leaving, but my aunt would relish some company."

Not willing to be undercut in this way, Trudy shook her head vigorously. "No, no, I cannot allow it," she said, turning to the viscount with an imploring expression. "You must convince her, Lord Verwood. It would be folly for her to venture into such a neighborhood with Robert."

"St. Giles Rookery?" he asked immediately, to Amelia's surprise.

Trudy shuddered and looked questioningly at her niece.

"Yes, St. Giles Rookery," Amelia admitted as she casually buttoned her pelisse. "There's no need for concern. The undernourished poor are no match for Robert, I promise you."

Since at this moment Robert appeared in the hall, resplendent in his livery, no one actually quibbled with this statement. He was certainly a strapping young fellow. His shoulders were as broad as a prizefighter's and his height surpassed Verwood's by a good four inches. Amelia thought he looked a great deal more civilized as well, this blond giant. Verwood's wild black curls and his fierce black eyes gave him the look of a pirate or a highwayman, hardly what one expected in the drawing room.

He was observing her now, the thick brows lowered thoughtfully over his eyes, and a rather odd twist to his lips. Amelia realized after a moment that this latter was his attempt at a polite smile. She had to bite her lip not to burst out laughing, though she sobered quickly enough when he said, "I would be willing to accompany Lady Amelia and Robert to the Rookery, Miss Harting, if it would set your mind at ease."

"Would you?" Trudy gushed over with gratitude. "How very kind of you, Lord Verwood! I wouldn't have a moment's rest the whole time she was gone. But you can see how determined she is! There's no stopping her once she has her mind made up."

"Is that so?" he asked, giving Amelia an amused look which she assumed was meant to quell any objections she might have.

And she had objections. Any number of them. Not the least of which was that she felt a trifle nervous in his presence. She had noticed it that morning, when he was making a particular effort to be pleasant to her. It was an unusual reaction for her to succumb to. Having enjoyed the benefits of society for some years now, there were few occasions on which she felt inadequate or uncomfortable, so it was difficult to explain the fluttery feeling she had in her stomach, or the way her hands were wont to tremble just because he was staring at her.

What could he do, after all? Scold her? Surely that wouldn't be so awful. Even his trick of turning the tables on her, of making her aware that he was laughing at her, couldn't really do her any harm. Who cared if he laughed at her? It was a unique experience, to be sure, but he never did it in such a way that anyone else knew, so there was no need to worry. Her daydreams from the early morning came back to her, and the unbidden thoughts she'd had in Hyde Park before he joined her. It was ludicrous to think she was forming some sort of attachment to him, and yet . . .

Better under the circumstances to accept his coming with them. Otherwise Trudy might positively forbid her to go, and Amelia was intent on seeing the Carson children. So she gave in with as good grace as she could manage, saying, "I'm sure it's unnecessary, but if you wish to accompany us, of course you're welcome."

She said good-bye to Trudy, tucked a strand of honey-colored hair under her bonnet, picked up her basket of food from the kitchen, and walked to the front door. Robert held it open for her, and for Verwood, of course, following them down the steps to where the carriage stood waiting. It was a maroon barouche with a crest on the door, the hood down owing to the fine weather. Verwood took one look at the open carriage and said, "The hood will have to go up."

Amelia frowned at him. "Why?"

"Because of the area in which we'll be travelling, of course. We'd probably do better to take a hackney."

The carriage would be stuffy with the hood up on such a day, and Amelia considered the possibility of remanding his order. But Robert had already sprung to do his bidding. It didn't help Amelia's mood any that Robert looked relieved about Verwood's advent, either. She allowed the footman to assist her into the carriage and reluctantly made room for Verwood on the seat beside her. Robert sprang up on the box with the coachman; she could see him through the windscreen talking with the older man.

"Blue becomes you."

Startled, Amelia switched her gaze to Verwood. If it had been conceivable that anyone but he had made the comment, she would certainly have believed it, since he sat rigid beside her, not even meeting her gaze. Nor was he observing her blue silk pelisse, but the tassels on his Hessians, which swayed with the movement of the carriage.

"Thank you," she said coolly.

"It might have been better if you'd dressed a little less elegantly to go into St. Giles."

"I don't own anything less 'elegant' than this."

He nodded his head in noncommittal acknowledgment of the likelihood of this statement and moved his eyes to the window, where Brook Street drifted past. "Have you been to visit the Carsons before?"

"No, I've dealt only through Reverend Symons."

"You may be disturbed by their living conditions."

She lifted her shoulders slightly. "Their situation has been described to me. I'm not likely to suffer from a fit of vapours, if that's what you imagine."

Verwood suddenly turned the full impact of his black eyes on her. He had a most unnerving habit of not blinking very often, and Amelia, as though to make up for this oversight, blinked several times in rapid succession. "I've seen poverty before, Lord Verwood," she said.

"In the country?"

"Yes."

"It's not the same. People in cities . . . Well, just be prepared for something of a shock."

There was a note of real concern in his voice and Amelia felt the irritation that had risen in her abate. Suddenly she wanted to tell him about Tommy and his family, though the night before she had tried so hard to give him as little information as possible. But she was afraid he'd think she was trying to make herself out as a Lady Bountiful, that she was asking for his approval rather than his advice, and she remained mute. He wasn't likely to know more about what to do with a family like the Carsons than she was, after all.

They had left behind the better area of London now and were driving farther and farther into a scene of raggedly dressed children, strong odors of decay, and worse. The stately homes of the West End had given way to ramshackle buildings and edifices that could be described as nothing but hovels. Their progress was slow, kept to a walking pace by the straggling animals, the bedraggled carts, and the press of wretched humanity. Amelia saw a blind beggar with a one-legged child and dug for her reticule.

"No," Verwood insisted, staying her hand with a firm grip. "If you give alms to one of them, we'll be so inundated we won't make it to our destination. The whole street full of people will crowd around the carriage begging for money, and such a group can turn ugly."

"But they're so pathetic!" she exclaimed, slipping her hand from his hold but making no attempt to get at the coins in her reticule. "Could we give them something on our return?"

"Perhaps."

Amelia felt he only said it to placate her. "You think I'll forget, don't you?"

"No," he said slowly, "I don't think you'll forget, but you can't help all of them, Lady Amelia. The way you've been doing it, through the reverend, is the best way to handle charity. There are any number of unscrupulous villains out there begging, men who would blind a baby or maim a child just to provide a ghastly spectacle for the likes of you. Encouraging that kind of crime doesn't alleviate the real suffering that goes on."

Amelia could feel the blood drain from her face. "Surely no one would do such a cruel thing! You're horridly cynical, Lord Verwood."

"You're understandably naive, Lady Amelia," he retorted. "People who have to fight for every crumb of bread haven't your sensibility or your refined sense of what is acceptable behavior. And there are wretched human beings among the poor just as there are among the rich."

Her stomach churned with nausea and she turned her head away from him. Though she felt sure he wasn't lying, she was upset with him for so bluntly forcing the ugly knowledge on her. Outside of the slowly moving vehicle she now perceived the malevolent or sullen gazes directed to her luxurious carriage and through the glass to her elaborately costumed self. The dirt, the squalor, the suffering humanity—all seemed suddenly frightening to her. Her small efforts to relieve a few families were hopelessly inadequate, the chances of turning the tide of poverty surely nonexistent. Amelia wished fervently that she'd never ventured forth from the house in Grosvenor Square.

St. Giles Rookery was notorious for its distasteful

conditions and its criminal activity. The Carsons lived there, in a dismal basement, because the lodging cost so little. When the carriage halted in a dark alley where the smell of rotting garbage assailed her nostrils, Amelia bit her lip and straightened her shoulders. Not for the world would she show Lord Verwood how overset she was by his words and her own observations. A motley group of youngsters straggled after the carriage and hooted as the viscount assisted her to the muddy street. There was no evidence of the beautiful spring day she'd left behind in the West End. No sun penetrated to warm the scantily clothed children or dry the ooze at her feet.

There was a flurry of movement behind her, accompanied by more raucous cries, and she felt the reticule she had firmly gripped in her hand torn abruptly from her fingers. Before an exclamation could escape her lips, of either pain or surprise, Verwood had spun and collared a minute urchin who now had her net purse clasped tightly under his arm. The boy was sprinting past, and his rag of a shirt ripped under Verwood's grasp, leaving the viscount with only a piece of cloth in his hands.

It seemed to Amelia that the child would get away then, and she almost wished that he would. There wasn't all that much money in her reticule. Was this the sort of thing Tommy Carson had done before Reverend Symons had urged his plight on her? Amelia's hands stung from the ripping of the purse out of her grasp, but she had already seen enough ugliness for one day. In horrified fascination she watched Verwood bound forward so automatically that he doubtless had forgotten his injured knee.

The child was small and wiry and fast, but his pursuer had a tremendously long stride. Before they reached the corner, Verwood had extended one of the gleaming Hessians, its tassel swinging wildly, and brought the child down with a thump. Amelia's reticule skittered from under his arm and into a puddle, where Verwood immediately rescued it, since the horde of boys was rapidly descending on them. Robert managed to put himself and his gigantic

stance between the two groups, frowning menacingly at the
tattered ranks. Not even for one of their own were they
willing to test the footman's size and temper. In a moment
they had scattered, leaving only the footman, the viscount,
and the cringing urchin.

Verwood reached down and drew the boy to his feet,
keeping a firm hold on one arm when the youngster made
an attempt to flee. Amelia had walked a little ways toward
them, but he stopped her progress with a scowl. There was a
brief discussion between Verwood and Robert, none of
which Amelia could overhear, and then Robert took hold of
the boy's arm and led him away. Amelia wanted to protest,
but the implacable expression on Verwood's face deterred
her. About this time she no longer even wished for the
comforts of Grosvenor Square; she would have settled for
sitting down in the middle of the muddy road and weeping.

Instead she stood poker-straight, trying to summon up the
courage to accept her disgustingly dirty reticule from the
viscount. He didn't offer it to her, however, but slipped it
somewhere inside his blue superfine coat and led her to the
Carson's door. There was no knocker, of course, and he
rapped on the unpainted wooden panel with his knuckles,
since he carried no cane, despite the bad leg.

A thin woman with spectacles and an astonishingly long
nose answered the door to them. Clustered behind her were
all four of the Carson children, exhibiting various degrees of
anxiety and hope. Tommy came forward to introduce
Amelia to Mrs. Didling, who dropped a startled curtsy and
looked unsure as to whether to invite them into the
dilapidated building.

"I've just come to see if you need anything for the
children, and bring you a basket of food," Amelia said
kindly. "Is there any further word of Mrs. Carson?"

"Doctor says she be better," the woman replied, stepping
back so Amelia and Verwood could come into the one low-
ceilinged room. There were no decent chairs to sit on, but
Mrs. Didling drew up a stool, wiped it with a decently clean
cloth, and offered it to Amelia, who took it more out of

thoughtfulness than any real desire to sit down. " 'Twas something she ate, he thinks. Perhaps a bit of meat gone bad that poisoned her system."

"Butcher gives us bad meat sometimes," Tommy explained. "Charges just the same for it. We always have a bit of meat on Sunday, if there's the money."

And not a day goes by when I don't have all the meat I could wish, Amelia thought helplessly, her eyes straying to Verwood's face. She could read nothing there. He stood at his ease, allowing the youngest child to play with the muddied tassels on his Hessians. When the baby lifted his arms to be picked up, Verwood stooped down and lifted him with one arm.

Though she had intended to visit with the children, get to know them, she found now that she only wanted to leave. She turned back to Mrs. Didling. "Have you enough money to see that they're well taken care of for a few days, ma'am?"

"Oh, yes. The man Robert left enough for a week. You're not to worry, milady. We'll get along just fine." She appeared a little nervous in Amelia's presence, eyeing her gown with only partially disguised awe. Amelia looked about the room, where there were simple pallets on the floor and an open hearth for cooking. The smoke from many fires had blackened the open beams overhead, but the walls had been washed down sometime recently. All was ragged, but clean, and Amelia rose to leave. "You have only to send word if you need something, Mrs. Didling."

"Thank you, milady."

Verwood transferred the bouncing child to the woman's arms and followed Amelia to the door. Her one last look around the room nearly overcame her, at the discrepancy between the way the Carsons lived and the way she did. Why, even the poorest of the cottagers at Margrave lived a great deal more comfortably. Tommy blinked wide eyes at her, saying formally, "Thanks for helping my ma, Lady Amelia." She nodded, unable to speak, and squeezed his shoulder before stepping out into the rank alley once again.

The carriage had remained unmolested, with the coachman sitting warily on the box, his eyes shifting from side to side. There was no one else in the alley at the time, except Robert, who strode toward them from the direction in which he'd left.

"What have you done with the boy?" Amelia asked.

"I left him with the reverend, as his lordship requested." He turned to face Verwood before continuing. "Mr. Symons said he knows the boy and will keep him until the family can be contacted. I told him you'd be in touch with him."

"Thank you, Robert." The viscount motioned him back onto the box and addressed the coachman. "To Hyde Park, and stop to put down the hood when we get there, please." His look was only faintly questioning when he handed Amelia into the carriage, and she felt too drained to question his high-handed treatment of the rest of her afternoon. She allowed him to hand her into the barouche and slumped back against the blue velvet squabs with a sigh of relief.

"You didn't have Robert take him to the constable."

"Of course not. If the case came to trial, they'd either hang him or let him go, neither of which is a decent solution, and you'd be called to give testimony."

"It's unlikely his family has any control over him."

"No, I don't suppose they do," he agreed.

Amelia studied the hands that lay clasped in her lap. "But you aren't going to pursue the matter further?" she asked, hopeful.

"I'll do what I feel is right."

Hardly a satisfactory answer, she thought, but allowed the subject to drop. They rode in silence through the noisy streets, gradually drawing out of the impoverished neighborhoods into the wealthier sections of the city. When they entered the park it was late afternoon, almost time for the daily promenade. The carriage stopped long enough for Robert to jump down and lower the hood, allowing the full impact of the sun and breezes to bathe Amelia with much-needed refreshment.

— 9 —

Various members of the ton were beginning to filter through the gates behind them, in carriages, on horseback, some even strolling in the delightful weather. Amelia knew a fair number of them and nodded or spoke as the carriage moved forward at an incredibly decorous pace. Over the past few years she'd driven out with any number of men and not one of them had she had to introduce on two occasions, as she did with Lord Verwood, so little was he known to the ton. He seemed to be making some effort to be charming to the people with whom they spoke, though he said little to her.

Amelia tried to recapture her exuberant mood of the morning, but her daydreams of the man beside her were an embarrassment. In her fantasies she'd pictured him as warm and affectionate, not merely attentive. His fierce black eyes weren't softened, but gazed about him with apparent fascination, and perhaps a wry amusement, at the ton disporting itself in this unlikely pastoral setting. She was about to tell him she was fagged to death and wished to return to Grosvenor Square when they encountered her brother.

Peter's curricle was drawn by two high-spirited, well-matched chestnuts, its body painted a gleaming black. The tiger who stood at the back was so small he looked as though he couldn't possibly handle the ribbons if the need should arise. But what drew Amelia's attention was not the vehicle, nor the tiger, nor even her brother. It was his companion that caused an involuntary exclamation to escape her lips.

Seated beside him, her cheeks flushed with excitement, was Mlle. Chartier. She wore a demure blue driving gown that merely served to accentuate her sparkling blue eyes and convince one that she had a perfect figure. It was possibly her first drive in the park during the afternoon converging of the ton, and her eyes were wide with the wonder of it all. Amelia found it difficult, in her jaded state, to believe that anyone could derive such pleasure from watching a bunch of grown people parade about in their finery.

Peter drew up beside the barouche and halted his chestnuts, indicating that his coachman should do the same. He was smiling almost as broadly as his passenger, something he hadn't done much of in the last few years. Amelia was used to seeing him serious, concerned, but rarely lighthearted.

"Amelia, you'll remember Mlle. Chartier from last evening," he said cheerfully, bestowing a smile on each of them. "And you, Alexander."

Verwood was all smiles and rusty charm. Amelia found it disgusting, though she kept a friendly expression pinned to her lips, even managing to ask Mademoiselle Chartier if Peter's driving made her nervous.

"Oh, not at all. He is very skilled in his handling of the horses, is he not?"

"So he says," Amelia responded, grinning at her brother. "I've known him to take a corner on one wheel."

"It takes a certain amount of skill to do that and not overset your curricle," Peter rejoined. "Amelia, you won't mind if I don't escort you to the Bramshaws' this evening, will you? Mlle. Chartier has kindly agreed to allow me to accompany her and her brother to the Warnboroughs'."

Verwood spoke before Amelia could open her mouth. "I'll escort Lady Amelia and Miss Harting to the Bramshaws'."

Peter immediately said, "Excellent! Rollings would have done it, of course, but I'd prefer he didn't." This with a rueful gleam in his eyes.

With this detail settled, Peter gave a jaunty wave of his whip, called a casual farewell, and drove off. His companion smiled shyly at Amelia as they drew away from the barouche.

Disgruntled, Amelia informed the coachman that she was ready to return to Grosvenor Square. What was the use of a perfect spring day if everything seemed to go wrong on it? She leaned back against the squabs and stared at her hands, missing two gentlemen on horseback who lifted their hats to her. "He's making a terrible mistake," she muttered.

"In what way?" Verwood asked, his face a polite mask. He had turned to observe her, his knee so close it was almost touching hers.

"Nothing. I was just thinking out loud."

"Think out loud a little more. Why would it be a mistake for Peter to see something of Mlle. Chartier? Such a delightful girl."

Amelia could detect a note of mockery in his voice, but whether he mocked her or the Frenchwoman, she couldn't begin to tell. "Being such a close friend of her brother's, of course you would see no harm in it."

"I scarcely know M. Chartier."

"It didn't seem that way last night."

"Many things aren't what they seem."

"So I've noticed," she sniffed, looking him squarely in the eyes.

Verwood laughed. "You're still convinced I'm some sort of nefarious character, aren't you, Lady Amelia? You must consider me something of a genius to be able to pull off such a stunt with not only your astute brother but also all the members of the ton."

"You don't know all the members of the ton."

"Thank God!"

Amelia couldn't resist a chuckle. "Well, you know enough of them."

"More than enough," he assured her as he discreetly rubbed his knee.

"And what is your opinion of M. Chartier?"

"I should like to think him a liar," he murmured, more to himself than to her, an appraising light in his eyes. Amelia felt momentarily uncomfortable under his scrutiny, but when he continued, his comments were crisply impartial. "I have some reason to believe he's not quite what he seems, either. And because he's French as well, that leaves me with a few unsubstantiated suspicions. Perhaps your brother shares them, though I've never mentioned my doubts. He could be ingratiating himself with the sister in order to learn something more."

"I don't think so," Amelia mused, allowing her gaze to wander thoughtfully over the carriages they passed. "I hope you will warn him about the Chartiers. She could very well be intent on gaining information from *him*."

"That innocent little thing? Surely you jest."

"How can you be so blind?" she demanded. "If Chartier is a spy, there's every chance his sister is working with him. She may very well be a consummate actress, for all you know. No one could possibly be that wide-eyed at eighteen."

"I dare say you were yourself," he teased, reaching out to tuck back a strand of her honey hair that had blown loose from her bonnet.

"Not at eighteen!" She looked about her nervously to see if anyone had noticed his familiar gesture. "Perhaps at fourteen."

"But then, you spent a great deal of time in London, even when you were a child," he reminded her. "I doubt Mlle. Chartier has had the same opportunities."

"Or perhaps she's only fourteen."

His lips twitched with amusement. "I shouldn't think so, considering her . . . ah, build."

As he was considering Amelia's ". . . ah, build" at the moment, color crept up into her cheeks and she glared at him before turning away. His disconcerting habit of putting her to the blush was becoming more familiar to her now, but no less effective. "Her build notwithstanding," she said in frosty accents, "she could be assisting her brother in his spying endeavors."

He was instantly serious. "Very true. What do you suggest we do about it, Lady Amelia?"

"As I said before, you might warn him."

"It's very difficult to persuade a man who's that forcefully struck."

Amelia's shoulders slumped. "So you think he's quite taken with her, too?"

"Oh, yes. One gets to recognize the signs. I will, however, mention the possibility to him."

"Thank you. I don't think he'd listen to me."

The carriage had emerged from Hyde Park and turned briefly into Park Lane before swinging onto Upper Grosvenor Street. "What time should I come this evening?" he asked.

"At nine."

He bowed his head in acknowledgment and opened the carriage door as it drew to a halt. "I don't believe I know the Bramshaws," he remarked as he descended and held out his hand for hers.

"Naturally," she sighed, and wearily climbed the stairs to the house.

Though South Street was only a few blocks from Grosvenor Square, Verwood took his time in traversing the minimal distance. His knee was aching painfully from the earlier exertion of capturing the urchin who had grabbed Lady Amelia's reticule, and if he'd had the choice, he wouldn't even have walked the few blocks. By that evening, when he would be forced to stand up with Peter's sister, his knee would likely be abominably stiff and unusable. How was he going to explain *that* to the imperious Lady Amelia?

At least he had discovered to his own satisfaction that her mission with regard to the Carsons was wholly motivated by charity, and not something that involved clandestine espionage. Whether the Reverend Sidney Symons had any other fascination for her than his acting as an intermediary for her good works, he would attempt to discover on the morrow. He had no intention of venturing into St. Giles Rookery twice in one day.

There was nothing particularly imposing about Verwood House in South Street. It was built in 1751 by Isaac Ware and was much smaller than Chesterfield House, though it had something of the same grace. A delicate wrought-iron railing protected it from the street, and the warmth of the red brick was added to by three floors of tall windows, which seemed to invite the casual passerby to inspect the interior. Not that Verwood had ever asked a casual passerby to inspect his house. For the most part it had been shut up during the last decade, and his own inspection of it on coming to town had been rather discouraging.

Protected for years with holland covers, the furniture still managed to look old and sad, the draperies moldering at the windows. He had instructed his housekeeper to do what she could with it, within reason, thinking possibly he would sell it one day and take on something even smaller. As he ascended the three shallow steps to the door now, he thought it unlikely he would sell it in the near future, and that sprucing it up even more might be worth the expense. At least the exterior window trim could be painted, and the fake balconies. It wasn't likely he'd be doing much entertaining, but people he knew might well be driving along South Street and think the place something of a shambles. Not that he cared, particularly, what they thought of him or his house, but the cracked chimneypot should definitely be replaced, and the other work could be done at the same time, surely.

Wilkins took his hat and gloves and handed him a message that had come an hour previously, marked "Urgent." Verwood carried it with him to his study, calling back over his shoulder, "I'll have a brandy, Wilkins, and you'd best send in some hot, wet towels for my damn knee."

He pushed a hassock in front of his leather chair and groaned as he stretched his leg out to rest on it. It had been intolerably foolish of him to strain it that way. Catching the little hellion had only further complicated his life, and certainly hadn't restored Lady Amelia's purse in any condition that it could likely be used again. But it was hard to deny years of training, a developed instinct to react on an instant's notice. He had also no doubt wished to pass himself off as a man of action in the young lady's eyes, he decided wryly as he massaged the aching joint.

The letter was sealed and he picked up a letter opener from his desk to slide under the hardened glob of wax. It was a single sheet, in familiar handwriting. Every message from Kinson was marked "Urgent," but then, almost everything he had to communicate with Verwood *was*. This epistle read:

Imperative we meet tonight at the Shorn Sheep at ten. Cancel any engagements. Interesting development in the matter you raised last Wednesday. You should be prepared to travel.

Kinson

Devil take the man! There was nothing Verwood wanted less to do right now than leave London. But the matter they had discussed was Chartier, and the viscount was not likely to let anything to do with the Frenchman escape him, especially now. What was he to do about Lady Amelia and her aunt, though, at this short notice? If Peter had been accompanying them, it wouldn't have mattered if he withdrew with some excuse or other, but he had so pointedly agreed to be their sole escort.

Exasperated, he looked up to find Wilkins standing in front of him with a glass of brandy on a silver tray, several steaming towels in his other hand. Verwood raised the glass to his lips, took one healthy sip, and set it down on the table beside his chair. Then he grimaced at the towels and sighed before unfastening the buttons on his pantaloons and pushing them down below his knees. Wilkins spread a discarded newspaper on the hassock before laying one of the folded towels on it. Verwood gingerly lowered the injured leg onto it, with a hiss of indrawn breath, and Wilkins covered the knee with another painfully hot towel. They would cool in a few minutes, of course, but the initial shock of the heat was enough to make Verwood run his fingers distractedly through his hair.

"Thank you," he said stiffly. "Have Huser pack enough clothes for a week for me. I'll probably be travelling this evening, but I won't need him to accompany me." As Wilkins turned to leave, he added, "And have him set out

something that will be appropriate for the Bramshaws'
party. I'll be going there first."

"Very good, milord. I'll bring more towels in half an
hour."

Verwood made a face at his efficient departing butler.
Trust the old fellow to know he needed more than one
dressing of the moist heat to restore some flexibility to his
injured knee. Verwood would have liked to forgo the ritual,
but felt sure he'd be unable to move in another hour or two
if he didn't go through with it. And how was he going to
explain leaving Lady Amelia and her aunt in the middle of a
party? He took another sip of the brandy while he considered the matter.

At precisely nine o'clock he thumped the brass knocker on
the door at Grosvenor Square. His two charges were just
descending the stairs to the hall, laughing at something one
of them had said. In the flickering light he was momentarily
frozen by the delightful picture Lady Amelia made, the
honey-colored tresses gleaming in the candlelight, her eyes
lit with a mischievous twinkle. She sobered immediately
when she caught sight of him, assuming a formal smile that
felt surprisingly chilly to him.

"How prompt you are, Lord Verwood! It must be your
military training. Aunt Trudy and I have to wait for Peter as
often as he has to wait for us. Not tonight, of course. In his
eagerness he was ready early, and off before it was really
necessary." Amelia allowed Verwood to assist her into her
cloak while Bighton swathed Trudy in the folds of her
voluminous mauve cape.

It seemed to the viscount that he was called upon to make
some comment on his companions' toilettes, but no glibness
came to his tongue, nor was he able to simulate ardent
admiration for Miss Harting's odd collection of shawls and
scarves and brooches pinned in a row across her bosom.
Lady Amelia's ensemble did appeal to him. Very much.
Still, he could hardly compliment her on the rose-colored
gown if he couldn't think of anything kind to say to her

aunt. So he said nothing at all except, "Shall we go?"

Despite the afternoon's treatment, his limp was particularly bad that evening. Lady Amelia stared pointedly at his leg, as though questioning the necessity for the heavy irregularity in his gait. Obviously she had forgotten his exertion in the alley, remembering only his playacting of the night before. He had brought a cane but now used it discreetly. Drat the woman, anyhow!

The Bramshaws' house in Portman Square was a pretentious old stone pile with inane turrets at the corners. To do it justice, it would have had to sit on at least a hundred acres of parkland, with a working moat. Verwood wasn't particularly impressed with the Bramshaws themselves, either. Sir William was an incredibly stiff fellow, and his lady so overwhelmingly loquacious that none of her guests got a word in edgewise.

In the ordinary course of things, Verwood should have stood up with Lady Amelia for the first dance, but he begged off on account of his knee.

Her eyes told him she was skeptical, wondering if he was trying once again to embarrass her by pretending his injury was more serious than it was.

"I'm in a certain amount of pain tonight," he confessed. "Because of darting after that little ruffian this afternoon, you know."

Immediately her eyes clouded with concern. "Of course. I'm so sorry. You shouldn't have told Peter you'd escort us."

"I thought my knee would have recovered by now."

"Well, as it hasn't, I think you should take yourself home and give it a rest. Standing about on it isn't likely to do it much good."

The perfect opening, and yet he was reluctant to grasp at it. Beneath her politeness and concern there was something more. A stiffness born of hurt feelings? Surely Lady Amelia Cameron didn't give a fig for his behavior, or for himself. Did she expect him to be like some Bond Street beau, bemoaning his injury but gallantly standing by his promise to escort her for the evening? Reluctantly he said, "I think you might be right, Lady Amelia. I'd be better off at home, if you will excuse me. Before I leave, I'll ask someone to escort you and your aunt home after the entertainment."

"That won't be necessary," she assured him, frowning. "I can find someone responsible."

It was getting perilously close to ten o'clock. His travelling carriage would already be waiting at the Seymour Street corner of Portman Square. Verwood gave a frustrated tap of his cane on the exquisite hardwood of the dance floor and studied her. Yes, he was sure she believed him and that her sympathy was genuine. "Very well. Please make my apologies to your aunt. I'm truly sorry for the inconvenience."

"That's quite all right," she replied, and turned from him to the gentleman (Rollings, Verwood thought) who patiently awaited her attention.

Verwood watched the fellow lead her into the set that was forming. Lady Amelia smiled and batted her eyelashes at Rollings (if it was), and the viscount swung about so fiercely that his cane nearly tripped a matron standing behind him. His apologies were accepted with cold disdain and he stumped from the room in disgust.

— 10 —

Trudy was nearly apoplectic when she heard of Lord Verwood's defection. "His leg!" she snorted. "Really, he has the merest limp, and the weather isn't such that it would cause his injury to act up. I cannot believe it necessary for him to leave."

Amelia hadn't disclosed the incident earlier in the day, and she had no intention of doing so now. It would only alarm Trudy unnecessarily. But she did defend Verwood by saying, "Apparently he strained it sometime during the day."

"Balderdash! He rode with you this morning, and he drove with you this afternoon. What could possibly have happened since then?"

"Any number of things," Amelia returned stoutly. "He told me he was in pain."

Trudy refused to be satisfied. "If his leg was falling off, he shouldn't abandon us when he had promised his escort. And don't think," she admonished, waving a finger under Amelia's nose, "that I will accept Rollings as a substitute on our return home. Far sooner would I make do with the coachman and the footman."

After Verwood had vanished from sight, Amelia had ceased her flirting with Rollings, since she really had no wish to appear interested in the fortune hunter. When he responded to her flirtatiousness, she felt inordinately cross with him. He was simply too easy to twist around her little finger.

Why was it always the gentlemen you were least attracted to who found you enchanting, and the ones you were intrigued by who thought you were a nuisance?

It wasn't that she didn't believe Verwood was in pain, but she couldn't help feeling a little rejected by him. If he had really had some interest in her, he would have stayed despite the discomfort, wouldn't he? Nonetheless, Amelia was determined to convince her aunt of the necessity of Verwood's leaving, since it was important to her to believe it had been a logical decision on his part.

"Now, Trudy," she said sternly, "I haven't the least desire for Rollings' escort. And you must understand that I wouldn't have wished Lord Verwood to stay on my account when he was in such distress. Didn't you see that he was using his cane this evening? Here the poor man was wounded in his country's service, and you want him to suffer for a useless point of gallantry."

"Well, perhaps you're right," Trudy conceded, looking slightly mollified. "I dare say he was disguising his discomfort out of respect for us. Now I think of it, there were definitely lines of strain about his eyes. If I had had any reason to suspect, I would have insisted on his leaving, of course. Naturally you did that yourself."

"Yes, I did."

"That's just fine, then. He will know what a considerate young woman you are. There are too many flibbertigibbets who would have insisted on his staying. This will show one more instance of your maturity. I'm quite sure that's what he so appreciates in you, my dear."

Amelia thought it unlikely that he found anything whatsoever to appreciate in her, but she didn't say so. In a moment she allowed herself to be led into a country dance by Lord Stratfield, who was one of her admirers, though not a favorite of hers. Long before the end of the evening Amelia felt weary and jaded. It was just one more social event, like all the others, and all the ones to come. Helping Peter had added a little spice to the usual round of entertainments, and now that outlet was denied her. Not that there were all that many suspect people floating through the London ton, but the possibility of encountering one of them had always made her feel on the edge of adventure. She might as well have gone to Bath as Peter had suggested.

"Lady Amelia?" A voice spoke at her elbow and she realized her name had been uttered several times. Mr. Woolbeding stood there nervously rubbing his hands together, looking wretchedly apologetic for interrupting her thoughts.

"Forgive me, Mr. Woolbeding. I'm afraid my mind was a hundred miles away." Amelia smiled at him, the warmest effort she had made so far that evening. He was such a shy creature, and tremendously self-effacing because his family had made their fortune in trade only three generations previously.

"If you'd rather not dance this set, I'd quite understand," he said.

"No, no, of course I wish to dance it." She folded the ivory-and-lace fan she'd been using and placed her hand on his arm. This dance had been promised the day before, when she'd run into Mr. Woolbeding at Gunther's. Making a mental note of it at the time, she had been careful not to accept the next-to-the-last dance with anyone else. Mr. Woolbeding would never have been so presumptuous as to ask for the last dance. But Amelia hadn't seen him earlier in the evening, and now smiled and said, "I thought perhaps you hadn't been able to make it after all."

"I was a little late," he explained earnestly. "As I was arriving, I happened to see Lord Verwood standing at the corner by his travelling carriage. One of his team had just thrown a shoe and he was in a bit of a pucker about getting somewhere on time. Of course I offered him my assistance, which he reluctantly accepted. Such a thoughtful gentleman. He was afraid I'd miss all the fun if I took him to the Shorn Sheep before I came here, but I told him it wasn't *perfectly* necessary that I be here until almost the end of the evening." He concluded this speech with a bit of a flush, having revealed that the most important aspect of his evening was his dance with Lady Amelia.

"A travelling carriage?" she asked, astonished. "You mean Lord Verwood was leaving on a trip?"

"He thought almost certainly, but felt he wouldn't need the carriage right away, if he could just get to the pub by ten. While he conducted his business there they could either have the horse reshod or one brought up to replace it." Mr. Woolbeding ducked his head in embarrassment as he added, "He said he'd send round an invitation for me to dine with him when he returned to town."

"How very kind of him," she muttered, barely able to repress the rage that filled her bosom.

"If he forgets, I shan't remind him, of course," Woolbeding said. "It's the thought that counts, isn't it?"

Amelia mumbled something in reply, but it certainly wasn't "yes." If her thoughts about Lord Verwood counted, he would be horridly maimed at that moment. The audacity of the man! To tell her he was going home to nurse his knee, when he was in actuality setting off for a strenuous journey. Amelia had been willing to forgive and excuse his duplicity in the past, perhaps, but she was no longer willing to do so. There was something decidedly wrong with the fellow—and she intended to find out what it was.

Peter smiled up from his morning cup of coffee. "What? Up at this hour, my love? I felt sure you'd be abed for another two hours at least."

The sideboard was stacked with plates of cold meats and fruit. Amelia chose a warm muffin and a peach before allowing a footman to hold her chair for her, and watched as he poured cream, tea, and hot water into her cup. "I won't want anything from the kitchen this morning," she informed him.

His newspaper discarded, Peter studied his younger sister for a moment in silence, before dismissing the servants. "Is there something wrong, Amelia?"

"Just how much do you know about Lord Verwood?"

He raised his brows in tolerant amusement. "Surely you're not still convinced he's a spy. I can't think what put that idea in your head to begin with."

"Nobody knows anything about him. He's just popped up in London out of nowhere."

"Not exactly," he assured her. "Look, love, I actually had a letter about him from Sir John Moore, you know. They're acquainted."

Amelia pursed her lips, unsatisfied. "Perhaps Sir John Moore knows the *real* Viscount Verwood. That doesn't mean the man who poses as him is one and the same."

Her brother's amusement had disappeared. "You're not being logical, Amelia. How in the hell could Verwood live in his town house, with old servants, if he weren't the real thing?"

"Does he? Have you ever been there?"

"Well, no," he admitted, "but he's talked of an aging butler who's been with the family forever."

Amelia smirked at this patent deception. "Neither you nor anyone else would know whether an old butler had been with his family forever. Peter, you've been entirely too trusting with this man. Absolutely no one knows him at all. That's hard to account for. The Candovers, Ellis Winchfield, all say they remember him, but they're so vague. Anyone who looked the least like the real Verwood would pass for him with them. Say the real Verwood was actually killed in Egypt and someone had the clever idea of replacing him with a lookalike. It wouldn't have been at all difficult to do, would it?"

"It would have been impossible." Peter was adamant. "Our army doesn't just lose track of its soldiers, Amelia. Verwood was wounded and took the next ship home. That's all there is to it, nothing the least mysterious. Is it because I won't let you help me anymore? Is that why you're seeing problems where none exist?"

Amelia flung her hair back in a gesture of haughty disdain. "Consider, if you will, my dear brother, just how little you know of Verwood and you won't be so sure he's what he seems. Yesterday in the park he offered to escort Aunt Trudy and me to the Bramshaws'."

"Didn't he?"

"Why, yes, he did. He arrived here promptly at nine, rode in the carriage with us, refused to stand up with me because of his 'injured' knee, and immediately abandoned us."

"Abandoned you?" There was a quizzical tilt to his brow now, and he shook his head ruefully. "Surely you didn't quarrel with him, Amy. You're much too old to be bickering with a fellow just because he won't dance with you."

"I didn't 'bicker' with him. He told me his knee was troubling him and he thought he would go home to care for it."

Peter frowned. "Not particularly gallant, I agree, but not the least suspicious, either."

"He didn't go home," she informed him, triumphant. "Later when I danced with Mr. Woolbeding he told me he'd run into Verwood at the corner—with his travelling carriage. Mr. Woolbeding took him up and delivered him to the Shorn Sheep because one of the horses had thrown a shoe. Now, that has a ring of authenticity to it, don't you think? That Lord Verwood would be going to a place called the Shorn Sheep?"

"I'm sure there was a reasonable explanation," Peter replied, ignoring the aspersion cast on Alexander's character. "It must have been necessary for him to travel rather suddenly."

"And why wouldn't he have explained that to me, instead of dredging up the tired excuse of his poor injured knee?"

"Because it may have been . . . business that he didn't want you to know about."

"Your own sister? Ha!" Amelia laid down the knife she'd been using to butter her muffin and eyed him implacably across the length of the table. "There's something amiss with him, Peter. Until we find out more, I think you should be cautious in what you disclose to him."

"Until *we* find out more? Now, Amelia, there's no need for you to concern yourself about Alexander. He is undoubtedly Viscount Verwood, he's no more a traitor to his country than I am, and he *does* have an injured knee."

Amelia sighed. "I should hate to see all your hard work go for naught because you trusted an impostor. Please, at least consider the possibility."

"You're dead wrong, Amelia. Just because he's not perfectly agreeable, and hasn't the polished manners to which you're accustomed, doesn't mean he's some sort of impostor. Why, if the French were going to substitute someone for Verwood, you can be sure they'd put a consummately accomplished gentleman in the spot, not someone as gruff and disinterested as Alexander." He grinned at her. "Is it that your pride is suffering because he hasn't shown any interest in you?"

"Don't be ridiculous! I wouldn't want him to show any interest in me! The man is decidedly peculiar, Peter."

"You're too used to receiving adulation. Just because a gentleman doesn't bow and scrape to you doesn't make him peculiar."

"He deliberately sets out to embarrass me at every turn."

"Not without reason, I imagine." He cocked his head at her, a smile tugging at his lips. "Do you think only a French spy would try to take you down a peg? You can be insufferably haughty, Amelia, to say nothing of your impulsiveness."

"So we've degenerated to a dissection of my character, have we? You'd rather do that than consider the possibility of Lord Verwood's duplicity."

Peter was infinitely patient. "There's nothing wrong with your character. I never said there was. Occasionally, when you're annoyed with someone, as you appear to be with Verwood, you have a tendency to act a trifle high-handed. You can't expect a man of Verwood's elevated rank to let you get away with that."

"I expect *nothing* from Lord Verwood," she assured him with a sniff. Her tea had grown cool but she managed a sip before she remembered something else that had happened the previous day. "Did he speak with you about Mlle. Chartier?"

Two lines instantly etched themselves between his brows. "What about Mlle. Chartier?"

"Well, if you think Lord Verwood is aboveboard, I'm sure you will wish to hear his comments on the Chartiers. We have both, independently, formed a grave suspicion of M. Chartier, and if he's involved in some underhanded activities, it wouldn't do for you to be spending a great deal of time with his sister. After all, your own sister has been diligent in helping you in your work, and there's no reason to believe the delightful Mlle. Chartier couldn't do the same."

Peter stared at her, his hand gone slack around his coffee cup. "You must be mistaken. Alexander's never said a word to me about Chartier. On what does he supposedly base his suspicion?"

"He didn't confide in me."

"Well, then, on what do you base yours?"

"None of the other French émigrés know him, for a start. That's really very suspicious, Peter, if he's what he says he is. And when I talked to him, he almost came right out and said he has ways of getting into France to get at his fortune. Ways where he's not in the least danger."

"When did you talk to him?" her brother demanded.

"Oh, some little while ago. I had intended to find out more, but after that evening he avoided me."

"Why didn't you tell me you'd talked to him? Was this before or after I told you you weren't to do any more clandestine investigating?"

"Before. And I didn't tell you because I hadn't gotten enough information."

Peter looked skeptical. "That never stopped you any other time from telling me what you learned. What it is, Amelia, is that you don't want me involved with a French girl and you're exaggerating. If Alexander had any suspicions, he would have brought them to me."

"He certainly should have! All you have to do is ask him!"

"You just said he's out of town."

Amelia felt inordinately frustrated in her attempt to warn him. "Well, he's bound to be back, and when he is, you have only to ask him. In the meantime it would probably be best if you didn't see Mlle. Chartier."

"I'm escorting her to a masked ball this evening."

"Two nights in a row? Oh, Peter, you shouldn't."

He regarded her with steady eyes. "I have no choice. And besides," he said as he rose from the table, "I want to escort her."

Amelia's shoulders slumped as she watched him stride from the room.

There was no way to tell if he had taken her message to heart. He might have, even though he'd scoffed at it. Perhaps, even while he escorted Mlle. Chartier, or stood up with her at dances to which he hadn't escorted her, or brought her refreshments at musical evenings, he was only pursuing further information on her and her brother. Amelia didn't really believe that, of course, but it was painful for her to watch Peter become more and more enamored of the young woman. If only Verwood hadn't disappeared from town before he spoke to Peter, this might not have happened.

Amelia developed an annoyance with the viscount that grew with each passing day he didn't show up again in London society. This had nothing to do with how insipid her entertainments seemed when he wasn't there to challenge her. It was entirely based on what she could see of Peter's mental state, which was deteriorating rapidly. He was absolutely smitten with the Chartier girl, with her sparkling eyes and her enthusiastic chatter. Personally, Amelia wanted to hate the Frenchwoman, but found it impossible. Almost as impossible as it was to believe there was any subterfuge in her. Her perpetual *joie de vivre* was infectious rather than irritating, her beauty so unaffected as to be stunning.

In addition to Peter, several other gentlemen were vying for Mlle. Chartier's affections. She was, in fact, very much in demand. M. Chartier stood on the sidelines and smiled enigmatically at all this interest, looking more confident than concerned. He carefully skirted Lady Amelia, but made no attempt to ward off the Earl of Welsford's attentions. Amelia almost wished he would, though it might have gone some ways toward proving he wasn't the French spy she suspected. Far rather would she have been proven wrong than find her brother married to a woman who was not at all what she seemed.

Trudy was no help in the matter. She went around the

house murmuring, "Charming, charming!" Not for a minute did Amelia believe this referred to herself. Though Trudy had no more reason than Peter or Amelia to approve of the French, she seemed completely taken with Mlle. Chartier.

"You don't think perhaps she's a little young?" Amelia asked one morning as they sat together in the Velvet Drawing Room, each engrossed in a mending project of her own.

"Young? My dear child, she's eighteen. Hardly a sophisticated eighteen, I grant you, but more than mature enough to find herself in front of an altar before long." Trudy snipped a loose thread and held the napkin she'd been edging with lace out in front of her for a final inspection. Dissatisfied with the way the lace bunched at one corner, she patiently set to work at it again. "The earl is very fortunate she seems to favor him, you know. A charming girl."

"Yes, charming," Amelia agreed. It wouldn't have occurred to her to share her suspicions with her Aunt Trudy, and Mlle. Chartier *was* a charming girl.

"I wonder what has become of Lord Verwood," Trudy mused next, as though there were some possible connection between the two thoughts. "We were used to see him everywhere we went. I do hope his leg isn't still bothering him."

"I believe he's out of town."

"At this time of year?" She gave a tsk of disbelief. "Mrs. Shipton was saying just last night that Geoffrey Lovell was recently come to town, and that he was in the army with his lordship. Lord Verwood would hardly leave just when a great friend of his was due, would he? No, I shouldn't wonder if it is just a ploy to see if absence makes the heart grow fonder," she suggested, coyly eyeing Amelia over the spectacles she used when doing handwork.

"Out of sight, out of mind," Amelia sniffed, stabbing her needle unnecessarily violently into the handkerchief she was monogramming.

— 11 —

Trudy's mention of Geoffrey Lovell did not escape Amelia's attention. Nor did the fact that Lord Verwood had managed to leave London just on his old friend's arrival. Here again was a highly suspicious circumstance which, when mentioned to her brother, only made him shake his head at her and wander off to his library. Amelia determined to meet Colonel Lovell without delay.

This proved a little more difficult than she had expected, and eventually she had to go to Clarissa Shipton to discover where he was most likely to turn up of an evening.

"My word, Amelia, you've done nothing this entire season but try to track down various gentlemen! It won't do, my dear." Clarissa twirled a bracelet around her wrist, inspecting it for any loose stones. "First Lord Verwood, now Colonel Lovell. I can't imagine what has possessed you. If you'd wanted to marry so badly, there was Lord Ashley last season. But I think you were wise to turn him down. He's much more interested in horses than he is in people. And Rollings won't do, of course. Still, this passion you've developed for military men in quite inexplicable."

"I have *not* developed a passion for military men," Amelia protested. "My aunt mentioned that Colonel Lovell was in London and I simply thought I should like to meet him. You seemed the most logical person to ask where I might find him."

"Not I! Mama perhaps, but then, she knows where everyone is, doesn't she?" Clarissa grinned at her. "Well, she did say she expected to see him at the Earnleys' tomorrow. I suppose you could just pop in there on your way to the Swinbrooks'." Clarissa lowered her eyelids demurely over brilliant blue eyes and murmured, "He's quite striking in his regimentals, Amy. I cannot say when last I've been so struck by a gentleman's appearance. A great deal more polished than your Lord Verwood, too."

"He isn't my Lord Verwood, and I would be the first to point out his deficiencies to anyone who cared to hear of them."

Clarissa offered a sly wink. "Many a gentleman has been known to smooth his ways for the sake of the right lady. I dare say even Lord Ashley would have made some effort."

They were sitting in the Shiptons' drawing room sipping languidly at cups of tea. Amelia helped herself to a rhubarb tart. "I can't think Aunt Trudy would mind stopping in at the Earnleys'. Will you be there?"

"Oh, yes. Mama is convinced Colonel Lovell is an eligible parti. A younger son, but from the Suffolk Lovells, who are without a doubt one of the most prominent families of the county. To say nothing of being one of the wealthiest."

Amelia laughed at her companion's mockery. "Ah, yes. An important point. Promise to introduce him to me, Clarissa."

The young lady sighed. "Well, I will, if you will promise not to dazzle him with your dimples."

"I don't have dimples," Amelia retorted, dusting her fingers on the minuscule napkin with which she'd been provided.

"That's true. It's your nose that intrigues them."

"My nose?" Amelia asked in astonishment.

"It twitches," Clarissa explained kindly. "When someone has caught your interest."

"Nonsense."

"But it does. I shall watch to see what your nose does tomorrow night."

Colonel Geoffrey Lovell might have made nine noses out

of ten twitch, but Amelia was interested in him only for what he could tell her of Lord Verwood. It was true that the colonel was an attractive man: medium height, with wavy brown hair and sincere brown eyes, regular features, and a warm smile. When Mrs. Shipton sailed into the room beside Clarissa, she immediately took note of where he stood with a group of gentlemen and nodded in satisfaction. "I told you he would be here," she whispered (rather loudly) to her daughter.

"Yes, Mama," Clarissa agreed, not allowing her own eyes to stray to the group. As Colonel Lovell detached himself from the other men and headed in her direction, she waved Amelia over to join her. During the introductions she paid particular attention to Amelia's nose, which remained quite unmoved by the signal honor, and she smiled with relief. After soliciting Clarissa's hand for the first set, the colonel politely requested Amelia's for the second. A very satisfactory arrangement to both young women.

Colonel Lovell was an accomplished dancer, possessing a grace which Lord Verwood might well have envied, had he been of such an inclination, which Amelia doubted. Since there was little time to lose, she began her interrogation immediately, with no diminution of her skill in managing the boulanger.

"I understand you are well known to my brother's friend Lord Verwood," she remarked, smiling pleasantly at him.

"Yes, indeed. It's the greatest ill-luck he should have been out of town when I arrived."

"Did you serve with him in Egypt?"

"I was there when he took the ball in his knee. Lord, he was lucky not to have the kneecap shot right off. Does he still have trouble with it?"

"A certain amount," Amelia said dryly.

Colonel Lovell apparently didn't notice her skepticism. "They weren't sure it would heal properly. I dare say he limps."

"When necessary."

"Not all the time?" the colonel asked, surprised.

Amelia repented her flippancy. "I suppose he does limp all the time. One simply doesn't notice after a while."

"Of course," he agreed.

"Have you known Lord Verwood long?"

"For several years. We joined the regiment about the same time. A shame we weren't sent to join Sir John Moore." He shrugged. "But then, I suppose we're both lucky just to be here now. Apparently Fraser's army has been blockaded in Alexandria."

"I take it you share Lord Verwood's admiration for Sir John Moore."

His eyes lit with enthusiasm. "You bet I do! And I've been lucky enough to be reassigned under his command. Alexander will envy me. Do you know when he returns to town?"

"I'm afraid not." Amelia was trying to find some way to ask a question that would prove beyond doubt that Verwood was or was not the viscount he claimed to be. Anyone could fake an injury, or profess devotion to Sir John Moore. "Did Lord Verwood know you would be here?"

"No. I had intended to surprise him."

The dance was drawing to a conclusion. Amelia wanted to ask him if Verwood was tall, with unruly black hair and fierce black eyes, but she knew he'd think she was crazy. "Did you stop at his house in South Street?" she asked desperately.

"Oh, yes. His butler couldn't say when he'd be back."

"You probably knew the butler from a previous visit."

"Perhaps." Colonel Lovell looked thoughtful for a moment. "Alexander didn't have the house open when we were last in London together. He had rooms in Clarges Street, as I recall. It may have been the same fellow then. I think he recognized me."

"You mean he called you by name before you gave him your card?"

He lifted his shoulders in a negligent shrug. "Really, Lady Amelia, I don't recall. Does it matter?"

His amused eyes made her immediately protest, "No, no,

of course not. I'm forever in admiration of these old family retainers who can remember a face from one's childhood, you know. Better than I do, usually."

"Yes, indeed," he agreed, giving her a rather skeptical look.

Amelia was relieved to be delivered to her aunt on the sidelines. Lord Verwood probably was who he claimed to be. Certainly he could prove it to her satisfaction by returning to town and facing Colonel Lovell. And she imagined he had every intention of returning to town. Though not to pay any attention to *her*. Which didn't mean she didn't look for him at every entertainment she attended. It wasn't a conscious decision on her part to search the masses of people, looking especially closely when a tall gentleman entered the room. She was only vaguely aware that she did it at all, until she felt the subtle disappointment that the dark-haired fellow would turn out to be Sir John Brewster or Mr. Alistair Hoffing. Surely she had much more important things to worry about than where his lordship had disappeared and when, or if, he would reappear. Amelia forced herself to concentrate on them.

There was Peter, of course. He was becoming more and more enamored of Mlle. Chartier. Not an evening went past when he didn't stand up with her at least once, usually twice if he could manage it. And Amelia had seen him driving in the park with the young woman on several occasions. M. Chartier was usually somewhere about, hovering within chaperone distance of his sister but never being more than civil to Lady Amelia.

Then there was the Carson family. Dr. Wells had sent Mrs. Carson home from hospital and Amelia couldn't bear to think of her recuperating in that shabby room in the Rookery, where she would doubtless only work herself into illness again amidst the foul air and unsanitary conditions. What the whole family needed was to live in a place where there was fresh air and decent housing and enough undemanding work for Mrs. Carson to support them. Somewhere in the country, perhaps.

It was after this thought had germinated in Amelia's mind

for a while that she came up with what she conceived as a brilliant solution to the majority of her current worries. She would move the Carsons to one of the cottages on her brother's estate in Sussex. There was bound to be an empty cottage there, and some work the woman was fit to do. Amelia would insist that she needed Peter's escort, and would manage to keep him in the country for a while, to let his ardor cool. Perhaps in the meantime some worthy swain would offer for Mlle. Chartier and be accepted.

The other advantage her plan had was that it got her out of London. She was becoming annoyed with herself for her constant awareness of Lord Verwood's absence. She was thoroughly bored with the London season, which was beginning to wind down in any case. None of her "suitors" had been encouraged, and none had come up to scratch. In the country she might find something useful to do, at least. Rumors of smuggling or invasion were always rife in the neighborhood. Surely Peter wouldn't mind her doing a little clandestine research on the subject. Nothing dangerous, of course, just something to keep her busy.

When she suggested the excursion to Trudy, her aunt was horrified. "You're not serious! You haven't had a single offer yet this year. And this was the year you were going to accept someone! No, no, it won't do. We can't be rushing off to Margrave until this matter is settled."

Amelia glared at her. "I'm not going to marry just anyone, Aunt Trudy. If I haven't found someone yet, another few weeks aren't going to do the trick. Surely you must see that."

"But you *have* found someone," Trudy insisted, clasping her pudgy hands together in an excess of torment. "It will only take a few weeks to bring him up to scratch. Trust me in these matters, my dear."

Since Trudy had never been married, it was the height of folly, so far as Amelia was concerned, for her to profess knowledge in the ways of men and matrimony. "Nonsense," Amelia replied briskly, and steeled herself to add, "If you are speaking of Lord Verwood, I can assure you you're fair and far out, my dear aunt."

"But he's shown a decided interest in you recently!"

"Pooh! The only interest Lord Verwood has in me is to embarrass me whenever possible."

Trudy looked astonished. "Whatever can you mean? Don't think I didn't notice that he attended every event we did for weeks. And he danced with you, when he seldom dances at all. He rode home from the park with you and took you on that ill-conceived expedition to the East End. Then he drove in the park with you. He escorted us to the Bramshaws' ball."

"And disappeared without a by-your-leave," Amelia reminded her.

"Nonsense! His leg was bothering him. You can't have forgotten that. I've given it a great deal of thought, and I'm convinced if he hadn't felt the greatest affinity for you, he would never have been so ungallant as to leave us there without an escort. Why, he hasn't been in town since, has he? It had nothing to do with you, my dear. But if we were to leave and go to Margrave, why, he'd forget who you were before we returned."

"I'm sure that's precisely as I would wish it."

Trudy studied the stubborn face across from her. "I see how it is," she grumbled. "You've taken one of your pets, and now you'll turn the whole household upside down so you can have your way. And what of Peter? This is a most important time for him to be in town. If we leave, he certainly won't come with us."

"Oh, he must. I can't like travelling without him. He can come right back, of course."

Her air of innocence did not fool Trudy for a moment. She gave a low moan and slumped back against her chair. "Oh, wretched girl. I can't think what's gotten into you." Her eyelids, which had fluttered down to cover the astute brown eyes, suddenly popped open again and she stared at her niece for an uncomfortable length of time. Eventually she nodded, as though satisfied with her conclusion, and said, "Very well. I'll ask Peter if he won't accompany us to Margrave."

* * *

Trudy was as good as her word. It wasn't even necessary for Amelia to speak with her brother, because her aunt had already handled the matter. All that was left for Amelia was to send her regrets to the hostesses they would be forced to disoblige, and to arrange through Robert for the Carsons' agreement. This latter never seemed much in doubt to Amelia, though she was relieved when the footman brought her word that the family would be ready and waiting whenever Robert had arranged for their transportation.

As their travelling carriage left the crowded city behind, Amelia gave a sigh and leaned back against the upholstery, smiling benignly out the window at Peter, who rode alongside them, not looking the least perturbed at being so abruptly wrenched from his beloved. Matters could not have progressed to such an advanced stage as she'd feared, Amelia thought, hearing his merry whistle as he rode. Probably he was as relieved as she to be headed once again to Margrave. Even Trudy seemed smugly satisfied as she napped in the corner, a beatific smile on her face.

Their route lay through River Head and Tunbridge, and everywhere the countryside around them sparkled with the freshness of spring. At Flimwell they stopped to dine at the Golden Arms, where they were greeted with warmth and shown to a lovely private parlor that Amelia remembered from far back into her childhood. She could recall going with her mother to freshen up, and returning to find her father and brother already quaffing a pint to wash the dust of the road from their throats. The memory made her own throat ache, but she smiled brightly at her companions and said, "Oh, isn't it the perfect time to be out in the country again? Have you smelled anything so rich and wonderful as this farmland? I can hardly wait to see Margrave again."

No one disagreed with her. Peter nodded amiably and Trudy helped herself to a second portion of salmon, saying, "You don't get fish this fresh in London."

It was only midafternoon when the carriage bypassed Rye to turn toward Winchelsea. Margrave was located approximately halfway between the two towns, set off the military road, and hidden from it by an enormously high hedge.

There was a broad piece of water beyond the hedge, where the Brede was adapted as part of the Royal Military Canal, with elevated banks designed as defensive works. The road crossed the water by a bridge, where most traffic doubled back to mount the height to Winchelsea — and a secondary road turned to the left, where it eventually passed through the gates of Margrave, seat of the Earls of Welsford for more than two centuries.

The date 1601 was carved above the east doorway, which had been the entrance front until forty years previously. Possibly the building would have appeared flat, with its three superimposed tiers of enormous mullioned windows extending across a facade almost two hundred feet wide and ninety feet high, but there were subtle changes like the porch and wings, or the Flemish-type gables, or the shallow bay windows at the ends of the wings, that gave it a real excitement. And there were the marvellous Elizabethan pavilions flanking the original forecourt, purposeless but beautiful, in which Amelia and Peter had played as children.

It was the west front they approached now, however, the brilliant conception of their grandfather. He had bought the porch and ornamental features of a late-Tudor house in the area that was about to be torn down, and fitted them between the two wings of the west front. Not only was the stone a perfect match for that of Margrave, but the detailing was so exquisitely smiliar it would have taken an expert to tell the difference. The adaptation was not only a work of beauty, however. By adding it to the front of the building the third earl had achieved internal corridors on the first and second storeys where previously one had had to pass through one bedchamber to reach another.

There were still inconveniences in the place, of course, such as the seventy-yard walk from the kitchens to the family dining room, but the house was wonderfully light and airy, for all its heavy stone. Each huge room had huge windows, where sunlight glinted through the glass at marvellous angles, making everything sparkle within. Amelia could see the light flashing off the diamond-shaped panes as they drove up to the porch, and she was the first one to leap down from the carriage and rush up the three shallow steps to the front door just as it was opened by Bighton.

Amelia grinned at him, knowing he must be as delighted as she to once again be at Margrave. "How does everything look, Bighton?" she asked, casting a loving glance about the Great Hall. The hardwood floors shone, the ancestral portraits gleamed in the light from the windows at the end of the room.

"As always, Mrs. Lawson has everything in perfect shape, Lady Amelia," he replied. "She's already preparing the extra chambers."

"Extra chambers?"

Trudy and Peter had followed her into the hall and watched her confusion with perfect equanimity. When Bighton made no attempt to enlighten her, Trudy said comfortably, "Yes, we'll need the rooms by tomorrow for M. and Mlle. Chartier."

"And Verwood, of course," Peter added, allowing Bighton to relieve him of his gloves and hat.

— 12 —

From any one of the four windows in the library, Amelia could see the carriage drive that led to the west front of Margrave. She felt sure the eager Chartiers would be the first to arrive. The Carsons wouldn't arrive by the carriage drive at all, of course, but by the back road that would take them around to the smattering of cottages nearer the old Camber Castle ruins. Robert had arranged for their transportation, and was to accompany them all the way from London. Amelia wasn't likely to hear of their arrival until they were settled into their new home.

It would have been quite enough for Amelia to cope with the Chartiers' unexpected visit without the added burden of knowing that Verwood was coming. She stared at the rainbow created on her hands by the colored glass armorial bearings in the upper rows of the windows, wondering how on earth she was to behave with the viscount. Surely he would think Peter had invited him to court her, and the very thought made Amelia cringe with despair. Even if he gave no such interpretation to the invitation (and Amelia supposed that was possible, considering his total lack of social finesse), what in the name of all that was dear was she supposed to do with him while Peter spent his time with Mlle. Chartier?

Since Trudy had had an obvious part in the underhanded scheme, she could be the one to entertain *both* M. Chartier and Lord Verwood, for all Amelia cared. All her clever

124

plans were going awry and there didn't seem to be a thing she could do about it. Except spend a great deal of time with the Carsons, helping them adjust to their new surroundings. But Amelia couldn't really imagine they would need much assistance from her, or that they would welcome her interference.

A distant clattering of hooves made Amelia raise her head and sigh. She rose and walked to the largest of the windows, where she could see out beyond the green parkland to the gates. A carriage was just coming through them, but it wasn't the travelling carriage she had expected. It was a curricle drawn by a pair of fine-looking bays. Now, how had he managed that? she wondered. Those were never post horses. He must have spent the night on the road and driven only a stage or two this morning. As he drew closer, she could see that he wore a drab driving coat with two shoulder capes, a rather elegant piece of apparel—for him.

She did not intend to go down and greet him. Let Trudy or Peter be the one to welcome him to Margrave. Heaven knew *she* wasn't glad he was here. But the patter of footsteps rapidly approaching the library ended in Trudy bursting into the room, an enormous smile on her face. "He's here!" she announced almost breathlessly. "I heard the carriage from my room. Come along, dear. You look lovely."

Did she? Amelia managed to catch a glimpse of herself in the mirror above a mule-chest in the hall. There was still some color in her cheeks from her early-morning ride and the jaconet muslin gown's shade of pale blue looked satisfactory on her, she supposed. There wasn't time to do anything with her hair, if she was to follow Trudy's clattering progress down the broad stone staircase. Her aunt hadn't stopped talking since she poked her head into the library.

"Imagine his being so early! I had no idea anyone would arrive before this afternoon." She swung around to impress a coy look on Amelia, who was several steps behind her. "It just shows how eager he is to be here. I hope you've been thinking of ways to entertain him, Amelia. After the bustle of London, a gentleman expects a little diversion."

"He hasn't spent much time in London recently," Amelia grumbled, nearly tripping over the skirts of her gown on the quarter-landing.

"Well, he was certainly back in time for Peter to invite him, wasn't he? And accepted with alacrity, I haven't a doubt in the world. Now, you're not in the habit of being especially pleasing to gentlemen, my dear, and you'll have to take my advice in how to handle him. I should have sat up with you last night to go over a few things, but, there, I was so tired from the journey. Never mind. I'll just coach you as the visit progresses."

Amelia conscientiously held back a sharp retort. As they had emerged from the north staircase into the hall, Lord Verwood was just being shown into the house. He looked devilishly handsome in the driving coat with his unruly black hair barely tamed by the hand he drew through it as he removed his hat. Trudy twittered happily as she trotted over to him.

"How nice it is to see you again! You've never been to Margrave, have you? Well, we've set aside one of the loveliest suites for you, Lord Verwood. There's a view of the water, of course. Your own property is inland, so I thought you would especially appreciate that."

"Thank you, Miss Harting, that's very kind of you." His gaze moved back to the foot of the staircase, where Amelia still stood, and he inclined his head in acknowledgment of her.

She found herself piqued at this small gesture and moved stiffly forward to say, "I hope your knee is no longer troubling you, Lord Verwood."

"Very little. I've had the opportunity to rest it for the last week or so."

Amelia found this a very unlikely story, and her cool stare told him as much, but he merely grinned at her. "So long as you don't have me chasing any more thieves, I dare say it will heal entirely in no time."

"I wasn't the one who set you to chasing thieves," she reminded him. "That was your own idea of proper conduct under the circumstances."

"You'd have had me let him get away with your purse?" he asked rhetorically as he drew that item, carefully laundered, from the pocket of the voluminous driving coat and extended it to her. "I think you'll find everything intact."

As Amelia reluctantly accepted her property, Trudy swung a suspicious gaze between the two of them. "Thieves? You don't mean to say someone tried to steal Amelia's reticule when you went to that distressing area of London?" Verwood nodded and Trudy dredged up a prodigious frown with which to regard her niece. "You see? Didn't I warn you it wasn't safe to go there? And you never mentioned a word of all this to me."

"There wasn't the least need for you to concern yourself. Under Lord Verwood's protection," she added, her voice rich with irony, "I was never in any danger. Why, you would have been enormously impressed with how heroic he was, Aunt Trudy. The child who grabbed my purse stood almost to his waist. A dangerous ruffian, I promise you. And his lordship strained his knee in giving chase to the lad. Truly a commendable act of bravery."

"You exaggerate, Lady Amelia," Verwood protested, a gleam of amusement in his eyes. "I doubt the child came up to my waist."

"Perhaps not," she conceded graciously.

Not knowing quite what to make of this story, Trudy asked the viscount, "Did you press charges against the brute?"

"No. I consigned him to the care of Lady Amelia's reverend friend, Mr. Symons. When I returned . . . That is, when I was able to speak with him, he suggested such an arrangement as Lady Amelia has with the Carson boy, to keep him off the streets and in school." He turned a benevolent smile on Lady Amelia. "I told him I was sure you'd wish to undertake the matter, perhaps even move his whole family down here, as you're apparently doing with the Carsons. There are fifteen of them, I understand."

"You didn't!" Amelia cried, before she realized, by the rueful twist of his lips, that he was teasing her.

"No, I didn't. Actually, I did agree to arrange for some of

his older brothers and sisters to be trained for household service, and for him to go to school. He seems young to be a hardened case, but the reverend didn't hold as much hope for him as for Tommy Carson. He's learned a great deal from the older boys, I gather."

"What," Trudy asked faintly, "has Tommy Carson done?"

Her niece glared at Lord Verwood, but said, "He tried a little pickpocketing. It's not uncommon for boys in the Rookery."

"Well, it is *most* uncommon for boys in Sussex, and I hope you will tell him so." Trudy pressed a handkerchief to her perspiring brow and upper lip. "I shan't feel comfortable with him around, wondering when he'll nab my pocket watch."

"He stole to support his family," Amelia assured her, "and since there will be no need for that here, you may be sure he'll behave quite decently."

Verwood looked skeptical. "To be on the safe side, I'll keep an eye on him while I'm here, shall I?"

Just as Trudy was saying, "Oh, yes, please," Amelia was saying, "That won't be necessary." She glared at both of them. "The poor child has enough to concern him without being spied upon. I think we can safely let him be."

"Well, well, we shall see," Trudy placated. "In the meantime, I'll have someone show Lord Verwood to his chamber. We've kept him standing here in the hall far too long. Peter will be back from Rye by early afternoon, my lord. We didn't expect you this early. Perhaps after you've had a chance to freshen up you'd like Amelia to show you around the house and the grounds."

"That would be . . . charming," he agreed, his black eyes alight with mischief. Before she could find some excuse, which she certainly intended to do, he followed a footman up the stone staircase.

Amelia was waiting, alone, in the Summer Parlor when Verwood entered the room. Trudy had refused to stay with her, insisting that she was needed to show Mrs. Lawson precisely what she wanted done with the winter draperies from her bedchamber. Though most of the rooms at Margrave were panelled, the Summer Parlor had cool apple green plastered walls and light curtains at its windows, and French doors. The doors were open at the moment, allowing a warm breeze to play through the room, carrying on it the scent of mowed grass and salt water. Amelia looked up from the book she hadn't been reading when the viscount strolled into the room.

His outfit was far less formal than she'd heretofore seen him wear—buckskin breeches with top boots, and a navy short-tailed coat that had the comfortable flavor of a shooting jacket. The walking stick he carried was a whimsical affair, carved so intricately that one doubted it was the least use in sustaining any amount of weight. He sported a Belcher handkerchief instead of a cravat, and he was smiling.

"Wonderful old pile," he declared, walking straight across the room past her to the open doors. "I hate to waste such a glorious day inside. Would you mind showing me around the grounds first?"

"Not at all." Amelia snapped the book shut, not bothering to put a marker in it, since she had no idea what it was even about. She rose with her usual grace and glided over to where he stood. "The house was completed in 1601," she began, stepping out onto the terrace, "and is constructed of stone from a local quarry."

Verwood patiently listened to her detailed description of the free-standing columns (which matched the columnar structure of the chimneys above), of the curved cornices and scalloped canopies, of the indentations where terra-cotta medallions had never been placed, of the classical entablatures (including the one with the triglyph frieze). He murmured approval of the balustrade with obelisks and the statues of the Nine Worthies. He praised the tawny ochre stone and the grassed forecourt. He strolled off the gravel path to inspect the flowerbeds on the low walls and to study the obelisks and stone lanterns on the balustrade that matched the one on the roof. He was quite overcome with the gracefulness of the pavilions that flanked the courtyard, expressing his admiration of the ogee roofs and the oriel windows.

"Let's go in," he suggested.

"There's nothing in them," she said firmly, suspecting him of mocking her with his abundance of appreciation. Somehow Verwood didn't strike her as the sort of gentleman who would ordinarily be the least bit interested in the details she was giving him.

"That's why I think we should go in," he retorted.

Confused, Amelia argued, "But you said you wanted to be outside on such a nice day."

"They're outdoorsy enough for me, sort of like a folly. I want to find out what you can see from them, how Margrave looks through those diamond-paned windows, what the inside of that grotes . . . the unusual roof looks like."

He was regarding her challengingly, daring her to step inside the strange little hideaway with him. Amelia squared her shoulders and marched to the door, rather hoping it would be locked. He reached around her and pushed it open, chuckling at the eerie screech of the heavy oak door that made her shudder. It was years since she'd been in one of the Elizabethan pavilions, or had the desire to enter them. As children it had been fun, a kind of playhouse to explore, but now it smelled musty to her and a sticky cobweb clung to her face and hair as she stepped into the cool, dim interior.

"Very interesting," he murmured so close behind her she almost jumped.

It wasn't interesting; it was spooky. She wiped the cobweb off her face and grimaced at the dusty earth floor. There was as much lichen on the interior walls here as there was on the exterior, instead of the creamy satin texture of the stone inside the house. Only the middle of the one large room felt the least bit acceptable to her, with the weak light coming through the dusty panes from all sides.

Verwood had followed her to the center and stood beside her, his hand falling on her shoulder. "We have a few things to discuss," he said.

"I can't imagine what," she muttered, moving out from under his hand.

"First, there's the matter of Mlle. Chartier. Apparently you spoke to Peter about her."

"Well, you certainly didn't."

"No, I had to leave town rather abruptly. It wasn't my knee, you see."

"Oh, I know that," she sniffed. "Mr. Woolbeding mentioned your travelling carriage and the Shorn Sheep."

"My knee *was* hurting rather abominably that night."

Amelia made a face at him. "You'll never convince me of that again."

He sighed. "No, I don't suppose I will. Never mind. I would have preferred your letting me speak to Peter first."

"How could I?" Amelia was incensed by his denseness. "Every day he was becoming more and more attached to her. I had to do something to put a rub in his way before it was too late."

"I fail to see how this expedition served your purpose." He regarded her quizzingly, both hands curled easily around the head of his walking stick.

"They tricked me," she admitted. "He and Aunt Trudy. We were supposed to come here to separate him from Mlle. Chartier. I thought perhaps if I could keep him here long enough, she would find someone else, and you might turn up something damaging enough against her brother to make Peter see reason. I didn't know until we got here that they'd invited the Chartiers . . . or you."

He'd known it all along. She could tell by the way he stood so very still, observing her, listening so intently, as though it was really the sound of her voice he wished to hear, rather than her words. There was something strange about his eyes, too, in the gloom of the ridiculous pavilion. They made her feel uncomfortably warm and excruciatingly nervous. For a long time he simply stared as a fluttery sensation grew within her.

Finally he asked, "Would you like me to tell you what I learned about M. Chartier?"

"Of course."

"Absolutely nothing of any significance," he admitted. "I spent a great deal of time sitting behind a hedgerow outside Bournemouth. There's some suspicious activity around the manor house the Chartiers live in there, and a revenue officer took it into his head that I might have something to do with it. When I'd finally convinced him who I was, he could provide very little information. He's been on the lookout, but he can't say for sure whether it's spying or smuggling or something quite innocuous that's going on. Mr. Selsey, the revenue officer, had made a raid on the beach just before I got there, as it turned out, but someone had warned off the boats and they didn't land. Which meant absolutely nothing happened while I was there, of course. A completely wasted journey. It needn't even be Chartier who's involved."

"Is that . . . where you went when you left London?" she asked.

"Yes. An associate had sent me word that something was going on. Unfortunately, he was in London talking with me when Selsey raided the beach, or we might have spared ourselves a great deal of time."

Amelia nodded and took a few steps away from him, feeling the need to be outside the strong field of attraction which seemed to surround him. She wanted to break that unnerving pull toward him, but, not watching where she was going, she stubbed her toe on a piece of stone, and bit back the cry of pain that rose to her lips. With her back to him, she stood wiggling her toes inside her shoe, trying to work the ache down to something manageable. He must have spoken to her, but she didn't hear him.

When he spoke again, it was to press her. "Well, have you?"

"I'm sorry," she said, reaching down to pick up the offending stone and toss it into a corner. "I didn't hear what you said."

"I asked if you had stopped doing any investigating on your own, as Peter suggested."

"Peter didn't suggest; he *told* me to stop. So naturally I have," she informed him self-righteously. Her toe still hurt, so she added, "And I'm well aware that you were the one behind his ever questioning the practice."

"Are you?" He had come up with her now, a slight smile playing near the corners of his mouth. "He didn't tell you so, did he?"

"No, but I assure you I'm quite clever enough to have found it out for myself." She glared up into his watchful eyes. "It's a great waste, you know. I was able to pass along some useful information."

"But at what cost, my dear Lady Amelia?"

His gaze was unnervingly intent, and there was that about it which made her feel somehow self-conscious. She turned her face aside, saying dismissively, "Cost? There was no cost at all, I assure you."

"I see. These unscrupulous fellows talked to you just for the sake of your beautiful violet eyes, did they?"

Amelia found she couldn't make her beautiful violet eyes meet his fierce black ones. She lifted one shoulder in a careless shrug. "Men are notoriously muddle-headed when they're dealing with women, Lord Verwood. Perhaps you've noticed that."

He gave a bark of laughter and reached out to touch her cheek with a tender finger. "Yes," he said, "I've noticed that, especially when the woman is you."

The sound of a carriage could be heard on the drive now. Without looking at him, Amelia headed for the open door. "Our other guests are arriving," she called back. "I should be in the house to make them welcome."

She didn't check to see if he followed her as she scurried along the gravel path of the house.

Verwood had discovered that his room was in the same wing as Lady Amelia's, though a fair distance away. Not that this provided any unique opportunity for him. For the first day of his stay, after their original walk together, he never saw her except in the company of her family and guests. He didn't see much of Peter, either, since his friend was determined on making Mlle. Chartier comfortable and providing for her entertainment. This didn't necessarily mean that he neglected his other guests, but it certainly limited the time he could spend with them.

But Verwood was enjoying himself immensely. He had three unique encounters before noon on the second day. First, he ran into M. Chartier on the north staircase, headed down to breakfast. The young man was dressed rather formally for a casual house party, with shirt points high enough to make it uncomfortable for him to turn his head very far. He had a unique way of overcoming this obstacle; he seemed to stand a little higher on his toes, as though this would raise him above the collar and make it possible for him to converse with his head at a forty-five-degree angle.

"Ah, Lord Verwood," he said, bouncing slightly to get even more leverage. "I was delighted to find that you form part of the house party. This last week in town I didn't see you at all."

"No, I was called away, unfortunately." There didn't seem much chance of M. Chartier having heard he'd been in

Bournemouth, so he decided against informing him. "To come here, I don't mind missing a part of the season, but for a business trip . . ."

"Ah, just so, just so." Chartier lowered his voice conspiratorially. "All the same, it was a dangerous week to miss. A young girl's affections are quickly attached, I fear. And I am not a brother who would stand in the way of his sister's happiness, you understand. Still," he added in a more encouraging tone, "I feel sure there is time. Veronique is not one to make a hasty decision. You mustn't let her carefree air fool you. She has a practical streak which will, I believe, allow her mind to guide her heart."

The gist of this declaration was, if not alarming, at least slightly unnerving to Verwood. "But surely Lord Welsford is by far the most desirable parti," he demurred.

Chartier dropped his voice even lower, bouncing more agitatedly now, though Verwood was directly before his eyes. "Indeed, it would seem so to many. Perhaps to everyone but me." With a flip of his hand he dismissed such material considerations. "It was you who gave me good advice on my sister's behalf, you who took a personal interest in her welfare. To me that is no small consideration. The earl . . . well, he is a handsome fellow, possessed of a fine old title and sufficient funds to make a young girl's head turn. This I know. But has he served his country in battle as you have? I think not. Has he led aught but a life of privilege and frivolity?"

Since Chartier paused at this point, Verwood murmured, "No."

"And he is young, yet. Several years your junior, if I am not mistaken. With an understandable pride in his family. He would give grave consideration to the matter of marrying an unknown girl such as my sister. Not that she hasn't perfect breeding! But . . ." He shrugged. "There is no way for us to prove this with documents and registries, you see. You, I think, would not be so concerned with such details, eh?"

"I trust my own judgment," Verwood assured him.

The Frenchman's head bobbed up and down enthusiastically. "I knew it! Just as I myself do. So take heart, *mon ami*. Nothing is settled as yet." And he bounced down the remaining stairs in an ecstasy of rational optimism.

Verwood's next *tête-à-tête* occurred directly after breakfast, when he was trying to figure out a way to manage a ride alone with Lady Amelia. She had spoken with him briefly in the breakfast parlor, but had left before he was finished eating, explaining to the others that she had several household matters to execute before she would be free. This disturbed no one at all, since Peter was already arranging to drive Mlle. Chartier into Rye and Miss Harting had offered to give M. Chartier a guided tour of the house, which Lord Verwood was invited to join if he hadn't seen enough the previous day.

His guide of the previous day refused to meet his amused look, and promptly excused herself. When he was finished eating, he had every intention of tracking her down, but as he left the breakfast parlor, Miss Harting waylaid him on his way across the hall. "In here," she whispered, motioning toward a small vestibule off the large room.

Curious, he followed her.

It was a room where Peter met local petitioners, and was consequently furnished only minimally, and with none-too-comfortable chairs, to discourage a lengthy audience. Miss Harting seated herself on the most agreeable of them, and waved him onto a ladder-backed item that had all the luxury of a fourth-form seat. He waited patiently for her to speak.

"She's not easy to manage," she began. "I think you will just need a few pointers from me. Peter wouldn't be the least help to you. That's not saying she's stubborn, you understand, just a trifle strong-minded, which no man of principle should object to in the least."

"Of course not," he agreed, folding his hands casually in his lap.

"The first thing to remember is that she's been given a lot of freedom in her life, and it wouldn't do to threaten that. Though she doesn't seem to realize that marriage would allow her an even greater latitude, you and I know that's the case." She glanced sharply at him to make sure he was paying attention.

"Indeed."

"Then you must remember that she lost her parents under very trying circumstances, and she has rather a 'thing' about the French. I don't believe she will be positively rude to Mlle. Chartier or her brother, but she isn't likely to be quite so warm and giving with them as she is with those of us who know her well."

"I quite understand."

"And there's her age, of course. She's attained her majority, and come into her fortune, and can't see that Peter and I have quite the authority over her which we were used to have. She's not disrespectful! It is just that sometimes she equates her own age with wisdom and experience which she doesn't have, and won't achieve for some time."

"How true!"

Trudy's brows rose at this fervent expression of agreement. Deciding that he was perhaps mocking her niece, she said sternly, "I daresay you were just the same at her age."

He bowed his head in acknowledgment.

Placated, she continued. "She won't marry without affection, so you will have to try your best to please her. That shouldn't be so very difficult. Mind you, I suspect she's already half-inclined in your favor."

At this Verwood's head came up abruptly. "What makes you think that?"

Trudy twitched away the details with her pudgy fingers. "Little things. I know her fairly well, my dear Lord Verwood. She's quite skilled at concealing her emotions."

"I shouldn't wonder," he contributed.

"And not at all reluctant to speak her mind. What you must understand is that she's a bit grumpy from time to time. I think it's a strain of her mother's melancholia. Nothing to be alarmed about! Just the tiniest bit, when she's thwarted or doesn't understand her own mind."

"Was Lady Welsford much afflicted?"

"Only occasionally. Once or twice a year she would be

sunk in gloom for a week or two before she perked up again.
Amelia isn't affected in that way. In her it is more often a
show of temper. She is not as placid a female as her mother
was."

"I see." Verwood shifted slightly on his hard chair. "Are
these shows of temper ever . . . violent?"

"Violent?" Trudy frowned at him. "Don't be ridiculous! I
warn you of them merely because you are likely to be the
recipient of a cross word now and then, not because she's
likely to run you through with a sword! In your case she
simply does not know her own mind, and it is bound to make
her a bit . . . edgy."

"Ah, yes, of course."

In a move of startling swiftness, Trudy hauled herself off
the chair and onto her feet. "I'm sure that will be enough to
guide you for the moment, Lord Verwood. As I watch your
progress with her, I may just point out something here and
there. I feel sure you are a man who will accept my guidance
with a good grace, else I wouldn't have offered it."

"I'm most grateful," he said humbly.

"Yes, I felt sure you would be." She marched toward the
door, but paused to add, "Of course, I wish you luck."

"I'll need it," he mused as she disappeared out into the
hall.

Just before the midday cold collation he was standing on
the terrace outside the Summer Parlor when he heard the
doors open behind him. For some reason he assumed it
would be Lady Amelia and he turned to greet her with a
smile. But it was only the elfin Mlle. Chartier, her eyes
gleaming with their usual excitement. He bowed a little
stiffly.

"A beautiful day, is it not, Lord Verwood?" she asked,
breathing in great draughts of the sparkling country air
much as though it were wine. "London is a fascinating city,
but no one would ever claim it is particularly clean, would
they?"

"No." For a moment he could think of nothing more to

say to her; then he remembered her morning's excursion. "How did you like Rye?"

"Delightful! So quaint, and more Flemish than English, I think. The earl showed me the parish church and the town hall and the Old Flushing Inn. He told me the inn is used by smugglers. Imagine! And there is a tower used as a gaol and a half-timbered building with gables that is used for a hospital. The English are so very practical."

"Smuggling is an old trade in this area," Verwood said, wishing to stick with the subject for a minute. "Not condoned by the authorities, but participated in by a goodly number of the natives."

"Lord Welsford said it is mainly brandy that is brought in from France, and that this goes on not only in time of war, but always. Is the excise tax so high, then, that it is worth men committing a crime?"

"It's high enough to make some men think so. Other goods come in as well, in time of war especially. Gowns, gold, even family heirlooms. There must be a certain amount of smuggling activity even near Bournemouth."

If he had hoped this suggestion would discompose her, he was disappointed. "I suppose there is," she said thoughtfully, "though it's farther from France than Rye is. Perhaps if I'd lived there all my life I'd know more about it. Not that I should particularly wish to."

This was said with perfect good humor, not a trace of anxiety or concealment evident in the delightful, open countenance. Verwood wondered if the girl's perpetual cheerfulness would drive him mad, were he to make some effort (as her brother encouraged) to win her affections. It was all well and good for Peter, who was himself possessed of a remarkably easygoing nature. But Verwood owned to a more saturnine disposition, and the girl's incessant optimism struck him as almost foolhardy.

Nonetheless, he decided, for the sake of pure devilry, or to see what information he could wean from her exuberance, to set up a bit of a flirtation with the girl. It would give him some much-needed practice, after all. Surely he had seen enough flirtations going on in London to have picked up a rudimentary knowledge of how they were conducted.

"Do you ride, Mlle. Chartier?" he asked, offering his most pleasant smile.

"A little. I'm just the tiniest bit afraid of horses," she confessed.

"They have a docile mare in the stables here. I was speaking with the stable boys just this morning. Perhaps I could convince you to have a ride with me after our meal. Nothing arduous, of course. Just a trot about the estate."

"That would be . . . lovely," she agreed.

"Good." He turned toward the doors then, thinking it must be close to time for their luncheon, and found Lady Amelia standing there. She wasn't smiling, but she spoke immediately. "Aunt Trudy sent me to find you. Won't you join the rest of us in the dining room? You must be famished."

She addressed the remarks more to Mlle. Chartier than to him, but Verwood hastened to say, "I haven't seen you around all morning, Lady Amelia. I hope no domestic problem has arisen."

She moved cool eyes to stare at him as though she'd never seen him before. "It was necessary for me to see that the Carsons were settling into their cottage," she said, before leading the way to the dining hall.

If this third encounter had not, perhaps, been as amusing as the other two, it was at least interesting. Throughout the meal Verwood divided his attention between the three women at the table, finding himself more often than not addressing only Gertrude Harting, as Peter captured Mlle. Chartier's attention, and Lady Amelia appeared pre-occupied. And even Miss Harting he had to share with Chartier, since the Frenchman still shied away from having much contact with Lady Amelia.

When the party started to break up after their meal, Peter learned that Mlle. Chartier had agreed to ride with Verwood, and gave his friend a speculative glance. The viscount maintained a bland expression and Peter invited

Chartier to try his hand at a little angling in the Brede. This left Amelia with no commitment for the afternoon, but Verwood did not include her in his invitation. Miss Harting scowled at him.

Amelia watched from her bedchamber as Mlle. Chartier and Verwood walked down the path to the stables. They had both changed into riding costume and seemed on the most agreeable of terms, chatting and laughing as though their time together was the most amusing of possibilities. Amelia told herself that it was for Peter's sake that she resented this instant camaraderie, that it threatened his own happiness with the young woman. It hardly mattered, at the moment, that the girl might be a French spy. Lord Verwood was obviously the most reprehensible of men for attempting to win Mlle. Chartier's affections from his best friend. (Probably his only friend, Amelia thought bitterly.)

When the two had ridden beyond her line of vision, she sat down to write a note to Clarissa Shipton in London, since she couldn't think of another thing to do with herself that might not advertise the fact that she was being excluded from her own house party. Not that she had invited any of these tiresome guests, but they were, after all, at Margrave, and she *lived* here, for heaven's sake. The thought of paying another call on the Carsons was not at all appealing.

By midafternoon she'd exhausted all the possibilities of directing Mrs. Lawson at her housekeeping duties, had given up on the book she'd tried to read, and had wandered out-of-doors with a basket purposefully slung over her arm and a pair of flower-cutting shears in her hand. Amelia was not particularly good at flower-arranging, but the task gave her something to do, and she thought she might catch Mlle. Chartier and Verwood on their return from their ride. It was her duty as hostess, she assured herself, to find something for the French girl to do which would keep her out of Verwood's clutches for the rest of the afternoon, or until Peter returned.

But the pair didn't pass her and she began to wonder just what they were doing out there on their horses for this lengthy period of time. Mlle. Chartier had said (Amelia had overheard her) that she was a little afraid of horses. Was Verwood using his nonexistent charm to convince her of the joys of equestrianism? Or was something entirely different happening? Really, it was too bad of Verwood to try to steal Peter's inamorata right out from under his nose at his own house!

She was bending over to cut her third tulip (her thoughts had decidedly slowed the speed of her activity), when she noticed a pair of top boots, with feet in them, directly beside her own feet. Startled, she straightened up to find herself staring into the viscount's amazing black eyes. "How did you get here?" she gasped.

"I walked," he explained. "My knee is hardly troubling me at all today. But I would have crawled if necessary."

Amelia was not going to let this sort of negligent flattery deter her from impressing on her mind that the man was incredibly light on his feet. Or he had an aversion to walking on the gravel path she herself had trod, which crunched under one's shoes. "Well, you can crawl back to the house," she informed him. "I would be greatly diverted by the sight."

"Undoubtedly." He lifted the basket from her arm, which he tucked under his own, without a by-your-leave. "I thought we might stroll around the grounds a bit."

"Did you?" Amelia left her arm where it was, but didn't move. "I'm rather busy just now."

"Your Aunt Trudy gave me to understand it would be expected of us." Verwood smiled at her, a quizzing, hateful sort of smile.

"My Aunt Trudy doesn't know what she's talking about sometimes."

"Perhaps not," he said agreeably, urging her forward.

There didn't seem any choice but to move with him. Amelia could have protested the need to cut more flowers, but she didn't think of it. With her arm tucked under his they moved toward the gate into a small orchard. It was a secluded spot, verdant now with the new leaves and springy grass. Verwood did not relinquish her arm as he pushed open the short gate, nor did he speak as they strolled along beneath the trees.

"Did you have a nice ride?" she asked at last.

"Very pleasant."

"How does Mlle. Chartier ride?"

"Not so well as you, but adequately."

They continued to walk through the trees, getting farther and farther from the gate and the house. There was no one about, just birds singing in the trees and the rustle of the wind through the leaves. Their own footfalls made no sound on the soft earth. Verwood stopped abruptly under an old apple tree, releasing her arm and setting the basket on the ground before leaning back against the bark. "I'm surprised you don't wear a bonnet of some sort out-of-doors, Lady Amelia. I thought all young women were fearful of getting too much sun."

"It's hardly the middle of summer," she protested, nervously toying with a lock of hair under his interested gaze. "I don't have fair skin, so I don't burn in the sun."

"Your skin has a marvellous golden tone. You would tan well, I imagine. I've never particularly liked pale skin on a woman."

Mlle. Chartier had a fashionably fair complexion, the sort most prized by the few magazine articles Amelia had read on the subject. She had repeatedly rejected Trudy's efforts to have her bathe her face with lemon juice or any of the other bleaching concoctions her aunt was fond of suggesting. There was an appreciative light in the viscount's eyes now that made her slightly nervous. Amelia moistened her lips and said, "Most men are supposed to prefer a fair skin."

Verwood nodded knowledgeably, and said nothing.

His eyes never left her face, and seemed to concentrate now on her wet lips. Amelia turned away from him, trying to dredge up some semblance of conversation, with her insides feeling very peculiar indeed. He had the most astonishing effect on her insides. And it was hard to think when the blood was throbbing in her temples. Not at all like the headache, in conjunction as it was with a delicate flutter in her breast and a pervasive warmth in her body. She thought that if she were to try to hold her hand steady in front of her face she would find it trembling.

"Do you know how long Peter intends to stay here?" she asked.

"Oh, as long as you would like him to, I suppose." He was wearing a faint smile.

"It doesn't matter any longer," she sighed. If Peter left, Mlle. Chartier would leave . . . and Verwood. Perhaps she could stay at Margrave with Trudy, just to settle herself down a little. This heady sensation, for instance, couldn't be good for a woman over a protracted period of time.

"Did you . . . ?" she began, and paused to clear her throat. "Did you see your friend in town?"

"My friend? Which friend?" He asked it languidly, appearing too distracted by her to pay much attention to the question.

Amelia was instantly alerted, however. She found it difficult to believe his lordship had all that many friends, and this one in particular it was very important that he had seen, or at least been seen by. For his benefit she assumed a superbly casual air as she said dismissively, "Oh, the one from the army."

He regarded her, unblinking, for what seemed a very long time. "Lovell, you mean?" he asked finally.

"Yes, that was his name." She could feel herself stiffen for what he would say next, her face hopefully a polite blank.

"Yes, I saw him briefly."

"And were you pleased with his new assignment?"

"Very. He'll do well with Moore."

Amelia let herself relax at last, and smiled at him. "He seems a pleasant gentleman."

Verwood had moved away from the tree to stand too close beside her. He took hold of each of her hands, which had been clenched at her sides, and massaged them with his strong fingers, as though she had told him they were aching. When she looked up to read what this meant from the expression on his face, he bent and touched his lips to hers. Perhaps it was the relief of finding that he really *was* what he said he was. Perhaps it was that she'd wanted him to kiss her again since that night on the balcony. In any case, she responded to that welcome pressure on her lips, returning it with an eagerness that surprised her. His kiss was long, firm, exciting, and she nestled closer into the circle of his arms, leaning against his chest for necessary support. Her knees felt trembly and her face flushed.

Verwood whispered something close to her ear, stirring the honey-colored tresses slightly with his breath. "Do you believe me now?"

Amelia drew back from his arms and met the softened black gaze. "Yes, I believe you."

"Good. No more trying to trap me with your questions?"

She shook her head.

His smile held a hint of amusement with her, but this was offset by the way his fingers traced the line of her determined chin and came to rest gently against her lips. "I think I'd better get you back to the house now," he said softly, and tucked her arm through his, forgetting the basket under the tree.

Amelia didn't notice it there, with its few bright red flowers, but hurried to keep up with his long-legged stride.

— 14 —

Gertrude Harting, for reasons known only to herself, invited a neighbor to join their gathering that evening. The only thing that gave Michael Upham respectability was his ancestry, and there was some question about that. He was known to have had Jacobite leanings in his youth, and in his more mature years to have consorted with smugglers. Trudy explained to her surprised relatives that as Michael was an old friend of her dead brother's, and a neighbor, he was a perfectly logical choice to add to their company after dinner. Her logic escaped the rest of the household.

Mr. Upham was a rather distinguished-looking gentleman, with grizzled gray hair and a moustache, but his green eyes had a subtly wicked gleam to them and he had a habit of staring at whomever he addressed. He was on the short side, a bit round, though not portly. Trudy knew his age to the day, and it was just over forty years.

To M. Chartier, Trudy explained, "I've known Mr. Upham my whole life. He lives just this side of Winchelsea and he and Rob, my older brother, were the best of friends. There are those who believe he's involved in the smuggling of brandy, but that's gossip, of course. He does, it's true, have access to the most incredible selection of French fabrics and French costumes. I've often been allowed my choice at wonderfully reasonable prices. Don't ask me how he manages to find them, for I don't know and I'm sure I don't wish to know!"

The gentleman in question sported a magnificent blue superfine coat and embroidered knee breeches, in addition to a pearl-gray cravat whose folds were a wonder to gaze upon. The gold buttons on his coat winked cheerfully in the candlelight. Trudy took the opportunity, in an aside to Amelia, to explain that she'd long had a tendre for Michael Upham. Amelia regarded her with astonishment. "You've never even mentioned him," she protested.

"Well," Trudy replied, affronted, "I'm sure I don't wear my heart on my sleeve."

"Then why are you telling me now?"

Trudy chose to ignore this question, turning to Mlle. Chartier to say, "Ah, my dear, I thought we would just get out some music for you. The gentlemen will wish to hear you play." The gentlemen sat patiently through her rather lack-luster performance, and through Amelia's more inspired, if less technically perfect, one. But the evening was too fine to be spent entirely indoors and Michael Upham's suggestion that they stroll in the gardens was met with general approval. The earl offered his arm to Mlle. Chartier (who seemed in the past few hours to have become "Veronique"), while Amelia found herself flanked by Verwood and Chartier, with Trudy trotting along beside Mr. Upham. This arrangement didn't last long, however, when Peter's two collies came racing up to the group, bounding with enthusiasm and a desire to play.

Somehow the group changed in the process of tossing sticks for the dogs. Amelia noted that Michael Upham and M. Chartier wandered off a bit from the group, talking earnestly but in low voices. Her own gaze hastily sought out Verwood's to assure herself that he too had noted this instant and suspicious meeting of the two. Verwood merely smiled enigmatically at her and assisted Mlle. Chartier in her attempt to get one of the collies to release the stick in its mouth. Trudy was explaining to the earl that Mr. Upham was really a reformed man, a worthy in the neighborhood, having given over his more youthful peccadilloes.

Peter looked skeptical but said, "I'm sure I have no objection to your having any of your friends here, my dear

Aunt Trudy. He wasn't, I believe, a great favorite of my father's, or I would have seen him around more when I was younger. Do you remember him, Amelia?" he asked, turning to her.

"Vaguely," she admitted. "Wasn't he married to one of the Broadwells? I seem to remember she died some years ago."

"Yes, very tragic it was," Trudy said. "A simple cough that developed into consumption. She was never a strong woman, of course. Everyone was surprised when he married a fragile lady, himself such a robust fellow. But that's the way men are. They like to think they can protect the weaker sex."

Involuntarily they all turned to look at Veronique Chartier, who was by far the most delicate among them. She was laughing as Verwood showed her how to get distance on an underhanded pitch, the delicious sound of her laughter bright on the balmy evening air. Peter smiled fondly and went to join them, just as one of the collies, in his excitement, accidentally tangled himself in Verwood's legs. The viscount's weak knee gave way and he fell forward onto the ground, despite Peter's attempt to catch him.

Amelia heard the thump of his body hitting the earth and his muffled grunt with a sick feeling in her stomach. Before she could reach him, Peter and Veronique were there, assisting him once again to his feet. The Frenchwoman's eyes were huge with concern and her fingers seemed to fly everywhere in her agitation, brushing the dirt from his cheek and his sleeve and the side of his breeches, all the while begging to know if he was all right. Amelia, unable to be of any assistance to him, grabbed the two dogs by their collars and dragged them out of the way.

"I'm quite all right," Verwood insisted, easing himself away from his benefactors. His face looked pinched in the pale evening light, but he offered a rueful smile. "My knee isn't up to much strain yet. It wasn't the dog's fault. He merely brushed against me when I wasn't expecting it."

It was apparent to all of them that he couldn't put his full weight on the leg, though he tried to stand normally.

Amelia watched him gauge the distance to the house before reluctantly turning to Peter. "I'm afraid I'll need your support to my room."

"Well, of course." The earl put an arm around Verwood's waist and the two men began moving off slowly.

"What will you need to put on it?" Amelia called, her voice sounding overly loud to her own ears.

Verwood paused to look around at her. "Boiled towels," he said with a grimace.

"I'll have Mrs. Lawson send them right up to you." She kept hold of the dogs' collars until the men were inside the house, then released them and hurried off toward the rear entrance, which led into the servants' quarters. The house-keeper's room still had a light shining under the door, and Amelia knocked lightly.

Mrs. Lawson appeared in her usual black bombazine, her hair still neatly gathered in a bun at the back of her head. "Lady Amelia," she said, surprised. "Is there something amiss?"

"One of the collies jumped on Lord Verwood, who has a bad knee. He needs boiled towels. Lord Verwood does, not the collie." Amelia felt she was doing less than justice to the situation. "His lordship suffers from a bullet wound in his knee, from when he was in Egypt with the army. He has a limp, and any strain seems to cause him a great deal of pain. Perhaps you would have some brandy sent up, as well."

"Of course, my lady." She studied Amelia closely for a moment. "I think you might have a sip yourself. You look a little peaked."

Amelia waved aside the suggestion. "No, no. I don't need a thing. Thank you, Mrs. Lawson." She had already turned to go, but stopped to confess, "I haven't always believed him about the knee. You'll see that he has everything he needs, won't you?"

"Of course." Mrs. Lawson followed her out into the hall but turned toward the kitchen when Amelia headed back for the gardens.

What she wanted to do was go directly to Verwood's room. She wanted to apologize for not always believing him, and to lay a cool hand on his possibly fevered brow. It made her furious to think that it had been Veronique Chartier who had brushed off his bruised cheek and discharged the dust from his coat and breeches. *She* should have been the one. Perhaps she was even strong enough to have had him lean on her as he hobbled to the house and up the wide stone staircase. But of course it was only reasonable that Peter should have done that. She couldn't very well help him out of his breeches and place hot towels on his naked leg.

She'd have liked to, though.

There were still several people in the garden. Trudy was chatting with Veronique, and Michael Upham and M. Chartier remained in close conversation. Amelia pushed back straggling strands of her hair and joined her aunt. "Mrs. Lawson will see that he has everything he needs," she said.

"The poor man!" Veronique exclaimed. "Your aunt was just telling me that he sustained his wound in the war, Lady Amelia. How frightful for him. I had noticed his limp but I had no idea the knee continued to trouble him. Miss Harting says you have yourself sent him home from an entertainment to which he escorted you when you could see he was in pain. How terribly kind of you! I'm not positively sure I would even notice."

Amelia frowned at her aunt, but merely nodded absently to the younger woman. "Shall we retire now? I dare say none of us feel much like further merriment when Lord Verwood is so discomforted."

"Certainly not!" Veronique agreed, twisting about to call musically to her brother. "Henri! We are going in now. Are you coming?"

Chartier bowed politely in their direction, smiled, and said, "Not quite yet, my dear, if you don't mind."

An exciting idea occurred to Amelia as she followed the other two women into the house. There was nothing to stop her from pretending to go to her room, then escaping back into the garden to eavesdrop on what the two men were discussing with such obvious interest. It might tell her something very important about Chartier, something she could

share with Verwood when he was better. And there was no
risk in it. She knew the grounds around Margrave as well in
the dark as in the daylight.

There was every need to hurry, however, for when Peter
returned the two men would doubtless join him for a glass of
brandy before Mr. Upham left for his own home. Amelia
separated from her aunt and Veronique at the top of the
staircase. When they were out of sight and their voices had
dimmed to a faint murmur, she tiptoed back down, de-
touring to the closet under the stairs to wrap a dark cloak
over her jonquil evening dress. She had rather hoped
Verwood would especially notice her gown, as it was one she
hadn't worn in London. But he hadn't seemed to pay any
particular attention. A pity. She was convinced it was the
most flattering dress she owned.

The hood of the cloak concealed her bright locks fairly
well if she drew it forward until it nearly blinded her. She
disposed of her shoes before peeking out into the hall to see
that there was no one around. The corridor to the back was
in almost total darkness because the kitchen area would
ordinarily be empty for the night. Amelia remembered that
Mrs. Lawson would be there now, though, boiling the towels
for Lord Verwood, so she slipped out the side door instead.
This put her in the courtyard she had shown the viscount the
previous day.

One wall ran along the ornamental garden where
Chartier and Upham should still be strolling as they talked,
and she avoided the gravel path as she made her way to the
five-foot balustrade. There was a good deal of vegetation
planted alongside the stone wall and she found the going
rather difficult in her bare feet (and because she didn't see
quite as well at night), to say nothing of the cloak being
continually snagged on the budding branches of straggly
bushes. Because she could hear no voices, she began to
worry that the men had wandered farther afield, away from
the forecourt toward the pond across the large lawn.
Peeking over the railing, she could see nothing but the
clipped yews and the serpentine balustrade around the
water.

Once her ears had become accustomed to the usual night sounds and to the relentless beat of her own nervous heart, she could distinguish the murmur of voices in the direction of the pavilion. The growth near the pavilion was at its thickest, and she found she could not penetrate it without causing herself a great deal of injury and making a great deal of noise. She regarded the stone pile with a sigh and decided the only way she was going to get close enough to hear them, in safety, was to enter the wretched building.

Amelia was beginning to wonder if this had been such a good idea after all. Probably Chartier was merely touting his sister's virtues, and the suave Mr. Upham was considering the possibilities of attracting a woman some twenty years his junior. Or they were discussing whether Chartier would be interested in purchasing inexpensive French material and fashions for his sister. Amelia reluctantly edged out onto the gravel path in front of the heavy oak door. That door creaked, she remembered with a shudder, and the interior was full of cobwebs and heaven knew what little crawly insects that would be waiting there for her to step on them with her naked toes. Besides, the windows didn't open. Probably she wouldn't be able to hear the men through the glass in any case.

The doorknob felt icy cold and damp in her hand. It was only the image of herself conveying important information to Verwood that gave her the courage to pull it cautiously toward her. From her childhood she recalled that if one didn't want a door to creak, one pushed hard toward the hinges, and she managed to swing the heavy portal far enough to slip through without its giving forth a wail of protest. Inside was total darkness, at least until her eyes became used to the creepy blackness. Then she could distinguish that there were faint panels of lighter hue, where the windows were.

Each footstep made her shudder with the anticipation that she would set her poor unguarded toes on a slimy snake or a crunchy beetle. Fearless she was not, but determination drove her on. She lifted and set down each foot with the slow deliberation of someone sloshing through oozing mud, but finally found herself beside the leaded windows closest to the garden. To her amazement and relief, she found she could hear two distinct voices, though their words were slightly blurred.

". . . fifty pounds, half beforehand . . . two trips . . . can't . . . there . . . not safe. Take it or . . ." Definitely Mr. Upham speaking.

". . . more than I'd . . . When could . . . ?"

"Thursday . . . give you . . . days. If you weren't there, they couldn't . . . Best I can . . ."

There was silence for a minute; then Amelia could hear a distant shout that sounded like Peter calling to them. Chartier said hurriedly, "All right. I'll have . . . by tomorrow. We can discuss . . . when I see . . ."

Peter's voice was closer now. "How about . . . brandy?"

Since Upham raised his voice to answer, Amelia could hear him quite clearly. "Sounds just right. How's Lord Verwood?"

She would have been glad enough to hear her brother's reply, but the three men walked off toward the house, leaving her to the spooky darkness of the pavilion alone. There seemed to be rustling sounds around her, and she made a hurried dash for the door, only to realize that she should remain there long enough for them to get out of hearing distance before she crept out and pushed the door closed. There was *definitely* something in the building with her, though it might have been as innocuous as any army of ants. She could *feel* it, and her back prickled with fright. Even a rat would have been too much for her to contemplate, so she slid out through the door and left it open. No one was going to notice, and if they did, they wouldn't think a thing of it, she assured herself.

Keeping to the grass just off the gravel walk, she hurried back to the side door she'd come through only a few minutes before. Really, it could only have been a very short time, though it seemed like hours. She could feel the perspiration cooling on her brow under the heavy hood. There must surely be a better way to serve one's country, she decided as she padded along to the closet. Perhaps she wasn't cut out for this kind of thing after all.

The men's voices drifted down the hall from the earl's library as she quickly disposed of the cloak and tucked her feet back into her shoes. Bighton must have left the door open when he carried in their brandy. If she hurried, she could be around the curve of the staircase before he came back out again. It wasn't all that comforting in the dark closet, either.

Amelia picked up her skirts and dashed across the short length of hall, feeling slightly ridiculous. There was no need for this cloak-and-dagger stuff in her own home, surely. If Bighton caught sight of her he was likely to say no more than, "Can I be of some assistance, Lady Amelia?" But she was fired with excitement now, and even the end of her expedition didn't seem to cool her down. She skittered up the stairs, flushed with her triumph. Most decidedly there was something to tell Lord Verwood.

In her room she couldn't settle down, but paced forward and back on the thick patterned carpet. After a while she decided the professional thing to do was to write down precisely what she had heard. Her mahogany escritoire stood against the north wall of her room and she sat down abruptly, drawing the inkwell toward her so quickly that the ink sloshed over onto the blotter. Undeterred, she whipped out a sheet of paper and began to scribble the half-sentences. When she sat back to look at what she had, she sighed. Not exactly a confession signed in blood.

The exercise hadn't exactly calmed her, either. She was bursting with the need to tell someone, preferably Lord Verwood himself. Hadn't she at least come up with more than he had, sitting behind hedgerows near Bournemouth? And she had done it at absolutely no risk to herself, so he could hardly complain, could he? There he was sitting in his room, no doubt in awful pain, nursing his bad leg and thinking that he was getting no further in his attempt to learn something of the Chartiers. And here she sat (well, actually, she had begun to pace the room again, waving the sheet of paper to dry it) with information which would so enthrall him that he would quite forget his pain. And possibly praise her for her efforts.

It was too much for Amelia. She knew he was in the same wing; he had been put in the Oriel Room because it was one of the largest of the guest suites, and one of the handsomest. She would just walk down the corridor and slip the sheet of paper under his door. He would find it in the morning and seek her out, eager to hear how she had accomplished such a feat.

There was light coming from under his door. Amelia convinced herself that if she put the paper under the door, he would see it and possibly hurt himself trying to walk over to pick it up. It would be much better if she simply handed it to him, with a brief explanation. Otherwise, he might wonder all night what the meaning of it was. And that was hardly fair to him, with his injured knee and all. He needed a good night's sleep.

She knocked on the door.

— 15 —

"Come in."

It didn't occur to Amelia that he wouldn't be decent. Peter never called to her to come in unless he was completely dressed. Of course, she had to admit, as she stared at Verwood, seated in a wing chair with his leg up on a hassock, that he probably hadn't expected the knock to be hers. Undoubtedly he expected it would be Peter, or one of the footmen bringing more boiled towels. And he couldn't very well treat his poor knee with his breeches on, could he? Still, she was rather taken aback to find him there in his shirtsleeves and drawers. No particularly important part of him was left exposed, to be sure, but . . .

"For God's sake, Amelia!" he exclaimed, making a desperate attempt to rise and find something to cover himself with.

"No, don't do that!" she insisted, turning her back on him. "I won't look. Just don't get up and hurt yourself." She'd already seen what there was to see, anyhow. Large feet, and strong hairy legs, and nothing more. She heard him sigh behind her.

"Why don't you hand me my dressing gown from the wardrobe . . . if you intend to stay?"

"Well, I had something to tell you. Something important," she said diffidently. "But if you want me to leave . . ."

"The maroon one, at the end."

Amelia walked stiffly to the oak wardrobe and pulled open the single wide door. His clothes, all neatly pressed, were hanging there in great profusion. Apparently he didn't travel light. Or he had intended to make a rather long stay. There were two dressing gowns. The one on the end was maroon. She lifted it down, holding it awkwardly away from her body, as though it were something not quite nice, and returned to him, her eyes studiously trained on his bed, where the rest of the clothes he'd been wearing that evening were strewn. Someone should have hung them up for him.

"Didn't you bring your valet?" she asked as she set to work gathering them up.

"No. You needn't do that, Lady Amelia. Peter's valet will be in later to get me into bed."

"I could do that."

"No, you couldn't."

There was a sharp edge to his voice, but she didn't face him until she'd found room for his coat and breeches in the wardrobe. "Are you ready?"

"Yes, I'm ready," he said, his voice sounding suddenly amused.

He was still seated in the wing chair, the maroon dressing gown with its black velvet collar now carefully tied about his waist. It came down past his knees, in fact almost to his feet. "Would you like your slippers?" she asked.

"Not unless my feet offend you."

"Of course not," she replied stoutly, retracing her path toward his chair, where she hovered uncertainly at his elbow. "Would you rather I waited until morning?"

"Not if you have something really important to tell me. And please sit down. You make me nervous standing there."

Amelia perched on the edge of the rosewood armchair he indicated, and gripped her sheet of paper tightly in her lap. "I was just so eager to tell you what I'd learned," she tried to explain. "About M. Chartier."

One brow rose skeptically. "You found it suspicious that he spent so much time talking with Mr. Upham."

Amelia remembered his blank look when she'd tried to call the matter to his attention, and sniffed. "I learned a great deal more than that. After you were injured and Peter brought you in, Trudy and Mlle. Chartier and I came in, too. Which left M. Chartier and Mr. Upham in peace to plot something between them."

"They don't even know each other," he told her reasonably. "I don't think you'd be able to convince me that they did, my dear. That would be far too great a coincidence."

"Of course they don't know each other. Did I say they did?" she demanded, annoyed with his skepticism. She dropped her voice to a conspiratorial whisper. "I spied on them."

The black eyes widened. "Spied on them, Amelia? God help us, what next? Just how did you manage this from your bedchamber? The garden's on the other side of the house."

"I think the pain has clouded your brain, Verwood." She made a negligent gesture with her empty hand. "Are the towels hot enough? Shall I get you more?"

"They're fine. Go on with your story."

He made it sound as though she was entertaining him with a fairy tale. Irritated, Amelia wiggled back into the chair, which was so deep her feet just barely reached the floor. She scowled at him, which had no noticeable effect. Finally she said, "I didn't go to my room. I put on a cloak and left my shoes in the closet and went out into the courtyard. Only the parapet on the wall divides it from the ornamental garden."

He frowned. "Did they see you?"

"No, certainly not."

"But what if they had?"

Amelia became very haughty. "There is surely no reason why I shouldn't take a stroll at night in my own courtyard."

"Without your shoes?"

"They wouldn't have noticed I didn't have shoes on." Amelia was feeling slightly impatient. "Do you want to hear what I discovered or not?"

"I'm all ears," he assured her.

"It's treacherous out there in the dark. I was extraordinarily brave. They were talking down by the pavilion and it was necessary for me to go in it to hear them, you

know. I couldn't catch everything they said. And then Peter
came along."

"So you actually heard nothing at all," he suggested,
impatient in his turn.

"I most certainly did. And I've written it all down." She
bent forward to hand him the sheet of paper. "That is
exactly what they said."

Verwood scanned the short entries quickly. "This is it?
This is what brought you to my room in the dead of night?"

Amelia flushed. "Well, it's highly suspicious, isn't it?
Perhaps you don't know that Mr. Upham is a smuggler and
could very easily arrange for transport for M. Chartier to
France."

The viscount once again read the hurriedly penned lines.
And shrugged. "My dear Amelia, they could as easily be
speaking of some shipment of brandy or clothing that
Upham could get for him. If Chartier wanted to get to France,
he wouldn't be likely to take a chance on a stranger."

"Yes, he would," she said stubbornly. "He's really not at
all bright, Verwood."

The viscount grinned at her. "I've noticed. Which is one
of the best arguments I can think of against his being a spy."

She thought about that for a minute, but shook her head.
"It could just be a trick of his. And English people think
anyone who speaks some other language is missing a little
something upstairs. Look, you told me the revenue officer in
Bournemouth was suspicious. If Chartier needs to get to
France, he really has to take a chance somewhere else right
now, doesn't he?"

"Possibly."

They sat in silence for some time, staring at each other. It
seemed to Amelia that for the first time he really noticed her
jonquil gown then, and the way it faithfully clung to her
figure. His gaze kept straying from her eyes down to her
bosom, to immediately swing back up. Eventually he cleared
his throat and said, "You really shouldn't have come here,
my dear. Your brother might misunderstand."

"Oh, Peter knows me very well. He wouldn't misconstrue
the situation."

He offered her a rueful smile. "I'm sure you overestimate his tolerance, Amelia. Even the most carefree of brothers wouldn't be best pleased to find his sister in a gentleman's room so late at night."

"Oh. Well. I shall go, then. But you'll think of how we can find out more about M. Chartier's activities, won't you? It would be a great pity to let my information go to waste."

"Indeed." She had left her chair and was passing by him when he caught her hand, gently pulling her toward him by drawing it up to his lips for a light kiss. His eyes, softened in the mellow light of the room, held hers as he said, "Please don't do anything foolish, Amelia. Desperate men are dangerous. Trust me, confide in me. Promise me you won't act on your own anymore. Being brave isn't all that important, you know. I'd hate to see any harm come to you."

Amelia smiled a little tremulously. "I wasn't really brave at all," she admitted. "The pavilion is bad enough in the daytime; at night it's positively threatening."

Verwood chuckled and drew her down onto his lap. His arms went around her in a tight hug, pulling her close against his chest. "Goose. Being brave is doing things that frighten you. If they didn't frighten you, it wouldn't be brave to do them, would it?"

"I suppose not," she whispered. She straightened abruptly, saying, "I'll hurt your knee."

"My knee feels just fine."

He tilted her head up and bent to kiss her. Amelia loved the warmth of his lips on hers, the urgent pressure that made her feel expectant and eager. She thought probably she could indulge in this kind of heady glory for four-and-twenty hours on end. So she was surprised, at first, when she felt his tongue tracing her lips, teasing at the corners, sucking little puffs of her lip into his mouth. It was a delicious sensation, one that made her feel giddy with pleasure.

Tentatively she extended her own tongue to taste his lips, and somehow his tongue slid right into her mouth. She thought, for a moment, that this was a mistake, that he hadn't meant to do it, that it had just slipped right in along the line of her own tongue. Her error was clear to her soon enough, as he explored the mysteries of her mouth, touching her teeth and the hardness of her palate, the softness of the insides of her cheeks. She felt literally dizzy from the stroking of his tongue, and then its playful darting about. But most of all she knew he meant it when he began a rhythmic inserting and withdrawing that made everything inside her strain with unfamiliar desire.

Her breathing became rapid but erratic; she found her hands clutching fervently in his thick black hair. Unconsciously she pressed her breasts more tightly to him, rubbing against the hardness of his chest. Her whole body felt tight to the bursting point. Dazed though her mind was, she knew this couldn't be quite the right thing to be doing. It felt far too good. She pulled back just as a knock came at the door.

"Alexander? Can I come in?"

Amelia didn't stop to think. A reflex action took her straight off Verwood's lap, and with only a second's pause she dived under his bed.

"Don't . . ." he started to say. There was a brief pause before he raised his voice and called, "Come in, Peter."

"How's your knee?" Peter asked. Amelia could see only his feet, but they headed straight for the chair she'd so recently left. So recently that it would still be warm?

"Not bad," Verwood replied. "The towels have cooled off but I don't think I'll need any more." A soggy mass fell to the floor with a wet smack. "In fact, I'm ready to call it a night. Don't bother to send your valet, old man. I can manage."

"Here, I'll help you. Do you want a nightshirt?"

Verwood hesitated. "I don't think I'll bother. If you could just give me your arm . . ."

Apparently Peter did so, because Verwood hopped on one foot over to the bed, which sank down dangerously close to Amelia when he lay down on it. "Is there anything at all I can get you?" Peter asked, now standing by the door.

"Not a thing. I can get the candle from here."

"Then I'll wish you a good night's rest. Hope your knee will feel better in the morning."

"I'm sure it will."

Peter paused when he already had the door partially open. "About Amelia . . ." he said.

"What about Amelia?" She could hear the tight note to his voice.

Peter interpreted it according to his own thoughts. "You mustn't think I invited you down here to court her, Alexander. I know Trudy's determined to believe that's why you're here, but I simply wanted your moral support." He was silent for a moment. "Are you interested in Veronique?"

"No." The single word came out flat and firm.

Amelia could hear the smile in her brother's voice. "Good. Well, good night, Alexander. If you need any help during the night, just give a tug to the bell rope. Someone's always on duty."

"Thanks."

The door closed softly and there was silence in the room. After a while Verwood asked, "Aren't you coming out?"

"No, I think I'll just stay here all night."

"Poor dear. You're that embarrassed, are you?"

"I'm *not* embarrassed," she muttered, wriggling out from under the bed. Her beautiful jonquil gown had gotten slightly rumpled in the process, and smudged with dirt. Instead of meeting his eyes, she stood up and cautiously dusted at herself. "I had already told you Trudy doesn't always know what she's talking about."

"Quite right, you had."

"I'll just be going now," she said.

"Yes, I think that would be wise."

She turned briefly to face him. "You *will* think about this information I've given you on Chartier, won't you?"

"Definitely. Let's find out a little more before we discuss it with Peter. All right?"

"All right."

His eyes were unreadable in the dim light, but his voice was soft when he said, "Good night, Amelia."

"Good night . . . Alexander." Just before she turned away, she saw him smile.

The smile lingered after she had left the room, but only for a few minutes. Verwood leaned back against the headboard, his arms folded under his head, and stared at the ceiling. He was inclined to agree with Trudy that Amelia had a fondness for him, if only to account for her ardent behavior when he took her in his arms. It was too painful to think that she had conducted herself that way with any number of other men, in her attempts to wrest information from them. The very thought made a muscle in his jaw twitch and his hands clench at his sides. What sort of thing did Chartier consider a "liberty," anyhow?"

Surely his intimate kiss had been a surprise to her, something new. But how could he really tell? It was no more proper for her to be kissing him, with nothing established between the two of them, than it was for her to be kissing anyone else. Yet she showed not the least reluctance. And he was sure he had convinced her that there was no need to press him further, to doubt him. It was possible that her earlier experiences had simply given her a taste for some degree of physical intimacy. Verwood groaned at the thought. How much physical intimacy?

His wild imaginings earlier about the Reverend Symons and the footman Robert were ridiculous, of course. Amelia had too much dignity and sophistication for that sort of intrigue. And where had she gotten all that sophistication, at one-and-twenty? Obviously from her encounters with the men she was intent on coaxing into revealing secrets to her. When he had pressed her the previous day in the pavilion, she had protested complete innocence. But her trick of luring men out onto balconies at balls was an established habit; he would have sworn to it. So, how much could happen on a balcony? She could have made other assignations with them. Like ones in that stand of trees in Hyde Park, where her groom waited patiently out of sight with her horse.

And what about the way she'd dived under his bed?

Perhaps that scene had been enacted before, in reverse, for her reaction to have been so quick. Verwood sighed. Perhaps it hadn't. With Amelia, one simply couldn't tell. She certainly wasn't going to answer his questions on the subject. The only way to find out was to see just how far she would let him progress with her. Which, since it was a matter of some importance to him, might or might not justify his own conduct with *her*. In any case, it seemed likely their association would not stand still, nor was it likely to regress. He could, of course, see that that happened . . . but he doubted he would.

Amelia had taken a firm hold on his mind, or his heart, probably both. There was really no going back, but there was a lot to discover before some resolution was reached. He assumed he was a tolerant enough man to accept a certain amount of impropriety in her past. After all, she had indulged in her activities out of patriotism. What was more difficult to assimilate was that she might have thoroughly enjoyed them. He, poor fellow, wanted her only to enjoy physical intimacy with *him*!

His candle was guttering and he reached over to snuff it. There was a dull throbbing in his knee, which he assumed would be gone by morning. He certainly hoped so. For a few minutes, in the darkness, he flexed the joint, then massaged it, willing himself to change his line of thought from Amelia to Chartier. But he had little success, and fell asleep with a small rueful smile on his lips.

— 16 —

Amelia had more difficulty getting to sleep. It was not every day that she experienced the sort of sensations she'd just encountered with Verwood. For one thing, no man had ever kissed her that way, though now she thought of it, Fernhurst had attempted to bring his tongue into play. She'd been so disgusted by the wet-fish touch of it, so sure he had nothing interesting to tell her, that she'd pulled back with a scowl and wiped her lips with the back of her hand. Even for her country she wasn't willing to undergo *that* sort of torture!

It hadn't been at all the same with Verwood. Somehow it had been the most exciting, the most intimate sensation she could imagine. Well, almost the most intimate. Amelia was not naive, in the purely mental sense. She knew what went on between men and women, though it would never have occurred to her that Verwood might consider her experienced in such matters. Raised in the country, curious about such things, she had managed to learn what she needed.

Peter had had mistresses, of course. Amelia supposed that Verwood must have, too. A lowering thought. She disliked the idea of his kissing other women the way he had kissed her. But it made her wonder what sort of women he was attracted to. He had told her that day that pale women didn't appeal to him. And he had, in the pavilion, though not in a particularly pleasant manner, called her violet eyes beautiful. It was just possible that he found her more attractive than he had as yet admitted.

Plenty of men had admitted to an attraction to her. Really, it became quite boring to be forever flattered with such unctuous nonsense. One got to be immune to it. Not that she would have minded a few compliments from Verwood. His actions apparently were a great deal more in evidence than his words. What it came down to was that he was either attracted to her or he was toying with her.

Now, though he didn't seem the sort of man who would toy with a woman, it did just occur to Amelia that he might be trying to teach her a lesson. Obviously he believed she'd let other men kiss her, and this might be his way of showing her the impropriety (nay, even the danger) of acting so incautiously. Certainly that was his intent on the balcony that night. Was he merely prolonging the lesson?

How she wished he'd said something more when Peter had mentioned her. It was comforting, of course, that he had adamantly disavowed any interest in Veronique Chartier, but he hadn't responded to Peter's assurance that he didn't expect Verwood to court his sister. Amelia rather hoped that was what he was doing, and would have felt certain of it (from his actions), if he hadn't seemed always to be poking fun at the suggestion. It couldn't, after all, be any more proper for him to behave as he was, than it was for her. Or not much. But he had such a strange concept of a gentleman's proper behavior, that it might merely be something he didn't understand.

These thoughts chased one another around her head for altogether too long. She could find no solution, and eventually determined she would be more circumspect in the future. Let Verwood give some indication of his intentions before he took her in his arms again. *She* certainly wasn't going to make a fool of herself. . . .

When she arrived in the breakfast room the next morning he was already there, along with Mlle. Chartier and Peter. The men rose as she entered and she waved them back to their seats, noting the cane beside Verwood's chair. Amelia spoke to the Frenchwoman and to her brother, then turned to inquire of Verwood's knee.

"It's better this morning, but I'll need to exercise it. I thought you might let me accompany you on a walk to the Carsons'."

She felt herself stiffen slightly. "Oh, I think that would be a bit too far for you, my lord. It's a good mile by the road, and you wouldn't want to walk across the fields. They're too uneven."

"A mile sounds just right. You won't mind resting with me now and again, I trust." His black brows rose quizzingly.

"Until your knee is healed, a shorter walk might be more desirable. We might walk to the church in the village, for instance."

"No," he said pleasantly, "I'd prefer to see the Carsons. You haven't forgotten that I've met your protégé, have you?"

Amelia couldn't understand his insistence on going there, any more than he seemed capable of grasping the fact that she didn't want him to go with her. "Very well," she said grudgingly. "This afternoon, perhaps." Something was bound to come up before then to distract him.

"Oh, I need the walk this morning. So my leg won't stiffen too much, you understand."

Peter had been watching the two of them with mild curiosity, and now interjected his suggestion. "You'd best go this morning, Amelia. We're planning an expedition to Winchelsea this afternoon."

Defeated, Amelia agreed rather curtly, concentrating on her breakfast to end the discussion. Verwood shortly excused himself, saying he would wait for her in the Summer Parlor. She would have liked to remain over her meal for a lengthy period, but once Peter and Veronique had excused themselves, she feared M. Chartier would descend on her, which was probably the worse of the two fates planned for her. Not that being with Verwood was such a bad fate, if it only hadn't involved walking to the Carsons'.

Sunlight filled the glassed-in Summer Parlor, sparkling off the green walls and the Delftware vases on the gate-leg table. Verwood was seated in a spoonback chair with his legs stretched out in front of him, the cane resting against one knee. His gaze was abstracted and thoughtful. He didn't hear Amelia enter the room through the open door.

"Really, I can't believe you're up to such a long hike," she began, nervously fingering the light shawl she'd thrown over her shoulders. "The church is Norman and rather interesting."

"I'll be fine," he assured her, rising slowly and taking a firm grip on the cane. "We're in no rush, I presume. We can walk slowly."

When they had started down the path that led to the road, she spoke again. "Have you given any thought to what might be done about M. Chartier? With your bad knee, you really aren't in a position to do much, are you?"

"I doubt if it will be necessary for me to run about, my dear," he said, sounding amused. "Let's look at the situation in the clear light of day. The conversation you overheard between the two men could have two possible connotations. One is that Chartier was bargaining for smuggled goods from Upham, the other that he was arranging for transportation to France. There may even be other possibilities, but we'll discard them for now. Say Chartier wants to get to France and Upham will provide the boat. In that case it sounds like they'd leave him and pick him up a few days later, right?"

"Yes, that's what I thought."

He smiled down at her, touching a finger briefly to a curl that rested on her shoulder. "Now, if you were a French spy, and you'd picked up information you wanted to have conveyed to Napoleon, doubtless you'd have a routine for conveying it."

"Yes, but his contact may have been unavailable," she protested. "Or having the revenue officer on the lookout in Bournemouth may have made it difficult for him to use his ordinary routine."

"True. One would think there would be some sort of backup, but let's not quibble on that point. He has decided to take the information to France himself, and he can see

Upham will do anything for the right price." They had come out on the road, which was narrow and dusty. Verwood stopped a moment and leaned more heavily on his cane. "Chartier could even have spun him some tale of smuggling of his own. Surely he wouldn't have trusted a stranger with the information that he's a spy."

Amelia glared at him. "You're mocking me, Verwood. He wouldn't have told him either thing. He'd have made up some story of a sick relative there, or something of that sort."

"You called me Alexander last night."

Her hands fluttered but she said nothing as they walked on.

"Very well," he went on smoothly. "He has told some story about needing to get there, in any case. The problem is that he seems to want to stay there for a few days. That's what I don't understand. If he were a spy, he'd have someone to hand his message on to within the hour, one would think. Why does he want to stay there so long?"

Amelia shrugged. "Perhaps he just likes the feel of French soil under his feet."

"A sentimental spy?" Verwood grinned at her. "Come, now, we'll have to think of something better than that. Does he want to take the message to Napoleon himself? Could it possibly be that important? I doubt it. And Napoleon isn't in France just now, in any case. He's getting ready for a renewed battle with Russia. It seems unlikely Chartier would have any information that would help him there."

They were walking slowly, but still the first of the cottages was in sight. The Carsons lived at the very far end of the village, a much farther walk. Amelia was still determined to terminate their excursion at the church, which was already in sight. "Well, what do you suggest?" she asked brightly, putting on her best such-an-intelligent-man-will-have-the-answer smile.

Verwood gave a doleful shake of his head. "None of that, Amelia. You may have noticed that Chartier never mentions where his home was in France before he immigrated to England. Fortunately, his sister is not so tight-lipped, though apparently she was brought here very young. Their family home was near Cherbourg, which you may realize is directly across the Channel from Bournemouth. But Upham isn't likely to be willing to make so long a crossing. His usual route is probably Rye to Boulogne-sur-Mer or Outreau. If Chartier wanted to get to Cherbourg and back, he would need time."

Amelia tried to look admiring. "Did you find out about Cherbourg from Mlle. Chartier yesterday when you were out riding?"

"I did."

They had come opposite the church and Amelia stopped. "Shall we have a look inside? It's still a distance to the Carsons', and I can see your leg is troubling you. There isn't really any need for me to see them today."

There was a puzzled tilt to his black brows, but he shook his head. "No, I'd rather continue."

"It will just make the walk back longer," she said desperately.

"I'm sure you won't mind stopping with me now and again."

Amelia sighed and walked on. "So you think it more likely he wishes to get to his old home. Why?"

"Because the timing is right. It's still possible he's a spy, but I'm beginning to think it's more likely he has business at his old home. Didn't you tell me he gave you the impression he can get at his financial assets anytime he pleases?"

"Yes." She frowned down at her dusty half-boots. "But if his money is there, why wouldn't he have taken it out long ago? Surely it would be safer in England."

"It probably isn't money. French banknotes wouldn't be of any use to him. Much more likely to be goods he can sell in England for a handsome sum. He couldn't manage to get much out at any given time without arousing too much suspicion."

Amelia stared up at him. "So you don't think he's a spy at all?" she asked, incredulous.

"I really don't know. He could be doing both things."

The Carsons' cottage was directly in front of them now, a neat whitewashed building with several windows open to the mild May morning. There was a bench alongside the green door. "Why don't you sit out there in the sun and rest your leg, Lord Verwood?" she suggested. "I'll be but a moment."

"And miss this opportunity to see how your pickpocket is getting along?" he asked. "Never."

"He's likely at the village school right now. Only his mother and the younger children will be here." She waited for him to seat himself, but he remained standing, raising his cane to tap authoritatively on the door.

There were muffled sounds from within. Eventually a voice was heard to grumble, "I'm coming, I'm coming. Can't a body have any peace?"

Amelia refused to meet Verwood's startled eyes.

The green door was opened to them by a woman of less than thirty, with suspiciously red hair. She wore a starched white cap and an old-fashioned dress that was far more elegant than most cottagers wore. It didn't look at all the sort of outfit which would be practical for milking cows. Amelia fixed a civil smile on her lips.

"Ah, it's you, is it, Lady Amelia," the woman barked. "Just the one I needed to see."

"This is Lord Verwood," Amelia said, trying to convey, by the narrowing of her eyes, that Mrs. Carson should show a little deference to his lordship.

"Mmm." The woman's sharp eyes took in Verwood's lanky height, his wild black hair and eyes, and his cane. Amelia fully expected her to utter something outrageous, like, "What a sorry specimen," but Tommy's mother merely shrugged and said, "He can come in."

Verwood said, "Thank you," in a tone Amelia couldn't quite identify. She refused to look at him as they were hustled into the spacious room that served as living and eating area for the cottage. There were two bedrooms on the same floor and another above in the gabled roof. Two children played on the plank floor, rolling a ball back and forth, while the youngest slept in a carved oak cradle that made Verwood raise his brows.

Mrs. Carson waved Amelia to one of the two chairs and seated herself in the other before Verwood could insist that she do so. He stood, leaning on his cane, behind Amelia's chair, towering over her. Amelia cleared her throat and said, "I trust you're well settled in now, ma'am."

"Not much to settle in to, is there?" the older woman grumbled. "I thought the kitchen would be better provided. And the coat of green paint they've put on the door already needs touching up. That's the problem with these country folk. They don't look ahead. If they'd given it a second coat of paint, the job would have lasted for years."

"I'm sure they did an adequate job," Amelia replied firmly. "I've spoken with the earl's estate manager and he feels there are several occupations you could set your hand to about the estate. You would report to Mrs. Lawson; she's our housekeeper and directs all the domestic chores. You've taken in laundry in the past, and she'd be willing to have you do it for her."

"Laundry?" Mrs. Carson was astonished. "Have you any idea how exhausting doing laundry is, lifting all those buckets of water, carrying about soaking clothes and linens? Why, I've just been at death's door! My constitution could never stand for it."

Amelia kept a firm rein on her temper. "Well, if laundry is too much for you, I'm sure one of the other suggestions would serve better. You can keep geese and a few pigs, and help with the brewing."

"Pigs? What do I know of pigs? It was pork that nearly caused my death, Lady Amelia. I couldn't possibly bring myself to learn about caring for *pigs*." She said the word with utter contempt, one hand coming up to adjust her unnatural red hair in a gesture of such vanity that Amelia felt like grinding her teeth.

"The brewing, then, and helping out in the dairy," Amelia insisted.

"I don't hold with fermented beverages of any sort," Mrs. Carson informed her self-righteously. "The Reverend Symons always spoke against drink, and I won't be helping the devil in his work. Now, the dairy . . . I suppose there might be some task there which wouldn't overtax my strength. Not milking the cows. I wouldn't be milking cows, would I?"

"I have no idea," Amelia muttered. "Whatever needs to be done, I'm sure you could learn."

Mrs. Carson sighed heavily. "There are the children, of course. I can't very well leave the little ones here alone when I go to the dairy. With Tommy in school most of the day there's no one to mind them, you see. It's difficult for a woman in my place."

"Yes, I'm sure it is," Amelia said as she rose, "but I think something can be worked out. Mrs. Lawson could have the laundry brought here for you to iron."

"Oh, dear me, no," Mrs. Carson protested. "Them irons are heavy and the little ones might burn theirselves. I couldn't think of ironing."

Amelia's eyes flashed. "Do think of it, Mrs. Carson. I believe it's the best solution."

"Well, perhaps," Mrs. Carson reluctantly agreed, sounding much put upon. "When I'm a little stronger."

"Next week," Amelia suggested.

"We shall see. Now, there were just a few little things you may have forgotten."

Amelia was edging rapidly toward the door, but Mrs. Carson was undeterred.

"I noticed the cottage down the way has curtains in the windows, so I should have them as well."

"Curtains don't come with the cottages. Anyone who has them has purchased them on their own."

"Not come with the cottages! Well, I never! And who comes in to cultivate the garden?"

If Verwood hadn't been there, Amelia would surely have exploded. "*You* cultivate the garden, and you teach your children how to do it as they grow. Tommy can help you." Amelia didn't wait for Verwood to reach the door but threw it open with an excess of energy that made the house shake. "And you teach them to feed and raise the animals, and to make bread and beer and bacon and butter and cheese and everything else that is needed!"

As Amelia erupted from the house and started to hasten
down the street, Mrs. Carson called after her, "But I don't
know anything about cultivating a garden! There is so much
dirt . . ."

Amelia wouldn't wait for him to catch up, but trotted
down the road as fast as her feet would carry her with any
dignity. There were very odd sounds coming from him,
much as though he were choking, which she could finally
hear when Mrs. Carson's plaintive voice was outdistanced.
There were muffled snorts and bursts of expelled air, a sort
of rumbling noise. Finally, when they reached the railing
outside the church, she heard him collapse against it, and
turned in alarm to see what damage he'd done to his poor
knee.

He was bent over, doubled up. Amelia's heart twisted
painfully in her bosom and she rushed to his side. And then,
unable to control himself any longer, he roared . . . with
laughter. Amelia had never seen anything like it. Peal after
peal of unholy mirth rocked right through him, exploding
out into the until-then-quiet village street. The whole area
was filled with his glee, so infectious that two laborers
walking by grinned, and then chortled, and finally burst out
laughing right along with him. Though he apparently made
some effort to overcome his excess of amusement, he could
do no more than shake his head and utter one word,
"Shrew!"

Amelia was not amused. She was affronted. However, the
general merriment proved too much for her, and her lips
began to twitch, her eyes took on a sparkle, her throat began
to bubble, and at last she, too, allowed herself to giggle.

Verwood clasped his hands at her waist and swung her
around, right in the middle of the street, saying, "She's a
shrew. My God, you've brought a shrew to Margrave. Oh,
Amelia, you are the most adorable, precious darling in the
whole world! A shrew. How positively wonderful! That will
teach you to play Lady Bountiful. I love it!"

When he set her down on her feet, her eyes were rueful.
"I'd never met her, you know," she explained between
lingering giggles. "I didn't want you to see what she was like.

Isn't she awful? I don't know what I'm going to do with her."

"Leave her to Mrs. Lawson," he suggested, clasping her hand in his and heading back toward Margrave. "Mrs. Lawson will know exactly how to handle her."

"I suppose so." She was silent for a moment, trying to gather the courage to speak. When he pressed her hand encouragingly, she moistened her lips and asked, "Do you really think I'm the most adorable, precious darling in the whole world?"

He continued walking, but his gaze caressed her upturned face. "Yes," he said, "I do."

He did not elaborate. They walked the rest of the way to Margrave in a companionable, if slightly uncertain, silence.

— 17 —

Since his home was on their route, and the excursion had been mentioned the previous evening, Michael Upham joined them. Martello House was named for the martello towers on the ruins of Camber Castle, which lay midway between his estate and Margrave. Amelia had never much cared for the design of Martello House, since it was a pale and pointless imitation of the fortress ruins. The duplication seemed almost a mockery to her, purporting to be something it wasn't, and making the accommodations within the house, she felt sure, quite uncomfortable.

Mr. Upham, however, was the most genial of hosts, inviting them to inspect his home before they passed through the Strand Gate and into Winchelsea. Amelia would have preferred to deny herself the treat, but the others appeared eager to inspect the place, so she tagged along, trying always to be close enough to Verwood to hear what comments he had to make.

The house was remarkable! Amelia had no idea Mr. Upham's home would be so luxuriously furnished or would give evidence of a very rich man with exquisite taste. If she had been asked her opinion beforehand, she would have guessed that the furniture would be overornate, the accessories vulgar. Trudy positively beamed at her as they wandered from room to room, exclaiming at each new and delightful vignette. Amelia was better able to restrain her enthusiasm, but she was not unimpressed.

And Mr. Upham was particularly genial and attentive. He joked with Peter about the extent of the marshland in the area, complimented Veronique on her lovely bonnet, wished he could remember when he'd seen as fine a pair of violet eyes as Amelia possessed, assured Trudy that he had seldom seen French cloth used to such advantage as in her gown, begged Lord Verwood to come again to take stock of his stables . . . and accepted a small packet from M. Chartier when the two lingered behind in his study.

Amelia saw this transaction, and nudged the viscount, who was standing beside her. "Not now," he insisted, grinning at her. His eyes gleamed with fervent admiration, or something of the sort, and he added, "Later, when we're alone!"

Of course she knew he was teasing, which both excited and frustrated her. "Did you see?" she hissed, unaware that her nose twitched.

"I saw," he assured her. "It's the most adorable nose I've *ever* seen."

"The packet," she whispered. "Did you see him give Upham the packet?"

Verwood pursed his lips thoughtfully, and winked at her, but walked off without answering.

This was not precisely the way Amelia expected a suitor to behave, especially one who was also a co-conspirator in a very serious affair. At least it *might* be a serious affair. Surely it was difficult enough for her to keep her mind on Chartier (when she would far have preferred giving some thought to just exactly what was going on in Verwood's mind), without having him act so perversely. Not until they were in Winchelsea opposite the Old Court House did it occur to her that his comment about her nose had something to do with its twitching. Clarissa had said that it twitched. Unconsciously Amelia reached up to touch it, flushing brightly when she caught Verwood regarding her with laughing eyes.

The group strolled across the square and down a short lane to a gate, which led to Greyfriars, once a monastery and now in a ruinous state, the house used as a farmhouse and the chapel as a barn. Verwood managed at this point to come abreast of Amelia and separate her slightly from the rest of the company. "Winchelsea isn't as large as I expected. Where do smugglers keep their goods?"

"In the old vaults." Amelia waved back toward town. "In the old days there was a thriving import trade in French wines, and the merchants had vaults built to store them. They haven't been used legitimately in ages, but the smugglers know where they are. At least," she said, casting a glance to make sure no one was close by, "I'm sure Mr. Upham does. There may even be some closer to Martello House."

"It seems unlikely. The old town spread out in the other direction."

"Camber Castle is just as convenient, really. It's full of dark underground passages."

His face showed interest. "Have you explored there?"

"Not since I was a child."

"Let's walk there tomorrow morning," he suggested. "Just the two of us."

Amelia felt her heartbeat increase, but she said only, "If you wish. I can't see how that will get us any relevant information."

He smiled lazily at her. "Oh, I think it could tell us a great deal."

Wednesday morning dawned as warm and sunny as each of the preceding days. Amelia couldn't see that Verwood had done anything to further their knowledge of Chartier's activities. When she had suggested that he search the Frenchman's room, Verwood had merely laughed. Nor had he spent any particular time with either Henri or Veronique casually attempting to extricate fresh tidbits that would be useful. He had, in fact, done nothing whatsoever except enjoy himself—riding, eating, playing cards, sipping at brandy, conversing on topics that didn't come anywhere close to inspiring confidences. He even had several seemingly amiable chats with Trudy. As Peter had remarked the previous evening, he was the perfect guest.

Everyone managed to be in the breakfast room at the same time that morning, which in itself was an unusual circumstance. Trudy and Chartier were both late risers as a rule. There was a cheerful buzz of conversation, broken only when Bighton entered with a sealed letter on a silver salver. Amelia expected it was something for the earl, and was surprised to see Bighton pass him by and pause behind M. Chartier.

"A letter by messenger, M. Chartier," he said. "The man is waiting for a reply."

Naturally Chartier looked quite surprised by this development, quickly snapping up the letter and breaking the seal with his table knife. A prodigious frown grew on his forehead as he read the contents, all the while making a truly admirable tsk-ing sound. "What a nuisance!" he exclaimed. "I shall have to go to London at once."

This did surprise Amelia. At once? Her eyes flew to Verwood, but he was watching Chartier, who continued, "How terribly vexing. Lord Welsford, I'm most dreadfully sorry, but this is a matter of some urgency. I do hate to break up such a delightful house party."

There was a general murmur of consternation. Peter was the first to speak. "I do hope this won't mean you must spirit off Mlle. Chartier. My aunt should, I think, make a perfectly acceptable chaperone for her, and we'd all hate to see her visit cut so short."

Deep lines of concern etched themselves on Chartier's face, giving evidence of his profound interest in his sister's welfare and the propriety of the situation. His worried gaze settled on Verwood for a moment, and then on Lady Amelia. But it would be rude and ungracious to contradict the earl's assertion that Miss Harting was sufficient chaperone. He calmed himself, offered his sister a fleeting smile, and said, "How truly kind you are. If Miss Harting feels up to the responsibility . . ."

"But of course," Trudy insisted. "Your sister must stay with us."

Just so easily was it settled. Chartier went off to oversee the packing of his valises and Verwood disappeared on some

errand of his own. Amelia was disappointed, thinking he
had forgotten their planned walk to the castle. As hostess she
really had to stay in the house until Chartier departed, anyhow, but it was the principle of the thing. She moped
around the major reception rooms, sitting down at the
pianoforte to play a few tunes before springing up to wander
about once again. Finally there was sufficient commotion in
the hall to signal Chartier's departure, and she came out to
bid him farewell.

Verwood was already there, shaking hands with the
Frenchman, who bounced about on his toes in his usual
attempt to get above his shirt points. "A few days, a week at
most," he was telling anyone who listened. "Be assured I
shall return as quickly as possible. If it weren't business of
the most urgent nature, I would never desert such a
delightful gathering. Take care of yourself, Veronique. Miss
Harting will guide you in how to go on. Lady Amelia,
farewell. Lord Verwood. Lord Welsford. And Miss
Harting," he concluded, kissing her hand, "I cannot thank
you enough for taking my sister in your charge. So very
amiable of you."

Amelia waited impatiently for him to actually climb into
his carriage and vanish down the road. She found Verwood
at her side, tucking her arm through his, with the soft
reminder, "We were going to take a walk this morning."

"Perhaps you have other things to do," she suggested, just
a little miffed with him.

"Nothing nearly so important," he assured her as Peter
and Veronique wandered off toward the conservatory, and
Trudy, humming cheerfully to herself, walked purposefully
toward the housekeeper's room.

Amelia took the time to find a shawl, just to keep him
waiting for a few minutes. He didn't even seem to notice.
When she returned he was standing in the open front door,
looking out over the lawns toward the castle. There was a
curious smile playing about his lips, which remained when
she spoke to him.

"Why do you suppose he left today?" she asked as they

descended the stairs. "I'm quite sure the day mentioned was Thursday."

"He may have to be in contact with someone before he goes. I'm having him followed."

"Really?" Amelia beamed at him. "Oh, I'm so glad. How did you find someone to do that?"

"Peter suggested a man I could trust. I was forced to tell him why. You don't mind, do you?"

"No, he would have to know sooner or later. But it's really too late as far as Veronique goes."

Verwood cocked his head at her. "In what way?"

"Peter's mind is made up. He's not likely to change it." She sighed and bent to pick a daisy from the bed along their path. "He's never been this devoted to anyone before, you know. I don't think even finding out her brother was a spy would deter him. And I'm sure he could never bring himself to believe *she* had anything to do with it."

"I doubt she does."

"No, I suppose not. Besides, she's young enough to be malleable."

He grinned at her. "That much younger than you?" he asked teasingly.

Unconsciously she had begun to pluck the petals from her flower. "I'm not very flexible, I suppose. But I'm not awfully stubborn, either. What I mean is, I try to learn from experience. My father used to point out the advantages of not becoming unbearably rigid. Of course, there are some things I'm more receptive to than others."

"Such as?"

"Well, I'm not very receptive to the idea of Napoleon ruling Europe."

"But what *are* you receptive to?" He stopped in the middle of the path to lean on his cane, eyeing her in a provocative fashion.

Amelia studied the cut of his jacket. "I've changed my mind about *you*. That shows I'm not totally unbending, doesn't it?"

"Perhaps." He rubbed a finger against her cheek,

tempting her to raise her eyes to his. "That may be merely a matter of expediency."

"How so?"

"You wouldn't want to look foolish holding on to a misconception that had lost its potential. The true test of your receptiveness would be if you were able to so overcome your dislike of me as to be swayed in quite the opposite direction. Now, that would be quite a feat of flexibility, in my humble opinion."

"I doubt if you can lay claim to such a thing as a humble opinion," she rejoined, tossing away the destroyed flower. "As to completely reversing myself in my feelings about you . . ." She shrugged her shoulders, offered a coy smile, and skipped off ahead of him, the shawl dangling temptingly after her from one elbow.

When worn with its lute-string spencer, her peach-colored walking dress was wholly demure, but Amelia hadn't chosen to wear it with the spencer today. So its faithful fit to her high-bosomed figure was admirably in evidence. She had never, to her recollection, felt the least inclination to disport her bodily attractions for a gentleman before this, but she had observed, with a sort of incredulous wonder, how the demi-monde conducted themselves in the boxes at the opera. Once, perhaps during her first season, when the sight of disreputable women was something of a novelty to her still, she had come home after such a musical evening and played the coquette to her mirror. The fluttering of eyelashes, the coy smiles, the languid gestures, the sensuous movements of the body.

This exercise hadn't made her feel the least ridiculous. In fact, it had made her feel inordinately desirable, calling forth hidden stirrings in her body that had intrigued and delighted her. If she had unconsciously used any of these tricks with the gentlemen she tempted to talk with her about their suspicious doings, she was unaware of it. She was not unaware of doing it now.

Her walk became a little sassier, her hips slightly swaying. Not too much. She had seen it overdone by the likes of Harriet Wilson, and had no desire to make herself look ludicrous. The trick, she'd discovered, was in letting all those undercurrents of passion stir her out of her usual well-bred carriage into a more tantalizing step. In front of the mirror she had sashayed back and forth, slowly removing first a shawl and then a pelerine, so the low cut of the white sarcenet corsage showed the fullness of her bust. She had put one foot up on a low stool and slowly drawn up her gown to release the silk stockings and roll them down her shapely legs.

Unfortunately, it was impossible for her to undress herself further, since it was a complicated gown, and her abigail had already appeared in the doorway without her noticing, and was regarding her with disapproval. Amelia had sighed and given herself over to the woman's ministrations, while enduring a lecture on the evils of behaving indecorously. The lecture had been unnecessary; Amelia had never come across anyone she wished to behave indecorously *with* . . . until just recently.

Verwood never took his eyes from her. And his eyes told her she was indeed arousing an interest in him. They had arrived at the castle ruins and she made a graceful, sweeping gesture with one hand.

"Erected as a fortress by Henry VIII. It was never meant as a residence, and the water receded shortly after it was built. Charles I commanded its demolition, but somehow it never got done. Parliament decreed the removal of the ordnance and ammunition, and that did get done. Nothing flourishes here but lichen and moss." She ran a hand along one of the thick, rough walls. "They board up the underground passages from time to time, but someone always removes the barriers. Maybe smugglers, maybe just curious folks in the neighborhood."

"Shall we explore?"

The way he asked it made it sound as though he were asking something entirely different. Or maybe not so different. Amelia swallowed nervously and nodded. "There are two ways to get down into the tunnels. The closest is behind that wall over there."

He followed her gesture with his eyes, then took her hand

and led the way to the crumbling stone steps that quickly disappeared into gloom below them. "I brought a flint and some candles," he said, digging into the bulky pockets of his jacket. "A lantern would be better, but I didn't want anyone to know where we were going, lest the word get back to Mr. Upham."

"What if we were to get lost down there?" she asked nervously. "Perhaps I should stay up here while you make a search. If you don't come back in a half-hour or so, I can get help."

"I don't think that will be necessary," he said soothingly, taking her hand and lifting it to his lips. "We'll stay close together."

"Yes, well, I suppose so."

He struck the flint and expertly caught the spark on a cone of paper which he used to light the two candles. When he handed her one he smiled reassuringly. "Why don't you follow me? I'll trust you not to catch my jacket on fire. Watch your step. These stairs are treacherous."

Amelia unhappily trudged down the stairs after him. Dark, dank places had never overly appealed to her. Especially ones where you felt tightly closed in on every side. The ceiling of the passage was so low Verwood had to stoop a little and he swung his candle about in a dizzying way to get a look at everything around him. The moss and lichen on the walls had been scraped off in numerous places, leaving long gashes in their place. The stone floor underfoot was uneven and she had to tread cautiously over the loose chips of stone.

They traversed what seemed like miles of passages, speaking rarely, and never coming across anything of the least interest. No kegs of brandy, no suspicious remainders of smugglers' meals, no trunks of French silks and satins. If it was a great disappointment to Verwood to surface into the fresh spring morning without finding so much as a clue to whether the passages served some secret purpose, it was a great relief to Amelia to rise again from the suffocating enclosure.

"Well," she said brightly, "that should satisfy your curiosity."

"Hmmm." He was ostentatiously thoughtful, rubbing a hand along his chin. "I think it would be smart of us to go through them again sometime at night, sometime when there isn't any moon. The times smugglers like best, you know."

Amelia shuddered. "You can do it alone. I'm quite satisfied."

At the head of the stairs there was a small square of reasonably smooth stone, bathed in sunlight and shielded from the wind (and from view) on every side by thick walls. Verwood took her candle from her and set it with his on the ground at the head of the stairs. Then he took her hand and drew her toward the corner, where he slowly untied the ribbons of her bonnet while staring intently into her eyes. Amelia felt a tremor run through her. He lifted the bonnet off her honey-colored curls and hung it on an outcropping of stone above their heads.

His hands came to either side of her face, his fingers weaving into the silky tresses. "You have beautiful hair," he said.

"Thank you." She was bristling with anticipation of his kiss, but he merely continued to gaze in her eyes and stroke her temples with his fingers.

"I don't believe I've ever met anyone with eyes that color," he continued. "They were what first drew you to my attention."

"Were they?" she asked, surprised.

"Yes, they were described to me as violet." He considered them judiciously. "I think it's an apt description."

Amelia was trying to think who could possibly have described her eyes to Lord Verwood. A small frown wrinkled her brow. "I cannot imagine Peter even mentioning my eyes."

"Oh, it wasn't Peter."

"Then who . . . ?"

His fingers had begun to trace the curves of her cheeks,

the slope of her nose, the softness of her lips. "Actually, it was Chartier. We were in one of the clubs and he was debating the wisdom of bringing his sister to London. Apparently he'd been much shocked by a young woman of the aristocracy who had allowed him to take 'liberties' with her. It was his considered opinion that if such a well-bred lady were so free with herself, his sister couldn't possibly emerge from London untouched by such loose principles."

"Why, the little toad!" she exclaimed, indignant. "*He* was the one who kissed me! And how very unprincipled of him to spread the tale."

"He didn't call you by name," Verwood assured her, his eyes more intent now. "And as I was new to London, I didn't have the first idea who it might be—an earl's sister with honey-colored hair and violet eyes. But I made a point of finding out."

Amelia's chin came up in a gesture of outraged defiance. "Because you were looking for someone who'd allow you to take liberties with her, I presume." She brushed away his wandering hands, her chin quivering slightly now. "That doesn't say much for *your* principles, Lord Verwood."

He made no attempt to defend himself. Instead he continued inexorably, "When I discovered who you were, I made a point of meeting your brother. Fortunately, we had a great deal in common and when I decided to join his efforts on behalf of the War Department, he became even more expansive about his methods, mentioning that you had actually helped him on occasion. It occurred to me that you were acting the *femme fatale* in order to weasel information from gentlemen you thought might have something of interest to conceal. A risky business, Amelia, both politically and personally."

Amelia swallowed over a lump in her throat. "Did you tell Peter what Chartier had said?"

"No. One doesn't, you know. And the same purpose could be served by simply making him see how inappropriate it was for you to be endangering yourself that way, so that he would insist you stop doing it. He was quick to agree; he's very fond of you."

Amelia nodded in silence and reached for her bonnet, but it was too high above her. "I'm sure you feel you've taught me a valuable lesson, Lord Verwood. Now I think I would like to go back to Margrave."

His voice became soft as down. "Don't go yet, Amelia."

— 18 —

Amelia stood poised to flee, but the gentleness of his voice made her feel uncertain. "You've indicated before that you think I behaved improperly when I was working with Peter. Perhaps I did." She lifted her shoulders in a shrug of bravado. "I've allowed a number of men to kiss me."

"The way I kissed you?"

"No, not the way you kissed me," she admitted, her voice a whisper. "But then, there isn't much privacy on a balcony, at least not for long. I might have."

Her defiance made his lips twist in a wry smile. "Do you really think so? If you had wanted one of them to kiss you that way, you could have arranged to meet him some-where—in Hyde Park, for instance."

"Hyde Park?" She frowned up at him, puzzled. "Why would I do that? I didn't even know someone could kiss me like . . . you did. There was one man who may have tried, but I thought it was disgusting! Even if he could have told me when Napoleon was launching his invasion, I wouldn't have put up with it. I have my dignity, you know," she sniffed. "There's only so much an inebriated gentleman will let slip. If he seemed promising, I told Peter about him and let my brother see what he could find out. Don't you under-stand that it would have been suspicious for someone in my position to allow a fellow much freedom? Flirting with them was something they could understand; letting them maul me would have been stretching credibility!"

"Ah. I see."

Amelia glared at him. "No, you don't. You don't see at all. You think if I let you kiss me like that, I must have let any number of men do it." Suddenly her eyes widened. "Why, you think I let them do other things to me, too, don't you? You think I let them—"

"No," he said firmly, "I don't think that. Perhaps I wondered, when I first met you."

"Nonsense," she scoffed, turning on her heel. "If you don't think it now, it is a very recent occurrence. Even in the pavilion you were pressing me on the subject. You're pressing me now. Well, I won't have it. I'm not interested in your small-minded opinion of me. Who are you, who is any man to question my right to behave as I see fit? I'm twenty-one years old and perfectly capable of being the judge of my own conduct."

She had managed to get a good ten feet away from him, but turned to ask, "How would you like it if I questioned *your* conduct? Which I never would, since I haven't the least interest in it!"

"Your bonnet," he reminded her.

She was tempted not to return for it, but gave a long-suffering sigh and stalked back to where he now stood holding it. When she reached for it, he clasped her hand, saying, "There's just one more thing I want to know, Amelia. Why *did* you let me kiss you like that?"

Her nose twitched; she could sense it. Feeling stubborn now, she said, "Because I liked it. Now, if you would just give me my bonnet, Lord Verwood . . . ."

"I rather enjoyed it myself. I had hoped we might do it again."

Drat her stupid nose! "I think not," she said stiffly.

"But a hedonist such as yourself must surely seek out every pleasure she can find," he argued, smiling wistfully at her. "I'd be perfectly willing to have you use me that way."

"You're too good," she grumbled, grasping the bonnet and plunking it at a ridiculous angle on her head. "I'm sure I can find someone else whose kisses I like every bit as well—probably better."

"I doubt it. You don't seem to have grasped the fact, my dear, that you like my kisses not because I'm so talented at executing them, but because you're fond of me." His eyes softened once again and one hand came up to stroke her cheek. "And the reason I enjoy kissing you so much is that I'm amazingly fond of you."

Not only her nose twitched now. Her whole face seemed to quiver with suppressed emotion, her chin, her lips, her cheeks. She found it impossible to speak, but when he opened his arms invitingly to her, she walked into them and felt them close tightly about her. The bonnet toppled off her head and onto the stone pavement, but she scarcely noticed. With a wavering smile she turned her lips up to him, to be met eagerly by his.

Oh, the wonder of that kiss. It was cool and hot, firm and soft. Their lips seemed to merge, their mouths to collide and mesh, giving off a dazzling display of multicolored delight. His tongue once again touched and teased, explored and excited. She clasped her hands at the back of his neck, holding tight to keep herself on her toes. His hands played along her back, stroking in ever-widening circles. Each area he caressed came alive under his touch, sensitive to the textured cotton of her gown and to the movement of his fingers above it.

She was pressed against the solidity of his body, oblivious of the buttons on his jacket that pushed against her soft flesh. Everything within her strained toward him, relishing the daring scent of him, the taut feel of his chest against hers, the echo of his breathing. When his mouth left hers to plant nibbling kisses on her eyelids and then her nose, she blinked up at him, breathless and near-mesmerized by the kindled light in the naturally black depths of his eyes.

There was a fire smoldering within her. She could feel it heating her face and her breasts and her very core, just as the sun beat down and warmed her back and hair. Amelia wanted his kisses to go on forever, to stoke the fire, to make it rage through every part of her. His tongue returned to seek out the hot moistness of her mouth, to play against the hardness of her teeth and rub against the velvet lining beyond. When she returned this intimate pleasure, running her own tongue deliciously around the cave of his mouth, he began the movement that had so disoriented her that evening in his room. His tongue slowly but firmly thrust forward and back between her lips until her body sang with the incredible sensation of it.

The blond hair had come loose from its pins and flowed down over her shoulders, framing her face like a halo. He stepped back for a moment to cup her face in his hands, and offered the most dazzling, endearing smile she had ever seen on his rugged face. "You're quite beautiful, Amy. And quite the most exciting woman I've ever met. I could stay here all day and hold you, kiss you . . . but I shouldn't," he finished with a sigh. "We're far too attracted to each other to spend much time alone together and preserve your innocence." He reached down to pick up her bonnet, dusting it meticulously before he handed it to her, as though the mundane act helped to calm him. "We should get back to Margrave."

"Not yet," she whispered, staring at the bonnet in her hands. Her mind was so befuddled with the intoxication of her arousal that she didn't know quite what to do with the simple straw confection and she absently handed it back to him. "It would be all right, I think, to stay just a while longer. No one will expect us yet."

"That's not the point." His voice was gentle and he settled the bonnet on her head, but removed it immediately, saying, "You should tuck your hair up."

Amelia reached absently to touch the silky tresses, but her fingers felt nerveless and she couldn't seem to find the pins. She gave a helpless shrug and stood expectantly before him. Verwood searched through the shimmering locks, discovering only two pins. "Perhaps some of them have fallen out," he suggested, crouching to look about them on the stone pavement.

The sunlight gleamed back from one of them and Amelia crouched down beside him to pick it up. But his face was so close, his lips looking so very inviting, that she bent forward to kiss him, and the next thing she knew, they were both sitting on the sun-baked stone, their arms once more around each other. His face was lost in her hair, the whisper of his breath against her forehead. Amelia found her hands were under this jacket, massaging his back through the crisp linen of his shirt. So easily did the simple touch rekindle heat in her body. His hand came to remove the shawl she wore and to caress the bare skin at her throat, sending a tremor down the length of her.

Don't stop now, she pleaded silently. Don't let this thrilling sense of imminent ecstasy fade out to nothing. She bent her head to kiss his wrist, and his thumb played softly over the rapid pulse in her throat. There was a handbreadth of bare skin from her throat to the sleeves of her walking dress and he brought his fingers to either side to gently knead the exposed flesh. The repetitious stroking made her breasts so close below ache for the same touch. They felt swollen to the point they would burst from her gown, straining against the material, too tightly enclosed to allow for their expansion.

He raised his head from her hair and stared directly into her hazy eyes, as though asking a question. Amelia smiled tremulously and nodded. He shifted her slightly in his arms until she was half-leaning against his chest and could feel the steady thumping of his heart, less erratic than her own. His lips touched hers, brushed against them, butterfly-soft, and his hands . . . They cupped her full, aching breasts with warm reassurance, remaining motionless there for several minutes as their lips merged in a sultry dance of heightening pleasure.

Then, slowly, slowly his thumbs began to move, almost as though he didn't even will them to. Through the thin cotton material she could feel them circling, swirling, confidently closing in toward the very tips of her breasts. Even under the cloth her nipples tingled to the pressure, stiffened to a solid knot of desire. Now every devouring flame seemed to be concentrated at three amazing points on her body, two of them in direct touch with him.

She opened her eyes to regain some sense of where she was, to place herself in his strong arms, to see the expression on his face. He was looking at her, his lips slightly parted, about to kiss her again. The unruly black hair and the bristling black brows over the enraptured dark eyes made her heart hammer with love. How very tender he was, this ordinarily brusque man.

"Should I be ashamed of myself?" she asked timidly.

"Ashamed?" His eyes snapped. "Of course not! We've both exceeded some typical bounds of propriety, but I can't see that will do the least harm. I don't think either of us knew quite how . . . ardent you would be, Amelia, but I for one," he said, smiling wryly at her, "am delighted."

"Well, I had no idea how . . . nice you could be." She rose to her feet and began to dust off her dress, not looking at him. "You've always been so gruff with me, or slightly mocking. You don't suppose the kindness could be a lasting thing, do you?" she asked, hopeful.

He considered her dolefully. "I very much fear it may be, where you're concerned, my dear." After shaking out her shawl, he handed it to her, along with two pins for her hair. "Can you pin it up yourself? It's not the sort of thing I've had any practice at."

Obviously there were other things at which he'd had plenty of practice, Amelia reminded herself. But that was only to be expected, and was undoubtedly to her benefit. She poked the pins casually into her curls and allowed him to settle the bonnet carefully on her head. When he had tied the ribbons at a jaunty angle under her chin, he kissed the tip of her nose and asked, "Shall we do things in a more orderly fashion from now on, my love? Why don't I speak to Peter first thing when we get back to Margrave?"

Amelia's heart leapt in her bosom. He had called her "my love." He really was going to offer for her! Her eyes shone with delight, but she lowered them demurely and said, "I'm sure I would wish you to do everything that's proper."

He laughed, and squeezed her hand. "Just as you would," he teased her as they wandered out of the castle ruins and back toward the house.

Peter regarded Verwood with some anxiety. "You're sure you're not feeling pressured into this, Alexander? I told you the other night I didn't regard your being here as in the light of a suitor."

They were sitting in Peter's study, in handsome leather chairs, with the window out onto the garden thrown open. Verwood stretched out his long legs, and when he spoke there was a trace of amusement in his voice. "The only thing that could pressure me into offering for your sister is my great affection for her, Peter. She's taken me completely by storm. I've never met such a delightful, intelligent, exasperating young woman in my life. I don't think I can live without her."

"I see." Peter leaned back in his chair, crossing his hands over his stomach. "Well, if you know she can be exasperating, you won't be much surprised in her, I dare say. It isn't everyone who would suit her, but I have a feeling the two of you will get on admirably . . . between your rows. Which is just as Amelia would have it, I think. She's a darling most of the time, headstrong occasionally, and downright feisty when pushed. Do you think she shares your affection? She swears she won't marry without it."

"Oh, I believe she shares it. We haven't actually come straight out and discussed that, you understand. But I did tell her I was going to speak with you." The viscount tapped one restless finger against the arm of his chair. "I suppose she will want to be married here, quietly, but if she prefers London, I'm not averse to that. If I can convince her, I'd prefer it be within the month. Once these things are decided, I can't see any reason for delay." He frowned across at his host. "You haven't made an offer yet to Mlle. Chartier, have you?"

"No, I'm not as precipitate as you." Peter laughed. But he grew instantly serious. "Actually, it's a matter of letting her get to know me a little better. I can't say your concern about her brother has made me one jot less determined to marry her, though. She's too young and too artless to be involved with spying, I'd stake my life on it. I know Amelia has helped me in the past; that doesn't mean Veronique is at all suited to the same sort of endeavor." He shrugged. "I can't say I'd like having a French spy for a brother-in-law, but I wouldn't be able to hold that against his sister. If you can possibly find out the truth about him, I'd appreciate your doing it soon. Exposing him as a spy should come before, rather than after, I ask Veronique to marry me."

Verwood nodded his sympathy. If indeed Chartier was a spy, and they were able to prove it, Veronique could well hold a lasting aversion to the earl, which had nothing to do with her obvious affection for him. There was no saying that she would marry him under those circumstances; indeed, it seemed unlikely. "Your man hasn't returned yet. I promise I'll let you know as soon as he does. Even then all we may know is that Chartier's gone to France on a smuggler's boat."

"I realize that."

The two men sat in silence for a while. Verwood finally rose and placed an encouraging hand on Peter's shoulder. "Things most often work out for the best."

"Thanks. Good luck with Amelia."

It was Verwood's natural assumption that there would be no question of luck about it. He felt certain Amelia shared his feelings and that she would be as eager as he to set a date for their marriage in the near future. When he and Amelia had gotten back to Margrave, she had been handed a letter, which she took absently, then noted that it was from a friend. "Oh, good, it's from Clarissa. I shall take it to the Summer Parlor to read."

Now there was little trace of Verwood's limp as he strolled confidently through the Blue Drawing Room to the door at its farthest end. If he wouldn't for a moment have believed two months ago that he would now be about to propose marriage to this intriguing young lady, well, any number of things happened in one's life that surprised one. He hadn't as yet given a great deal of thought to his future with Amelia —where they would spend their wedding trip, whether they would live in London or at his seat in Derbyshire. Those were questions for the two of them to decide together, after all. But he was impatient to discuss them, to know that they really would be planning how they would spend their lives together.

The door to the Summer Parlor stood partially open and he pushed it the rest of the way with an eager hand. She sat at a small table, her friend's letter open in front of her, but she was not looking at it. Instead she was staring off at nothing in particular, a strange expression on her pale face.

"Amelia?" Is there something wrong?" he demanded, hastening to her side. "Have you had bad news?"

She refused to allow him to take her hand, but stared stonily up at him. "You lied to me," she said.

— 19 —

Verwood searched through his love-clouded brain for a time when he had lied to her. Somewhere the nagging thought came to him that he had, about something a little more serious than the limp, but he was at a loss to put his finger on it. "It was probably just an exaggeration," he suggested, trying once again to take her hand.

This she would not allow, clenching her hands tightly on the table on top of her friend's letter. "It was not an exaggeration," she insisted.

"Perhaps you will refresh my memory of the occasion. I certainly wouldn't lie to you without provocation."

"Yes, the greatest possible provocation, I'm sure." Amelia drew forth the letter and read, " 'Colonel Lovell was much disappointed to hear that Lord Verwood had gone to Margrave without stopping in town to see him. He is much afraid he'll be posted before his lordship returns, and won't have any opportunity of discussing their army days together.' " She slapped the letter down on the table and regarded him coldly. "You told me you had seen Colonel Lovell in London. You even professed to know of his new assignment with Sir John Moore."

"Well, I did know of his assignment with Moore. I helped to arrange it for him through the War Department."

"But you didn't see him in town, or anywhere else."

"No," he admitted, running a hand through his disordered black locks.

"Then why did you tell me you had?"

"Because, my dear Amelia, it was your way of testing me. I could tell from the way you asked. God knows why anyone should ever have let the least bit of information slip to you; you were so utterly transparent. I knew if I said I had seen him, you would be satisfied that I was myself. Otherwise you were likely to continue your misguided cloak-and-dagger presumption that I wasn't. It was the simplest way to prove myself; anything else would have taken an inordinate amount of time." He smiled confidently and reached out to place a hand on her stiffened shoulder. "I didn't want to waste any more time, my love. Given the circumstances, I'm sure you would have done the same."

Amelia stepped away from his hand, which fell to his side. "You fail to understand the gravity of the situation, sir. It turns out you haven't proved your identity after all, in addition to which you lied to make me believe you had. That's not something I can simply overlook, you know."

"Certainly it is," he assured her, trying with a hearty tone to cajole her out of her absurd stance. "You know very well that I'm Verwood. For God's sake, Amelia, I'm in this room right now to ask you to marry me! How would that set with your idea that I'm not actually Verwood at all?"

"Not at all well," she said, gathering up the three sheets of the letter and stuffing them in her pocket. "Which is why I have no intention of accepting your offer. Since you lied to me, I have no compunction about refusing you. I can't imagine I would go on at all well with a man who would lie to me. Which is quite apart from whether you are indeed Lord Verwood or not. I shall be forced to mention this to Peter, of course, since your involvement in the Chartier affair has now compromised our chances of finding out the truth about him. For all I know, you may be associated with him in some way."

"Don't be ridiculous!" he snapped. The muscle in his jaw twitched, his eyes had become fiercely black again. "Peter knows who I am and you'll only make a fool of yourself by trying to convince him he doesn't. He's not going to listen to you."

"Then I may have to take matters into my own hands."

Verwood felt the most ominous foreboding. His own position with her was so weak now that he knew it would be completely useless for him to argue with her. The possibility of shaking some sense into her did briefly occur to him, but he immediately discarded it. What he really wanted to do was simply take her into his arms and profess his love, and have all this other ludicrous baggage disappear.

She stood rigid before him, one hand clenched at her side, the other stuck in her pocket with the letter. Despite her anger, her face was pale, the violet eyes enormous and moist. He had expected her to run from the room when she finished speaking, but she seemed incapable of movement. Verwood willed himself to a calmness he was far from feeling, forcing his hands not to reach out for her.

"Amy," he said softly, "I love you. That's not something I offer lightly. For years I've thought there was no woman I could possibly spend my life with, who would tolerate my sardonic tongue and my lack of interest in the ton. I believed there was no one who could be a companion and a lover and a helpmate to such a perverse man as myself. But then, I hadn't envisioned such a perverse lady as you." His tone was rueful, his dark eyes earnest. "Not that I would have you change the least thing about yourself, except your refusal to marry me. I didn't lie to deceive you, my dear, but to allow you to accept the truth."

Now she turned away from him, before the moisture could spill out of her eyes. In a strangled voice she said, "I couldn't trust you. Whenever it was expedient for you to lie to me, you would. Whenever it was easier for you to get your way by fabricating some tale, you'd do it. You wouldn't feel it necessary to deal honestly with me, and I won't have someone who doesn't."

"That simply isn't true, Amelia." He moved to stand behind her, carefully resisting the impulse to put his hands on her slumped shoulders. "There are times when absolute honesty doesn't serve to anyone's advantage. I apologize for that little deception; it wasn't, as it turns out, a wise move on my part, but it seemed harmless enough at the time. If I *had* seen Lovell, he would have confirmed my identity. Would it help if I sent for him now?"

"No," she whispered. "Nothing will help now but your going back to London."

"You told me you weren't stubborn."

Amelia refused to respond to this taunt.

The breath from his pent-up sigh ruffled her hair. He felt certain that if he took her in his arms, she would respond to him, would be won over by her physical attraction, but it seemed an underhanded way of going about convincing her. Did she really still believe it possible he wasn't legitimate? Or was she more hurt than suspicious? One thing alone was paramount, and he found himself asking, "Do you love me, Amelia?"

With a muffled sob, she fled the room.

Verwood made no attempt to follow her. There was no sense in creating a scene in front of the whole household. She would need time to staighten out the confusion he had inadvertently caused in her mind and her emotions. And he, too, was disturbed with a nagging sense of guilt at having created her dilemma. Though love was imperative, the element of trust was surely as necessary. He could understand her anguished feeling of betrayal, but he hadn't meant to cause it, and he had every intention of eradicating it . . . if she would give him the opportunity.

He had the most awful feeling that she might not.

After standing in the Summer Parlor for some time, ignoring the midday heat of the sun through the windows and debating his next move, he shook off the feeling of hopelessness and went to explain the situation to Peter.

Amelia was unfortunate enough to run into Trudy on the way to her room. Her aunt was gloriously attired in a purple cotton walking dress, a fall of blond lace scattered over her ample bosom. They met at the head of the stone staircase, Amelia hurrying upward as fast as her feet could carry her and Trudy padding slowly toward some unknown but unurgent mission on the ground floor.

"Wherever are you going in such a rush?" Trudy demanded. "It's not becoming to be seen in such haste. One loses one's dignity and grace of carriage, you know. You must always tread lightly, acting as though everything is under strict control, even if the house is afire. I'm sure I've mentioned it before."

"Yes, indeed you have. But there's no one about to see me except you, my dear aunt. I was on my way to my room."

"And where, pray tell, is Lord Verwood?" Trudy lifted one coy brow at her. "I believe the two of you went walking this morning."

"Yes. He's below, in the Summer Parlor."

"You mustn't be discouraged with him, just because he's a little slow to come up to scratch," Trudy said, sympathetic when she noticed the damp eyelashes. "He's not just your ordinary suitor, Amelia. One must make allowances for all that time he spent in the most amazingly uncivilized countries when he was in the army. Not that I hold with the aristocracy engaging in such dangerous pursuits. Where would we be if all our young lords went off to get themselves killed? But that's beside the point. Lord Verwood has managed to return with only an injured knee and I'm sure it would serve your purpose better to be a little more concerned about that. You shouldn't make him overextend himself by taking him on long walks. I noticed you were gone above two hours."

"He didn't complain of any pain."

"Well, he wouldn't, would he? It's for you to be aware of when he has tired, and suggest a brief respite."

"Oh, I gave him quite a long . . . respite," Amelia assured her, experiencing a most unnerving wave of remembered heat through her body. This might be the best time to inform her aunt that there was no longer any possibility of a marriage between her and Verwood, she decided stubbornly. "Aunt Trudy, I think I must tell you—"

A loud knock at the front door electrified the phlegmatic Trudy into action. "We'll speak later, my dear," she said, tripping down the stairs. "That will be Mr. Upham come to call on me." And she disappeared around the bend in the steps before Amelia could utter another word.

All to the good, Amelia decided as she made her way to her room. Trudy would have nothing but disapproval for her rejection of Verwood's offer, and wasn't likely to understand the reason for it, since she was convinced that Amelia held an affection for the viscount. And that was indisputably true. Amelia had been almost too impatient, waiting for Verwood to join her in the Summer Parlor, to open her friend's letter at first. But as the time lengthened she used it as a distraction, assuming her brother was delaying the viscount with his good wishes. She had been unable to believe her eyes when she came upon the incriminating sentence, and read it over and over until it was engraved on her mind.

Her room felt stuffy from the heat and she crossed to throw open a window, letting the cool breeze waft against her now-flushed cheeks. From feeling drained and cold, she noticed she had become slightly feverish. How could he have so callously lied to her, allowed her to base her trust in him on an acknowledged untruth? She had wanted so badly to believe him, had prayed he would make the right answer. Her relief had been like a weight lifted from her heart.

A sham, all of it. Oh, he probably *was* Lord Verwood. Amelia couldn't seem to think straight enough to decide if this was unlikely. She crossed the room to pour water from the pitcher into the basin and dipped her handkerchief in it and bathed her wrists. Then she lay down on her bed and put the cloth on her forehead, which had started to ache abominably. This brought very little comfort, though, since she was unable to stop the thoughts that raged through her mind. Eventually, out of sheer exhaustion from the emotional swings of the day, she fell asleep.

It was late afternoon by the time she woke. Cooler air was creeping through the open window, chilling her where she lay uncovered on the bed. Her stomach was also rumbling in protest against not being fed for so long, and she grimaced as she sat up and the clammy handkerchief dropped into her lap. The case clock on her mantel indicated it was still an hour until dinner, but she decided to dress now and go down to the drawing room ahead of time. Bridget came immediately when she rang, looking concerned.

"They sent me to look in on you when you didn't come for luncheon," she said. "We were all that worried. But you were sleeping peaceful as a babe. Are you feeling all right?"

"Fine. I'll dress now for dinner. When we're finished, have the kitchen send a bowl of fruit to the drawing room, please." As Bridget helped her out of her walking dress, Amelia tried not to think of Verwood's hands ranging over her bosom that morning. She was reminded, however, that she'd lost quite a few hours, which might have been important ones. "Has anyone left or come?" she asked.

"Mr. Upham called. That's all I know of."

"No one came for Lord Verwood? A servant, perhaps?"

Bridget shrugged her gaunt shoulders. "If one did, I never heard of it."

"Did his lordship go out riding?"

"Mercy, Lady Amelia, I can't be watching what all the guests do. If you'd told me you wanted me to, I'd have made it my business, of course. Far as I know, he stayed in the house all afternoon, but he could just as easy have gone out. I was mending with Mrs. Lawson in the sewing room, and pressing your dress for this evening. Shall I ask round?"

"Heavens, no! It was just idle curiosity. Ordinarily I would have seen to his entertainment. That will be fine, Bridget. If you'd just see to the bowl of fruit . . ."

Amelia walked rather nervously into the drawing room a few minutes later, assuming (hoping) that Verwood would not yet be there, or that if he were, there would also be someone else. Again she was out in her luck. He was there, alone, and he looked as though he'd been waiting for her. He was already in evening dress, his black locks still damp, either from a bath or from an attempt to coax them into some manageable style. His hair looked ridiculous to her, she was so used to its endearing disarray. If it had been any other time, she might have teased him about it.

"Are you well?" he asked, not moving toward her.

"Quite well," she said, though actually she did continue to feel a little weak and feverish.

"And are you still determined against me?"

The pain in his expression she found unbearable. But he had caused her a great deal of pain, too. The best she could manage, in all fairness, was, "I haven't found any reason to change my mind."

Bighton entered the drawing room bearing an enormous silver bowl filled with fruit, which he set on the spider-leg table nearest her. "I trust you're feeling better, Lady Amelia," he said.

"Yes, thank you, Bighton. Starved, though. I appreciate your bringing the fruit." She helped herself to an apple as he left. When the door had closed again, she turned to Verwood. "Has your man returned from following Chartier?"

"Not yet." He raked fingers through his hair until it looked quite normal again. "I thought about what you said, Amelia, and I can understand your disappointment and annoyance, your feeling of betrayal. And I realize it's asking a great deal of you to put your trust in me again, but I wish you could. Isn't there some way I can persuade you?"

Amelia was silent for what seemed a long time. When she finally spoke, it was to ask, "When your man returns and tells you where Chartier is, what do you intend to do?"

Verwood sighed, frustrated that she wouldn't respond to him. "If he's back in this area, I suppose I will go to him, try to catch him in the act of climbing into a boat. That would be evidence enough to press him for some explanation. Perhaps Peter could bring a little pressure to bear on Mlle. Chartier."

"Would you let me come with you?" It was not an idle question, nor one to which she expected an immediate negative. This was her answer to his question "Isn't there some way I can persuade you?" She made this perfectly clear by the steady way she returned his gaze, the defiant tilt to her chin.

"Dammit, Amelia, it could be dangerous. If he's planning to use one of the smuggling boats to get to France, there are going to be men there who don't want to be seen by someone like me . . . or you. You can't really expect me to take the woman I love into a situation like that! It will be dark in all likelihood and we'll have to be careful to catch them off guard. Be reasonable."

Amelia was not feeling much like being reasonable. She took a hard bite out of the apple, chewed it thoughtfully, and said, "I want to come with you."

"I can't allow it." He made a helpless gesture with one long hand. "Not even to earn your trust. Can't you see that? What kind of man would I be to endanger your life just so I could win you? It's not a reasonable request. How would I ever forgive myself if something happened to you?"

"That would be your problem, of course, for I should be dead," she rejoined callously. "If I weren't dead, I would marry you. Otherwise I shan't."

He muttered something that sounded very much like "Damned if I do, damned if I don't," and wandered off to the cold hearth. "I'll have to think about it," he said aloud, stalling. "After all, Amelia, you've told me you're not really all that brave. I can't think you would like to be in much danger."

Which was perfectly true. But she wasn't going to see him go into a hazardous situation himself without her by his side. The possibility that he could fend better for himself if she wasn't there never occurred to her. She had already put herself to a great deal of trouble to find out if Chartier was a French spy, and she wanted to be there when the solution was finally reached. It was Chartier who had blabbed to Verwood about her in the first place. Not that that had proved entirely without its positive side, of course, but the Frenchman certainly hadn't intended it to.

Amelia frowned at him. "I can be as brave as the next one. If you don't take me with you, I shall find a way of getting there myself."

"That's what I'm afraid of."

— 20 —

Mr. Upham had joined them for dinner again. Amelia had felt decidedly suspicious with the extraordinary amount of time the men took over their brandy and port. It seemed likely to her that during that period Verwood's man had come and the viscount had set about making arrangements for catching Chartier in the act of setting sail for France. But no one said anything throughout the excruciating length of an evening spent at cards. Not one of them seemed to cast furtive glances at the clock, or at his pocket watch. If there was an air of expectancy about their waiting, Amelia was at a loss to discover it. They seemed, if anything, in amazingly high spirits, and any little thing was a cause for amusement, which was not an uncommon aftereffect of having drunk more than was quite good for them.

The party broke up at just going on eleven, with Trudy announcing that she was for her bed. Amelia suspected that one of the gentlemen had induced her to make this move, but she hadn't been able to catch one of them at it. Trudy shepherded Veronique Chartier and Amelia off with her, waving a cheerful good night to the men, who remained standing about the drawing room as though they had nothing more significant to do than chat about the price of corn.

Amelia was loath to go but decided that if Verwood hadn't taken the opportunity to draw her aside and confide in her, she would have to make plans of her own. And the first thing she needed to do was to get out of her evening dress and into something more suitable for a ride to the coast. She allowed Bridget to undress her and slip her nightdress on before dismissing the girl.

Every riding costume she owned looked unusually cumbersome as she made her way down a row of them in her wardrobe. She had just decided on the emerald-green one when a knock came at her door. For a moment she froze, and then she tiptoed over to the door and whispered, "Who is it?"

"It's Alexander, love."

Well, really, it was a startlingly frank way for him to introduce himself at such a time. Nonetheless, Amelia opened the door to him. (It was a flannel nightdress she wore, singularly unrevealing, more was the pity.) The riding habit was slung carelessly over her arm and as he entered he said, "You won't want that. I've brought you a pair of pantaloons and a shirt."

"You're going to let me come with you?" she squeaked.

"Obviously I had no choice," he said with a sigh, setting the clothing down on the bed. "I couldn't very well let you go off by yourself, could I?"

Recovered from her initial shock, she said sternly, "I should hope not." She regarded the gray pantaloons and white shirt somewhat skeptically. "Is that all men wear?"

"Well, we wear drawers, of course, but I didn't think any of mine would fit you." He continued perfectly seriously, "We can roll the legs up on the pantaloons and tie a string round your waist to hold them up. And it doesn't matter if the shirt is too large. You'll have riding boots of your own, and I thought you could simply wear your cloak to cover it all."

"I suppose so," she said doubtfully. "Aren't you going to leave while I dress?"

"If you want me to."

"Well, of course I want you to," she said, blushing. "I mean, since you're letting me go, I suppose I shall have to marry you, but I haven't anything on under the nightdress, and . . . Well, something should be saved for when we're wed."

"Do you think so?" His eyes were wide with innocence. "You may need help with the pantaloons."

"I'll manage. You wait in the hall."

Verwood did as he was instructed.

In the end, Amelia decided to leave the nightdress on and put the other garments over it. Otherwise one could rather see through the shirt and that didn't strike her as particularly desirable. The waist on the pantaloons was far too large and she pulled the door open a few inches to ask, "Did you bring string?"

He dug in his pocket and produced a ball of twine, which he handed her without a word.

When she had accomplished her dressing to her own satisfaction, she opened the door again and waved him in. "How do I look?"

His eyes trailed from her flushed face to her booted feet. "Splendid. There was a tinker who used to come through the village in Derbyshire who looked remarkably like that. Baggy breeches, and a shirt stuffed with cloths to keep him warm."

"It's my nightdress," she explained. "I kept it on."

"Very appropriate."

His eyes were sparkling with laughter, though he tried very hard to keep his lips from straying into a grin. Amelia chose to ignore this *in*appropriate lightheartedness. They had serious business ahead of them. "What's happening with Chartier?" she demanded, breathless with excitement.

"He kept his carriage as far as Tunbridge, where he took a room at an inn for the night. Terwick saw him send off a messenger shortly afterwards and this morning the messenger returned. Then Chartier left the carriage there and returned here on horseback. He took a room at that unsavory inn southeast of Winchelsea right near the water and made an excursion up the beach about a mile on foot. Then he returned to the inn and has been there ever since. Terwick came just after dinner to tell me."

"Aha!"

Verwood shook his head at her, unable to resist smiling this time. "Amelia, you really are too much. Don't you think you'd be just as happy if you crawled between your sheets and had a good night's sleep? I promise I'll tell you everything that happened in the morning."

"Never!" she declared, inspecting herself one last time in the glass. "Should we go now?"

He was reluctant to leave. "Perhaps, considering the danger of the expedition, you would just give me a kiss before we do. I've never been kissed by a lady wearing pantaloons before."

"Aren't we in a hurry?" Amelia wanted to kiss him, needed to kiss him, but was anxious about the possibility of missing out on all the adventure.

"They're saddling the horses. You'll be on Cleo but I've had them put a regular saddle on her. They aren't to know at the stables that it's you going out at this hour of the night."

"I see." She considered this a minute. "Well, I shall pull the hood of my cloak forward so they won't see my face."

"That won't be necessary. Peter's bringing the horses round to the side of the house."

"Peter's going with us? And he agreed that I could go?"

"I explained the situation to him. He wasn't very happy with you, Amy, but he was forced to admit it was better than seeing you wander off on your own."

"I'm surprised he didn't just lock me in my room."

"He considered it; then he decided it was safer to take you than chance your breaking a leg trying to climb down on sheets or something."

Amelia wondered if she'd even have thought of doing such a thing, but she didn't tell Verwood so. Really, it was quite unbelievable that they'd decided to let her come. She felt a little uncomfortable with the power she'd wielded, and more than a little frightened of being out on the beach with dangerous smugglers and a French spy. What if they thought the revenuers were after them? Surely they would turn into thugs, or worse. She crept closer to Verwood and turned her face up to him for a kiss.

Obligingly he closed her in his arms and pressed her firmly against him. His kiss was almost nostalgic, sweet and tender, as though it might be their last. Amelia shuddered against him.

"Why don't you stay here and wait for me?" he whispered against her hair.

Actually, there was nothing, at the moment, Amelia would have preferred doing, but she pulled away from him with a show of indignation. "You won't fob me off, Alexander. If you go, I go."

"I shouldn't let Peter go alone. It wouldn't be fair."

As though he would ever seriously consider staying with her, she thought, outraged. He was just trying to make her feel guilt-ridden. "We'll all go."

He gazed deep into her eyes for long moments. "Very well," he said at last, resigned. "We'll all go."

Margrave was uncannily dark and Amelia was relieved that he held on to her hand as they descended the stairs. She found her cloak in the closet without any difficulty and he gallantly wrapped it about her, taking this last opportunity to hug her. They went out the side door into the brisk, moonless night. There were three horses on the riding path, one of them already with its rider mounted.

Amelia was a little nervous of her brother's reception, but he merely nodded to her as Verwood helped her onto Cleo. She had never ridden anything but sidesaddle, and straddling the horse felt unfamiliar. Cleo sidestepped a few paces, as unaccustomed as her rider to this unusual arrangement, but Amelia easily brought her under control, maneuvering the mare between Verwood's horse and her brother's. They walked the animals until they were out of hearing distance of the house, and then broke into a canter.

It was exhilarating to ride astride, to be a real part of the gentlemen's enterprise—or so Amelia told herself. Certain aspects of it made her rather dubious: the ominous roar of the ocean getting closer and closer, her inability to see exactly where they were going, the grave silence that came from each of the men, the fear of what lay ahead. If she hadn't been so wretchedly stubborn, she'd be in her own bed right now, dreaming of the viscount, no doubt, and feeling a whole lot warmer and more cheerful.

Verwood gestured, with a hand Amelia could barely see, that they were to slow to a walk again. This indication that they were getting close to the scene of action did not encourage her. She could feel a bolt of lightning fear shoot up her spine, which caused her to tremble all over. They followed the trail along the marshy land a little farther before dismounting and tying the horses to the stunted bushes along the way.

Her voice trembled as she asked, "What do we do now?"

Verwood came forward to lay his hand on her shoulder. "We wait," he said. "There isn't much cover here, so we can't get too close to the shore without being seen. When there's activity down by the water, we'll close in on them."

"Do you and Peter have p-pistols?"

"Of course." He patted the deep pocket in his dark coat. "Primed and ready."

"You wouldn't actually *kill* anyone, would you?"

"Only if necessary," he assured her.

Amelia was not comforted. Her hands were icy and shaking; she wished he'd take hold of one of them. But he had moved away to consult with Peter in hushed tones she was not able to overhear. She felt wretchedly isolated on the black marshlands, unable to see clearly as far as the water's edge, and therefore fearful of what might be happening without her knowledge. The men had ceased talking and for some time the only sound was the lapping of the water.

By the time she could make out some sort of movement on the beach, she was almost paralyzed by the wish to be in her own bed. Not that she wanted Verwood and her brother to be out here alone; she wished the comfort of their beds for them, too. Let someone else find out if Chartier was a spy. But she was impressed with the sheer confidence radiated by the viscount and the earl; they stood at their ease watching what for them must have been much more distinct activity down by the water.

"Now," the viscount said, drawing his pistol from his

pocket and grabbing hold of Amelia's hand. Peter instantly produced a pistol too, and took her other hand. Wonderful, she thought. If they shoot at anyone, and are shot back at, I shall be the easiest target of the three of us, right in the middle. But she assured herself she would prefer to be the one to receive some fatal injury, rather than either of them, her brother and the man she loved.

They were walking at a pace it was difficult for her to keep up with. Her feet seemed to stumble continually on the uneven ground. By now she could see the scene before them with more clarity . . . but even less fortitude. There seemed to be an awful lot of people there, far outnumbering the three of them. A small boat was being launched into the waves. Amelia was surprised that no one had as yet noticed their approach. Didn't they keep some sort of lookout?

Yes, they did. Suddenly there was a bellow that reached her with astonishing clarity. "Ho, revenuers!" The cry was taken up by what seemed a chorus of thousands, like a refrain sung at Covent Garden. Verwood and Peter never hesitated in their progress, dragging her along between them. There was a flurry of movement by the men on the beach as they scattered here and there. A shot rang out.

"Oh, my God," Amelia moaned.

"Are you hit?" Verwood demanded.

"I don't think so," she said.

Another explosion roared, and this time Amelia could see the flash from a pistol in a man's hand. For the briefest moment she thought she would faint, but she gathered her faltering courage about her and hurried on, since the two men still had not paused. She considered this foolhardy of them, but hadn't the breath left in her fright to tell them so.

"We're not revenuers!" Peter called. "We've come for the Frenchman."

There was more activity, another shot was fired, and the cry went up, "There he goes!"

Amelia could see a lone figure racing up the beach, ducking and weaving in an erratic pattern. Beside her Verwood spoke to Peter. "You stay here with the smugglers. They won't bother you now they know you aren't after them.

I'll take Amelia with me, after Chartier. It's only fair she be in on the capture."

She wanted very much to tell him she wouldn't mind not being there, but it seemed a cowardly thing to do and she didn't want him to think she was a coward. Besides, she didn't want to be separated from him. He kept hold of her hand as they ran after the diminishing figure. Amelia had never run so fast in her life, but the pantaloons helped. There was a freedom her skirts had never given her. And it was encouraging, if also nerve-racking, that they were gaining on the dark figure.

Her heart stood still when the man turned slightly and fired a pistol over his shoulder. Verwood reacted by firing the pistol in his hand, its report so loud she nearly cried out. The dark figure fell and she blinked in horrified astonishment. "Oh, you shouldn't! You shouldn't!" she wailed. "What if you've killed him?" She was panting as they raced up to the downed man, tears spilling over onto her cheeks. "He may not have been a French spy at all. Oh, what are we going to do?"

"Well, he shot at us," Verwood pointed out as she bent over the crumpled figure. "Is he dead?"

"I don't know. How do you tell?" Poor Amelia already sounded frantic, but when she had crouched down and gotten a look at the fellow's face, she thought *she* would die. "Oh, my God, Alexander, *it's not Chartier.*"

"How's that?" The viscount bent over the recumbent form and gave a tsk of annoyance. "So it's not. Well, these things happen."

Amelia stared at him, incredulous. Could a human being possibly be that callous? And then she saw that his shoulders were shaking, and she thought perhaps he had only spoken so offhandedly to make it seem that he wasn't upset. She was about to rise and comfort him when he gave one of his shouts of laughter, just as he had after they visited Mrs. Carson. Amelia had the most awful feeling she had been caught in a nightmare.

The crumpled figure stretched out his arms and legs and rose to his feet. It was Terwick; Amelia should have recognized him immediately, but she'd been too over-wrought, thinking it was Chartier. She allowed herself to slip from her crouched position to a sitting one on the ground, unable for a moment to take in exactly what had happened.

"Great sport," Terwick was saying. "Hope I didn't shoot too soon, milord, but I was right there in the spirit of the thing, you see. I thought about reloading, but you and Lady Amelia were gaining on me so fast I figured it would be better to just fall down then. She's a fleet one, for sure."

"Yes, she's going to lead me quite a chase," the viscount said ruefully, reaching a hand down to help Amelia to her feet. As Terwick moved off toward the group that waited by the water, Verwood asked, "So how did you like your adventure, my love? Was it as exciting as you'd hoped?"

Amelia was furious with him. She brushed away his hand and leaped to her feet, but her knees were a little weak yet and she swayed. Verwood's arm came around her waist, pressing her against him. "Now, don't be angry. It was your own stubbornness forced us to do it, Amy."

"Where's Chartier?" she demanded. But she didn't try to move from his sturdy comfort.

"Should be back at Margrave with Upham by now."

"And all this was for my benefit?" She waved an unsteady hand that encompassed the beach area.

"Yes, but don't feel guilty about putting everyone to so much trouble. They'll be paid for the night's work, and besides, I think they all quite enjoyed it. I know I did. There's a lot of thespian talent lying around unused, you know."

"What did you tell them you were doing it for?"

"We didn't give any explanations. These people are used to the eccentricities of the aristocracy."

They had begun walking along after Terwick, but Verwood halted and cocked his head at her. "Do you think I could have a kiss? Something to show your gratitude for all my effort?"

"You're lucky you don't get a kick in the shin," she muttered.

— 21 —

Peter insisted that she change into a dress before she joined them in the drawing room. "After all, Chartier is going to be my brother-in-law, and I won't have him seeing you in a pair of pantaloons, Amelia, even if he *is* a spy."

"But you'll start talking to him before I get back," she protested. "If I wear my cloak, he'll hardly notice."

"He'll notice," Verwood said, grinning at her. "If you hurry, we'll wait here for you before we go in."

This offer didn't seem to sit very well with Peter, who was anxious to get the matter settled, so Amelia dashed up the stairs before he could disagree. Getting out of the shirt and pantaloons wasn't all that difficult, but getting into a dress (heaven knew what one was expected to wear at two o'clock in the morning) took a great deal longer. She fretted over every stupid button and paid not the least heed to her hair, which had become hideously tangled on the ride. Instead she pulled a night cap over it, which made her look adorably young and innocent.

They were still there when she scurried down the stone stairs, and she smiled her thanks as she followed them into the drawing room, where Chartier and Upham sat drinking brandy as though it were the most normal occurrence in the world, this gathering in the middle of the night. On coming closer, however, Amelia could see the nervous strain in the Frenchman's face, and she felt almost sorry for him. Not as sorry as when she thought he'd been killed, but mildly sympathetic.

He wore rough, dark clothes, peasant's clothes, and he wouldn't meet Amelia's eyes when she gazed at him. The sleeve was torn off one arm, which was bandaged from wrist to shoulder. "Were you hurt?" she asked, alarmed.

Michael Upham answered. "No, it's to keep from being conscripted when he gets there. Any healthy-looking fellow his age daren't wander about the countryside in France."

Peter took a chair directly opposite Chartier, and Verwood seated Amelia beside him on a sofa, where his arm stretched behind her along the back. Her brother studied the Frenchman for a moment and then began the proceedings. "The reason we detained you from your trip, M. Chartier, is that the circumstances seemed suspicious to . . . some of us. There is the suggestion that you may be going to your native country in some effort to serve it. That is, a few of the people in this room believe you may be a spy."

Put so bluntly, it sounded ludicrous somehow. Chartier regarded the earl with astonishment, which appeared entirely unfeigned to Amelia. For a moment he forgot what he was wearing and attempted to straighten a nonexistent neckcloth. Before he managed to speak, Peter added, "Or a smuggler. No offense intended," he said in an aside to Upham.

"None taken, I'm sure," the smuggler replied easily.

Verwood, whose hand had dropped behind Amelia's head where it couldn't be seen toying with the tangled curls there, suggested, "Perhaps you would just tell us what your business was in France."

For a moment the only sound was the crackling of the fire, necessary in the middle of the night for such a gathering, despite the daily warm weather. Chartier appeared undecided and shifted restlessly in his seat. When he spoke, it was to say, "First, I can assure you my business had nothing to do with spying, nor smuggling, either, as it is ordinarily meant. All of my belongings were taken from me by this gentleman," he remarked rather indignantly, indicating

Upham, "and I'm sure he can tell you there was nothing among them the least incriminating."

Mr. Upham nodded his agreement.

Chartier fidgeted with the bandage on his arm, looking up at last at Peter. "It's a rather awkward matter to discuss, your lordship. One of family affairs, you understand."

"You have a wife there?" Upham offered.

"No, no, nothing like that! I have no living relatives in France at all. When I go there, I bring back family . . . belongings. Things that are hidden away near the old estate. A few at a time. Valuable things. It's dangerous, of course, but it would be even more so to try to bring much at one time. My sister may need a dowry soon," he said, avoiding Peter's gaze, "and I thought I must make a run now to have it when the time arises."

"How does it happen your belongings weren't confiscated when you came to England?" Verwood asked.

Chartier hemmed and hawed. His eyes bounced from one to the other of them, unable to find someone to light on with impunity. They were all regarding him with curiosity, if not suspicion.

"It wasn't because I agreed to spy!" he insisted.

Peter considered him for a long moment. "I'm very attached to your sister, but I think it will be necessary to clear up these matters before we come to some understanding on that subject. I can't very well be left in the dark. I have a duty to my country as well as to myself."

The bandage on Chartier's arm had started to unravel from his nervous picking at it. To give himself something to do other than look at any of them, he wound it off as he told his story. "My father was the Comte de Rocca. He was sixty years old in 1792, and getting a little senile, or at least, a little strange. He had the wild notion that the revolutionaries had right on their side, that the aristocracy had plundered the poor. For siding with their cause, Louis took away his title and would have taken away his riches, only Louis had problems of his own at the time, and my mother's family was still influential. Their family name was Chartier."

He fell silent for a moment, then sighed. "I was only a child of ten and didn't really understand what was going on, but my mother was shrewd. Before Louis was even executed she had spirited a goodly sum out of the country to her cousin in England, who bought the estate near Bournemouth with it. That estate is mine now that my mother is dead, but for certain reasons it has been left in her cousin's name. My father, despite his revolutionary principles, was guillotined; savage people don't listen to reason. He was a comte, or had been one, and comtes were executed. But my mother managed to flee the country with my sister and me, though she hadn't time to bring the rest of our belongings with her. They were hidden so well and so secretly that it took me several expeditions when I reached an age of understanding to find them, using her instructions."

Verwood continued to twine Amelia's curls about his fingers, though he listened with as much interest as any of them. "You never shared your father's revolutionary ideals?" he asked.

"Never," Chartier pronounced adamantly. "It was my mother who instilled a love of king and country in my mind. A respect for the position I should one day inherit. And I intend yet to inherit it."

Upham shifted restlessly in his chair. The tale, having little bearing on him, also held little interest. "How do you plan to manage that?"

The shifty-eyed look Amelia had long ago noted in Chartier appeared now. "I've planned since I was fifteen," he said, the proud tilt to his head looking incongruous with his disheveled clothing. "Our Louis in exile is constantly in need of funds. He hasn't the resources he would have in France. I have pledged him one-half of my hidden property, in exchange for the eventual restoration of my title. It is through his agents that the goods I bring into England are converted into money. Sometimes I think I am shortchanged a little, but . . ." He gave an eloquent shrug. "It is worth it for my title."

"Yesterday, to whom did you send off a message from Tunbridge?" Peter asked.

Chartier's brows lifted. "Ah, I was followed, was I? It doesn't matter. Always I send a message to the agents ahead of time so my goods are picked up immediately. This time, also, I explained the necessity of coming into my own rather promptly, in order that my sister should have a sufficient standing . . . should her suitor find it important."

"It isn't important," Peter said.

"Well, one cannot know. To me it is important. Veronique knows only that our family was once titled. She doesn't seem to care if we are again, and she doesn't know of my plans to bring it about."

The revelation of the truth of the matter was a bit of a disappointment to Amelia, but she tried not to show it, stifling a yawn behind her hand. She was very aware of Verwood's fingers stroking the back of her neck, but she didn't dare look at him. And she *was* tired. It had been an exhausting day. She was ready to excuse herself, hoping Verwood would follow her, when the viscount suddenly said, "None of this explains about the doctor's records. I saw you come out of Dr. Braithwait's surgery some months ago, but he had no listing of a Chartier ever having visited him."

A ruddy flush stole into Chartier's cheeks. "It was a delicate matter on which I saw the good doctor. I had no wish to use my rightful name. You will find I used the name Lavalette."

Verwood didn't press him, though he would have been intrigued to hear what "delicate matter" could bring a flush to the cheeks of a twenty-five-year-old man. "It's late. I shall see Lady Amelia to her bedchamber."

All too ready to go, Amelia bounded immediately to her feet. "It seems you are paying quite a substantial duty to your king, M. Chartier. I doubt the English would be justified in taking any more. Forgive me if I've been suspicious of you. I'm sure I wish you well."

The Frenchman had risen and came forward to clasp her hand, the old admiring look in his eyes. "Perhaps you had reason. Now you will understand. Tomorrow we could take a walk together."

"Tomorrow I shall be busy planning for my wedding," she

said, throwing an arch look at Verwood. "His lordship is an impatient, scheming sort of gentleman, but a lady doesn't go back on her word." With a bright smile at the assembled men, she glided regally from the room.

Verwood caught up with her in the hall, having been delayed by the others' congratulations. "Scheming, am I? I should like to know what you'd have done in my position. Do you wear that cap to bed at night?" he asked as he twitched it off her honey curls.

"Only when I'm particularly cold."

"Well, there won't be any reason for you to be cold in bed when we're married. Still, it's rather becoming, in a way. Makes you look almost demure."

"*Not* one of my favorite poses," she informed him, "but if it will get you to kiss me, I think I shan't mind wearing it now and then."

"You don't need to wear a nightcap to get me to kiss you." Which he proved right there on the stairs, gathering her lightly into his arms. Amelia felt the tremors of desire run through her again as his lips tasted hers. Only after several minutes did they continue their climb toward her room.

"How did you manage it, with Upham and all?" she asked.

"We put our case to him after dinner and he sent a message off to one of his men. Then he went and got Chartier from the inn. He wasn't at all happy about it, you know. Being a smuggler is one thing; being recognized as one is quite another. It broke all bounds of civility to lay the thing out in the open. Peter had to promise not to stand in his way if he made an offer for your Aunt Gertrude."

"Trudy? Good Lord!"

"Yes, well, she's a grown woman, Amelia. She does seem to have been rather . . . ah, flirting with him."

Amelia remembered Trudy telling her she'd long held a tendre for Michael Upham, and sighed. "And he does have the most beautiful home. But somehow I can't picture Trudy married to a smuggler."

They had reached the door to her room, and thoughts of her aunt rapidly disappeared from her mind.

He cupped her face in gentle hands. "Do you believe I'm Lord Verwood?"

"Yes."

"And do you think you can come to trust me again?"

His eyes were so very dark, and so very full of tenderness. She ran her fingers through the unruly locks above them. "I love you," she whispered, meeting his intent gaze. "I trusted you with my life tonight, or at least I thought I did. I wouldn't want you ever to deceive me again, but I understand why you did it. Don't ever think I'm so unreasonable that I won't listen to you. I want to be part of your life. Not just your hostess and your bedmate. I'm not very good at intrigues. Do you think you could do something I could work with you on?"

He grinned at her, and kissed the tip of her twitching nose. "I have just the thing, Amy. I'm going to take my seat in the Lords, and we'll go into politics together. The new government needs a lot of direction in how to pursue this war with France. We could make it our business to guide them. Would that please you?"

"More than anything," she said, her eyes sparkling in the dim corridor. "Oh, Alexander, you really are the kindest person in the whole world."

"Only when I limp," he teased, drawing her into his arms again.

When Amelia entered the breakfast room the next morning, the others had already finished and gone, but Verwood waited for her there, rising to hold a chair for her. There was no good-morning kiss in front of the footman, much to her regret.

"How are you feeling this morning?" Verwood asked.

"Marvelous!" She helped herself to a platter of eggs and ham, muffins and toast. "But I'm starving."

"I could tell."

She seated herself beside him and dismissed the footman, thinking perhaps they could have an intimate chat before they were disturbed. But no sooner had Robert left the room than Trudy came bustling in. "Ah, there you are," she said.

"I've never known you to sleep so late, my dear. You mustn't lie abed when you have guests."

Amelia blinked across at her. "I'm going to marry Lord Verwood."

"Excellent!" She smiled placidly at the viscount. "I told you she'd come round, didn't I? Now, then, I have news of my own."

"Mr. Upham has asked you to marry him?"

"Yes. How did you know? Well, my dear, it is just what I've wanted these twenty years past, you know. I was so very put out with him for marrying that mouse when he could have had me for the asking. All these years I've carried a grudge about it."

"A grudge?" Amelia asked, bewildered.

"It was *understood* we would marry, you see. Everyone thought so, including me. So I'm gratified that he's finally done the right thing."

"I wish you very happy," Amelia said a little uncertainly.

"Happy? Nothing in my whole life has given me the pleasure turning him down did! Imagine his thinking I would marry him and give him respectability. The very thought of it! One would have thought a smuggler had more intelligence than that."

It was a little more than Amelia could handle at that hour of the morning. She burst out laughing. "You can come to Derbyshire and London with us, love. We would be pleased to have you, wouldn't we, Alexander?"

"Of course," he agreed readily.

"Well, that's kind of you," Trudy replied, heading for the door. "But I shall stay here with Peter and Mlle. Chartier. They'll need me about the house a great deal more than you will."

They watched her go in silence. When the door had closed, Verwood sighed and said, "So much for long-standing attachments."

Amelia grinned at him. "I dare say it runs in the family. Do you really want to take a chance on me?"

He lifted her stubborn chin with a gentle finger. "I'm determined on it," he said, and kissed her waiting lips.

About the Author

Laura Matthews was born and raised in Pittsburgh, Pennsylvania, but after attending Brown University she moved to San Francisco. Before she sat down to write her first novel, she worked for a spice company, an architecture office and a psychology research project, lived in England for three years, had two children, and sold real estate. Her husband, Paul, has his own architectural practice, and they both work from their home in the Upper Haight Ashbury of San Francisco. Ms. Matthews' favorite pursuits are traveling and scrounging in old bookstores for research material. Her previous novels, A VERY PROPER WIDOW and LORD GREYWELL'S DILEMMA, are available in Signet editions.